I Want It Now

Books by Sydney Molare

SATISFY ME
(with Renee Alexis and Fiona Zedde)

SATISFY ME AGAIN
(with Renee Luke and Fiona Zedde)

SATISFY ME TONIGHT
(with Kimberly Kaye Terry and Fiona Zedde)

I WANT IT NOW

Published by Kensington Publishing Corporation

I Want It Now

Sydney Molare

APHRODISIA

KENSINGTON BOOKS
http://www.kensingtonbooks.com

All characters, companies, and products in this book have no existence outside of the imagination of the author. Events depicted are purely fictional and are not inspired by any person living or dead.

APHRODISIA BOOKS are published by

Kensington Publishing Corp.
119 West 40th Street
New York, NY 10018

All Kensington Titles, Imprints, and Distributed Lines are available at special quantity discounts for bulk purchases for sales promotions, premiums, fund-raising, and educational or institutional use.

Special book excerpts or customized printings can also be created to fit specific needs. For details, write or phone the office of the Kensington special sales manager: Kensington Publishing Corp., 119 West 40th Street, New York, NY 10018, attn: Special Sales Department, Phone: 1-800-221-2647.

ISBN-13: 978-0-7582-3896-2
ISBN-10: 0-7582-3896-7

First Kensington Trade Paperback Printing: August 2010

10 9 8 7 6 5 4 3 2 1

Printed in the United States of America

CONTENTS

YOU'VE GOT MALE

1

Secrets.

There are many types—big, small, inconsequential, and life changing. Mine is the latter: definitely life changing . . . for me, for my world.

I smoothed the foundation over my face and added eye shadow and blush. A touch of gloss to the lips and I was ready to get dressed. The panty/bra set was electric blue with lace frothing everywhere. I needed to lose a few pounds but I wasn't unhappy with the woman in the mirror. The dress I wore was an iridescent ecru, form-fitting and tasteful for the day ahead.

My mind whirled with thoughts of what I was doing. Was I crazy? Would my family and colleagues laugh their asses off? Was this the biggest mistake of my life? Who knew? I'd committed myself, and I prided myself on going through with my commitments; therefore, I was in until the sink capsized and pulled me along in its undertow.

The ride to the dock was sweet. The sun shone in the sky, the air was warm for a March morning, and traffic was light and moving well. Nothing to complain about. I found a spot to park in that wasn't far enough away to cause blisters to form on my heels from the walk. I took a few deep gulps of air to calm myself and gathered up the necessary papers before I exited. Armed with everything I needed to get this adventure under way, I lifted my chin and strode confidently toward Landing Dock 7.

Get ready, 'cause here I come!

I could see the large ocean liner, the *Bravado,* being secured to the dock by strong-armed, strong-backed men. I thought the name of the ship was fitting because what I was doing required tons of bravado on my part. From the first time I'd spotted the ad to the inquiry to the follow-through, no one would have thought I'd have this type of moxie. Not Dina Charles. My image to family and friends usually made them think cute, brainy, but definitely one to be overlooked. Not anymore, folks!

The ship's horn blew loud and long before the gangplank was attached. Family and friends of the passengers began cheering with expectancy of viewing their loved ones. As the first passengers disembarked, my heart began a heavy thudding against the back of my breasts. I had the fleeting thought to run, but I willed my feet to stay still.

I was jostled from behind. I shifted as a voice asked, "Waiting for your boyfriend?"

Startled, I turned and looked into a pale, sunburned face wearing sunglasses and a wide smile. It's true: smiles make you smile. And I did. Widely. "Not quite."

"That's a curious answer." The sunglasses were removed, revealing aquamarine eyes. "Usually the women proclaim loudly they are waiting for their husbands, boyfriends, fathers, or brothers." He tilted his head in question.

"I know. I like being a bit different." I was also feeling a bit unnerved by this inquisitive stranger. I don't mind chitchat, it just wasn't the day or time for it for me. Thankfully, the first passengers had reached the level of the dock, and the crowd surged toward them. I was torn away from the man and moved along with the tide of people.

Suddenly, I spotted him. There was no mistaking the hunk of a man standing a head taller than the others around him. He looked just like the photo he'd sent. Actually, he looked way yummier than the photo. Thank God. So many times, people used "old" photos of themselves in their prime. They failed to give you the new, gravity-dropped version, instead allowed you to be surprised by the variations present in the "current" them versus the "when I was in top shape" one. I waited, watching as he reached the platform. A man I hadn't noticed before—probably since he was much shorter and smaller—spoke to him and they both began scanning the crowd. I waited until their heads turned in my direction before I waved.

Our eyes locked. I could see his pupils dilate, nostrils flare from where I stood, and I swear, I felt a bolt of electricity zap through my body in response. Both of our feet moved simultaneously, first steps, then I was running into his open, waiting arms. As he leaned down, thick biceps enclosed me, picked me up, swung me around. I felt like I'd finally reached . . . home. I clung to him, a feeling I'd never experienced with anyone I hadn't known for a while.

Who knew how long I was spun, wordless, before we heard a throat clear and a heavily accented voice saying, "Well, this is one of the best first meetings I've ever seen." I pulled my head from wide shoulders as the blush crept up my throat. I kept my eyes downcast but the arms refused to place my feet on the ground. "This bodes well for your future. Very good indeed. Dubois, please let Ms. Charles down."

"Must I?" His breath blew against my still down-turned face, making me glance up. Yep, my first impression was confirmed: His parents must be artisans, because he was a specimen carved perfectly from muscle, blood, and bone.

"Yes. We have a tight schedule, and unless Ms. Charles has any objections, I plan to accomplish everything required today." The small man looked at me and bowed. "I'm Simon Daughter, Esquire, at your service. I'll be consummating the contract and handling any questions that may arise until I leave tomorrow evening."

Hands were on my waist, shifting me until I was face-to-face. I looked up, up, up into his twinkling eyes. "And I'm Dubois, your new husband . . . to be."

2

That's correct. I've bought me a bona fide, flesh-and-blood, hunky-as-hell, mail-order husband. Yep, this secret will definitely stun, amaze, trip out, and even irritate those in and around Dina's World. My grin could have lit up Grand Central Station during a power outage. "You sure are." We stood there grinning like we'd been together for a minute. I don't know, life *felt* right. If he was an axe murderer or wrong, I wasn't getting any negative signs from the heavens above.

"Shall we get started?" Simon asked.

"Sure," we both said together.

"Follow me, then."

"How was the trip?" I asked as we followed Simon to wherever. Simon walked fast and with purpose, so he'd obviously been here before.

"It was good. I'd never been on a ship for two weeks before, but the ride was good. No storms that made me seasick." I loved his thick British accent and concise English.

"You're better than me. I took a three-day cruise and spent most of it making love to the porcelain goddess."

"Who?"

There I go with that bad habit of using the slang language I'd picked up from my students. "The toilet. Sometimes when you are ill, people jokingly refer to the toilet as the porcelain goddess since we spend a lot of time paying homage during that particular time."

"Oh. The loo is the porcelain goddess. You Americans are truly . . . unique."

"Ye—"

"Could you two keep close?" Simon was standing ahead, tapping his gleaning shoe's toe on the ground. "We are expected in two minutes, and I do hate to be late." Censure was in his eyes.

This grown woman definitely felt chastised. "Yessir!"

Dubois squeezed my hand as I picked up the pace. "Simon is all bark. We are why he is here, not vice versa." He was correct. I slowed down.

Soon we found ourselves inside a small room that resembled a chapel. A ruddy-faced, bearded man conversed briefly with Simon before striding over to where we stood. "I'm Captain Mark Tooney and I'll be performing the ceremony."

"Good to meet you."

"Hello."

"Great. Do you have your paperwork, Ms. Charles?"

"I sure do." I opened my purse and pulled out the required papers. "Here you go."

The captain studied the papers for a few moments before he nodded and said, "Everything appears to be in order. If you will step this way."

When he began positioning us, I stopped him. "Please. I need a moment. Where is the ladies' room?" I knew my wedding was unconventional, but I wanted to look the best I could for it.

"Of course. It's out those doors and down the hallway. Take your time."

I thanked him and strode toward the doors he'd indicated. As I reached for the metal handle, a hand covered mine. "Allow me." I hadn't realized Dubois had followed, but I was more than happy to see that chivalry was not dead. I stood to the side as he opened the door, then followed me through and stopped just inside the hallway. "I need to freshen up a bit myself. But I'll be waiting here for you upon your return."

Damn! He was definitely winning cool points all around. Oops. Got to stop the slang, even in my mind. After all, if I think it, I'll eventually speak it. I nodded and entered the bathroom. I touched up my makeup, released my hair from the pins holding it, and brushed it out and straightened my dress. After spritzing on more perfume, I removed the gold band I'd purchased for Dubois. Ready.

He was relaxing against the wall as I exited but stood upright immediately. "You look wonderful," he said, eyes looking me all over.

"You do, too." He'd changed into a cream suit that set his dark skin off to perfection. In his hands, he held a bouquet of red roses. "For you. I didn't know if you'd bring your own bridal flowers, so I brought some . . . just in case."

I hadn't remembered the flowers, and they were just what I needed for the day. "I didn't remember, and they are lovely." I took the offered flowers, feeling my heart begin that now familiar thudding in my chest. "Thank you."

"You are more than welcome. Shall we?" He offered me his arm. I slid my arm into the crook. "Of course."

The ceremony was a bit of a blur since so many other thoughts were churning through my head. I do remember reciting the vows, but it was when Captain Tooney said, "You may now kiss your bride" that I truly focused. I was feeling quite shy about our first kiss. However, Dubois was not shy as he pulled me to his chest and his lips fit over mine. I was planning on a chaste kiss, and apparently so was Dubois. His tongue remained in his mouth as our lips slid over each other, softly, teasing with promise behind them.

We pulled apart—reluctantly—with big smiles on our faces. If this was the warm-up, the consummation was going to be the bomb! Drat! There I go again.

"Okay, you guys are officially married. Congratulations, Mr. and Mrs. Dubois Harrington!" Canned music began playing and we turned and walked back down the empty aisle and out into the hallway.

"Dina, I hope to make you the happiest woman alive." Dubois grabbed me up again, his lips on mine, but this time the kiss was a bit different. His tongue snaked out, twisting and flipping my tongue into complicity, and in no time I found myself sucking his tongue deep, biting his lips, running my hands up and down his back.

The clearing of a throat was the only thing that stopped us from peeling off our "good clothes" and doing the nasty right there. We turned to a smiling Simon holding papers in his hands.

"I'll need your signatures here." He held out the marriage certificate, which we both signed. I smiled at the Old World calligraphy penmanship of Dubois. "Now . . . let's have a celebratory dinner, and I'll need to go over the last-minute details."

We all loaded into my car and I drove to a restaurant across town, the Queen's Tearoom. After we'd been seated, Simon pulled out the contract I'd filled in more than six months ago and began. "Dina, Dubois, again congratulations." We nodded. "Dina, according to the contract, there is a thirty-day, half-rate, money-back guarantee with this marriage. If after thirty days, if *either* of you is not satisfied or wishes to leave this marriage, please let me know. The marriage will be annulled. Dubois will then return to Extania with you paying his return fare home. Are you both clear on that?"

Simon's talk was sobering indeed. *Either of you* . . . This was no one-way street. I could reject or be rejected. "I am." I turned to look at Dubois, who also was no longer smiling.

"I am also."

"Good. After the thirty-day period, no money is refundable and no passage home is guaranteed." He looked at each of us slowly. "You must then do as any other married couple does: Work hard to stay married." I gulped in spite of myself. "Any questions?" We both shook our heads. "Great. Let's eat!"

3

We dropped Simon off at his hotel before heading to my room. As was fitting for the occasion, I'd secured the bridal suite. The bellboy lifted Dubois's duffle bag and escorted us to our room. As I started to walk inside, Dubois stopped me with a hand on my arm. I gave him a puzzled look. "No, Mrs. Harrington. We are going to do this correctly." With that, he picked me up and walked with me in his arms across the threshold. He slowly placed me back on the floor. "I plan to do *everything* correctly," he whispered, eyes hooded, before planting another delicious kiss on my lips.

Blood whooshed through me. I was *so* ready for the bellboy to be gone, gone, gone! Dubois tipped him and closed the door. He turned to me, unbuttoning the top button of his shirt. "Ready for . . . us?" His fingers were soft as he stroked my chin and down the center of my chest.

My ears began ringing and my heart stuttered as his fingers rubbed my now hot skin. "I—I think so." He lifted his fingers and I leaned in, wanting them back in contact with my flesh.

"I think so, too." Dubois turned me, slowly pulled me to his chest. "I know we just met—*officially*—so . . . why not take it slow? Let's get to know each other before we jump into sex," he whispered against my neck.

Oooh. He'd read me well. Dubois and I had corresponded regularly, so I felt as though I *knew* this man, could trust this man. But I have to admit, I wasn't a jump-in-the-bed-at-a-moment's-notice type of girl. The fact is, the wedding night and what I would actually do had bothered me quite a bit. Yes, this was a far-fetched idea—one which I'd paid for dearly with my hard-earned money—but still, an unfamiliar penis just didn't sit well with me. So I was a bit relieved at the offer to go slow instead of consummating the marriage upon sight . . . even if my starving pussy *was* screaming for some hardness to marinate in its wetness. "I think that's a great idea."

I felt his smile spread on my neck. "I *totally* agree."

Fingers brushed against my lower back, sending frissons of excitement down my spine. "But . . . there are some . . . *skills* . . . I didn't mention." My dress was bunched in the back as his large hands roamed up and down my spine.

"Really? Like?"

"Making love to a woman with her clothes on."

I shivered in joy. I was happy I would actually get a "preview" of the sex, and thus his true character, before the actual sex.

His lips pulled at my earlobe, hands roamed across my back. My nipples puckered, clit began a slow throb. Dubois's tongue slid from my earlobe to the back of my neck, and he began to lick across my shoulder. Firm hands held me as his tongue reached the indentation in my throat, swirled around and around. I moaned.

Dubois turned me, let my back rest against his broad chest. My nipples, unmashed now, rose like frozen buttons in the cool room air. Dubois saw. I watched his hand slide upward, cover the stiff points, warm them with his fingers. I covered his hands, wanting to feel him milk my tits. He took his time strumming the soft mounds, teasing my nipples, whispering unidentifiable words in another language.

This felt better than I could have ever imagined. My head rolled around; my body hummed in anticipation of his next move.

Fingers tap-danced across my belly and down a thigh. He squeezed, then stroked my thigh, causing my dress to ride up. He hesitated when he felt the exposed flesh between my garter and hosiery. I smiled as he looked down.

"You weren't expecting that, huh?" I teased. No high-waisted pantyhose for this chick. The garter and hose might cost more, but heck, I'm worth it.

"Definitely not." The dress was lifted higher until my panties peeked out. His eyes roamed over me appreciatively. "God, woman, you are beautiful." He licked his lips, causing my clit to jump.

"Thank you," I whispered.

He groaned then, both hands rubbed up and down my thighs, agonizing rubs. I felt on fire. He nudged my chin, captured my lips beneath his. His tongue sizzled inside my mouth, taking me higher on this ride. His fingers grew bold, sliding over the skin before resting just beneath the level of my panties. I knew my panties would reveal how wet I was for him.

I held my breath as I felt his finger brush against the thin material, then my body lurched as he flicked across my clit. He leaned back, looked into my eyes. "Found your spot, eh?"

I nodded in assent. The fingers drove a torturous path around and around my clit, never touching but promising, nevertheless. My breathing was rapid, my pussy leaking copiously. I wanted this; it had been too long since I'd enjoyed this.

Dubois suddenly changed gears, let his hands drift to cover my tits again. My clit protested, but as he pulled at my stiff points, I growled deep in my throat. I loved having my tits milked and he was doing a damn good job.

His hands began moving downward again. I widened my stance, wanting to make sure he had room to work.

He noticed. . . .

I felt the smile in my hair as he cupped my mound, thumb stroking my clit. Soft kisses rained across my ear. I slid my hands over his bald dome, wanting the connection while he loved me. His cock was like an iron pipe pushing into my hips. My pussy began a steady stream down my inner thigh as he took his time. My clit throbbed furiously, wanting, no, *needing* Dubois's touch to soothe it.

He heard the wordless pheromonic call. . . .

His fingers reached out, covered my stiff clit. I panted as he diddled, stroked, and plucked. I held on to his head as a finger slid into my leaking pussy. He stabbed my hole constantly, made me juice all over his hand. Fingers pulled my nipples, made my head roll. I moaned, undulated on his hardness at the double assault on my body. When Dubois reclaimed my clit, I felt the pinpricks surge up my legs, across my shoulders.

I screamed.

My pussy geysered.

The marriage was officially under way!

4

We started out early the next morning. We had a five-hour drive before we reached my—or rather, our home. Dubois snored quietly as I navigated through the rush-hour traffic. I was not surprised. Neither of us could sleep last night. We talked—and lightly stroked—long into the night. I glanced over at his strong profile, still shocked at how this whole adventure seemed to be working out so well. I took the quiet time to reflect on how I got from there to here, conventional and conservative to unconventional and running with the wild mustangs.

It all began quite innocently: the latest blind date gone wrong and my determination not to be the sad sister everyone was trying to "hook up". . . for the umpteenth time. For some reason, once I'd reached a certain level of success, I was unable to find suitable counterparts to date. It was like I had a sign on my forehead: SHE'S TOO RICH AND INDEPENDENT FOR YOU, MAN! And those *not* reading it and having the courage to ask me out should have. I tell you, if another man invited me to dinner and we pulled up to another buffet—Chinese, Japanese, Ryan's or its counterparts—I would have screamed.

And my God! What's up with the men with poor manners: letting me help myself into cars, walking in front of me, letting me open my own doors, and the casual ease with which they asked me for sex? Like sex was as meaningless as grabbing a glass of water. Not me. I wanted sex to be the mind-numbing, commitment-driven act I always felt it was intended to be between partners.

So when I spotted this small ad in a women's magazine, it piqued my curiosity. It said simply, WANT THE MAN IN YOUR DREAMS? CONTACT US. 150-555-4398. I dialed the number, thinking it was probably a gag. But it was no gag. The representative was courteous and quite knowledgeable about the entire process. I gleaned as much information as possible, then visited their Web site.

Their site provided much more information. Each potential husband spoke at least three languages, was in perfect health, and had received "advanced training" in husbandship. I wasn't sure what the husbandship training included, but I figured it was a class in understanding a wife and his marital obligations and expectations better.

I viewed the photos of available men, read their profiles and biographies, then narrowed my search down to three prospects, kind of like the Match.com stuff I see on television, only with me completely in control of the selections.

I'd spoken at length to each contender before settling on Dubois. There was something in his voice that scratched at my soul, made me want to know him much better. Further conversations cemented this feeling and so, after much meditation, I filled out the contract and selected Dubois as my mate. I was hoping and praying I'd made the correct choice.

"Second thoughts?"

Dubois's question startled me because of the similar thoughts I was having about him. "Not really. You?"

"Definitely not." He smiled before continuing. "Honestly, I'd heard horror stories about things that could go wrong."

"Like what?"

"A person looking like Halle Berry on their photo actually looked more like a Harold Berry in person."

I had to laugh at the visual that popped in my mind. "That definitely could be a problem."

"You are telling me. How does one make love to a man-looking woman?"

"The same way someone makes love to a woman-looking man?" We both laughed. "Well, rest assured, someone probably is doing it right now."

"Perhaps. I imagine there is someone for everyone . . . I just don't think . . . let's just say, she would have gotten a refund with me on sight. I'd be back on the *Bravado* right now, thankful I got away alive."

I loved how "politically correct" he was. "Gotcha."

"So, your job . . . do you enjoy what you do?"

I was an anthropologist at the university and loved what I did. Yes, I visited exotic places for weeks on end, but it was the student interaction, the passage of my knowledge to the unknowledgeable that drove my engine. "I sure do. There is nothing more rewarding than sharing knowledge."

"Really? Explain, please."

I broke it down. "When students come into my classroom, they are, for the most part, a blank slate that I have the wonderful job of filling in with my words, their assignments, and taking them to the field. And if I do a good job, their slate becomes crowded with knowledge, historical facts that still apply to our lives today, and thus, allows them to place themselves in context to the world as it evolved."

"You help them find themselves by showing them how similar and dissimilar they are to those who have come before."

"Correct!" It was so refreshing to find someone actually

understanding my ideologies on the first conversation. "The meek become proud, the boastful become humble, because the realization finally dawns that there truly is nothing new under the sun. It's just new to *them*."

Dubois rubbed his hands together like a kid. "You've got me excited, that is for sure!"

"Oh, keep hanging with me. I've got a lot more excitement to come out." We broke into laughter.

We only stopped once to stretch our legs, grab some gas and food. I wasn't surprised to see Dubois surrounded by three animated women when I exited the bathroom. He *was* a sight to behold. When I advanced, the conversation I heard seemed innocent . . . but I knew women and went on guard anyway. But when he took my arm and introduced me to the women as his wife—earning pointed looks all around—I relaxed and smiled. They might not have been innocent in their motives, but Dubois surely was.

I pulled into the driveway just after lunch. My home was an old antebellum house I'd rescued from the foreclosure block and restored in a mixture of old charm and modern amenities. It was huge by today's standards, but I loved it and hoped Dubois would also.

His eyes grew large as I slowed in the circle drive. "This is home?"

"Yes. You like?"

He nodded. "It reminds me of the stately manor houses at home." He turned to look at the pasture just across the road where the cattle grazed freely. "Yes, it definitely reminds me of home."

"Really? I thought Extania was pretty urban."

"Some areas are. It's a small island, for sure. But where I lived wasn't very . . . urban." He turned back to me. "After we unload, would it be all right to walk into the pasture?"

I didn't know much about cows and definitely didn't know if there was a mean bull present, but I swallowed my own apprehension down and said, "Of course. This is your home, so I think you should get to know it."

"Great!"

I unlocked the trunk and Dubois grabbed all our bags in his hands and gestured for me to precede him. I took my time walking up the walkway with the pampas grass sprouting around it. I liked the look but I was well aware there could be unwanted "visitors" lurking there also.

Dubois sat the bags down in the foyer and stared up the winding staircase. "Wow. This is truly magnificent."

I clapped my hands in glee. "Glad you like it."

"And you did all this restoration . . . by yourself?"

I couldn't take all the credit. "Well, actually, I came up with the ideas, then hired contractors to do the actual work."

"They did a great job."

"Let me show you the rest of the house." I enjoyed the slow tour throughout the house, pointing out extra touches here and there I thought were unique. I paused when we reached the upstairs master/mistress suite. Taking a deep breath, I said, "These are our rooms."

Dubois took in the blue-green décor I'd used in the room in silence. When his eyes rested on the iron king-sized bed, he smiled appreciatively. "Nice." He pulled me into his arms and added, "Nice, indeed," before covering my lips with his. He released me just as I was starting to feel giddy. "I think we'll have a lot of good times in this room."

"Um," was all I could manage to eke out. I stepped back from all the maleness that was seeping into my pores and shook my head to clear it. "Hey, let me show you one of my favorite spots in the house."

"There is such a thing as a favorite place besides the bedroom?" His eyebrow quirked in amusement.

"For me, there is. Come along." I pulled him behind me as we navigated back down the stairwell and out onto the patio. Here I'd installed a hot tub with those wonderful shooting jets. I'd had more than my share of orgasms thanks to those jets. "This . . . is *my* favorite spot."

Dubois turned in a circle, taking in the hot tub, the gazebo and pergola, and the mini–botanical garden I'd been tinkering around with. "Are you the green thumb?"

"Yes. It's a hobby of mine." I walked him around spouting off the names of the different flowers and shrubbery I'd planted around the koi pond. The sun glinted off the exotic fishes' iridescent scales.

"You did a great job here."

"Thanks." Appreciation never sounded so good. "Hey, why don't you go . . . explore . . . and I'll get started on dinner."

"If that's all right with you. By the way, how close are our neighbors?"

"The nearest one is a half a mile in that direction." I pointed to the west. "On this side, the closest would be around a mile." I waved to the east.

"So who owns the pasture across the road?"

"I'm not sure. I think it's the family on this side." I pointed to the west again.

"Do you have a bicycle?"

Of course, it was his normal mode of transportation. I chastised myself for not thinking of buying one. "No. But we can get you one tomorrow."

A big smile broke out on his face. "Great. I guess walking will have to do today."

Suddenly, I heard the front door open and close. I frowned, wondering who it could be.

"Hey, Dina! You here?" My eyes widened. "Yeah, her car is out front, so she's around here somewhere," I heard her say before footsteps were clomping across the ceramic tile.

"Expecting company?" Dubois asked beside me. I was mute as a body walked into view, cell phone plastered to her ear.

Sleek black hair, black-rimmed eyes, a halter top that dipped down to *there* and shorts that rose up to *here*—my lifetime nemesis, aka Stacy, my younger sister. Brown eyes widened as they took in me and Dubois. "Let me call you back, Mom." She clicked her phone off slowly and took a moment to look Dubois from head to toe, licking her lips as she gazed into his eyes. "Damn, girl. Where'd you find him?"

It never ceased to amaze me how someone who had grown up in a small town could become ghettofied at the drop of a piece of lint. Today she was definitely in Ghetto Mode. "Hello to you too, Stacy."

Her eyes shifted to me, "Oh, my bad," then back to Dubois. "Hell-o." She held out her hand. "I'm Stacy, Dina's *younger*, *single* sister." If her meaning wasn't made obvious by emphasizing her words, the way she thrust out her high breasts and let a leg extend a bit in front of her sure made it clear.

Dubois took the offered hand and pulled it to his lips. I felt a tinge of greenness swimming in my blood as Stacy showed every one of her braces-perfect teeth in appreciation. "It is my pleasure to make your acquaintance, Miss Stacy."

"Oooh. Talks pretty, too." She gave me a look of shared conspiracy that I didn't return. "I think you and I will be getting much, *much* better acquainted, as you say."

Dubois flashed her a megawatt smile. "I would think so." Stacy gave me a look I'd seen many times before. "I'm Dubois. Dina's new husband."

I would have happily paid a month's salary to have a photo of the changed look on Stacy's face at that announcement. Priceless, indeed.

5

I changed into some shorts before heading toward the kitchen. Dubois had set out on his exploration after helping Stacy bring in her bags. While I defrosted chicken, I checked my messages. Two from my parents, one from my brother, and the last from Michael, a man whom I never hoped to see ever again. His message was typical of the men I'd dated: *Hey, if you aren't busy, let's "hook up."* Well, I'm busy whenever you call from here on out, buster.

A giggle made me turn around. Stacy leaned against the door, a hand over her mouth.

"What's so funny?"

"The fact that you suddenly have a husband nobody ever heard you mention, yet the man you *have* been dating and even brought to the family reunion is still leaving messages. That tells me a couple of things: one, you broke up with Michael but the breakup is so fresh, he still thinks he has a chance and has no idea you've really moved on." I felt the redness creeping up my neck. "And two, Dubois must be hella good in bed since you married him so fast."

I turned away from her, opened the microwave, and poked at the defrosting bird. "You are not as smart as you think you are," I responded over my shoulder.

"Really?" A perfectly arched eyebrow rose. "What part did I get wrong? I mean, Mom keeps me up on everything, and not once has she mentioned this Adonis with a British accent and you. So I'm definitely thinking she has no clue . . . or rather, *had* no clue."

I swung around then. "Tell me you didn't tell Mom and Dad." Stacy gave me a noncommittal shrug. Blood swooshed through my brain. I wasn't ashamed at what I'd done, but like everything in life, it was about timing. My *own* timing to keep and reveal my secrets as I wanted. The fact that Stacy had possibly preempted me had me seeing red. I moved closer to her. Stacy moved backward, eyes looking at my hand. The skewer I'd poked at the chicken with pointed straight ahead. I dropped it and got into her face.

"I want you to hear me and hear me well. My business is *my* business. Despite what you believe, I will live my life like I want, whether it meets with your, the rest of the family, friends, or the world's standards, understand?"

Stacy eyes were wide, but suddenly they narrowed and she burst out laughing. "Girl, that must have been some kind of sex to make your uptight ass get some backbone."

Her statement infuriated me further. I grabbed her upper arm. "I don't need hellified sex to give me courage. I just need you to understand that this is my life and I'll live it however I want, regardless of your opinion."

Stacy didn't back down. "You're just bluffing. Something's up and I plan to find out why you would hide this dude away, no mention of him at all to your family, and suddenly, you're married." Her eyes drifted down to my belly. "Pregnant?"

The urge to slap her was great. "If I am, that's none of your concern."

"So I'm right! You are pregnant." She moved until our noses almost touched. "How could you be so . . . *old* . . . and stupid?"

"You mean-spirited little heffa!" Stacy and I definitely have had our share of catfights. When I was still at home, she took great pleasure in parading around half naked, tempting my boyfriends. Truth be told, I suspect she actually did get with one or two of them because I'd found their numbers on her cell phone. I left them alone after that. But that was then. I wasn't letting her get away with jack now! "I will—"

"Wow! I could hear the yelling out in the portico," Dubois said as he strolled into the kitchen.

I released Stacy's arm and she rolled her eyes before placing a smile on her face and turning. "We were just chitchatting about some . . . things. You know, like sisters do."

"Yes. You were going at it like my sisters do all the time." Dubois stared into my face, a face I'd not managed to remove the scowl from. He gave me a smile. I gave him a halfhearted, lopsided one in return. He nodded before looking back at Stacy. "So, Stacy, how long will you be staying?"

Stacy's smile grew larger, feeling secure that whatever she wanted, she'd get. "Oh, I'm in the middle of a move and thought I'd spend a week"—she looked over her shoulder at me—"or two with Dina and my parents. Catch up and all."

Dubois nodded again. "No husband waiting for you anywhere?" He walked over and stood behind me.

"None." I could see Stacy's lips curling at the edge as they always did whenever she was about to smirk.

"Your parents live nearby?"

"Yes. They live across the county."

"Did you grow up in a large house?"

My parents were both schoolteachers and so we were definitely brought up firmly entrenched in the middle class—nice home, regular new cars, no hand-me-downs for their kids.

Image, after all, was important. As my father always told us, we were a reflection of them, and they wanted the world to believe they could give us a pretty good life. Stacy was their princess child. Spoiled rotten.

"Yes, a four-bedroom, three-bath ranch. There was plenty of room for us."

Dubois hugged me to his chest, placing a light kiss on my neck. "That's good." His eyes shifted back to Stacy. "Stacy, I think it would be a better idea if you stayed with your parents. Dina and I forgot you were to visit, but since we just got married, I would really appreciate if you would visit us another time—after the honeymoon. Then we would be able to give you excellent hospitality. Right now, we are focusing on . . . us."

I would have lost a second paycheck if someone had a camera at that moment. Stacy's eyes bucked, her face fell, and her mouth opened in astonishment. "You . . . you want me to leave?"

Dubois nodded. "I think it would be best, considering this is our honeymoon."

"B—but—"

"I'll be happy to help you get your bags back in the car." Dubois's tongue snaked out of his mouth and he licked my lips. "Sweetie, it won't take me but just a moment. Perhaps while I'm helping Stacy, you can give your parents a call and let them know when we'll visit them?"

I quickly jumped into my role. "Sure. Saturday or Sunday, you think?" Of course, I added a flashing smile for my gorgeous man—and to irritate Stacy.

"Either sounds splendid." He then turned and said, "Let's get those bags!" He placed his arm around Stacy's shoulders and guided her out of the kitchen and toward the stairwell.

When they were out of sight, I clutched my stomach and

sank into a chair. Stacy had her faults, but she was right on the money about this: Dubois *was* a hell of a man!

My parents didn't answer, probably because it was during their favorite soap opera's daily episode, so I left a message. I could hear Dubois carrying on a one-sided conversation as he rounded up Stacy's things and knew the lack of chatter from her meant she was past pissed. I smiled brightly.

I was seasoning the chicken as Dubois brought Stacy's bags back downstairs. In seconds, an engine started and the tires squealed as she pulled out into the road. Wonderful!

I headed out to the grill with the chicken, thinking about potential scenarios that would occur once Stacy told my parents. I sighed, knowing life would work out one way or the other. Just as I sat the meat on the patio table, I heard a rustle in the shrubbery beside me. Looking down, I saw one of my biggest fears: a snake. It didn't matter how long I'd lived in the country, I never, ever would be a fan of reptiles, so I did what I always did whenever I saw one: jumped sky high and screamed!

The snake moved, in my mind curling up to strike, and I tripped over a chair as I ran toward the house. Dubois met me running full tilt. "What's happened?"

I jumped on him and wrapped my arms around his neck, my legs around his waist. "A snake! There's a snake on the patio!" I blubbered as I squeezed his neck tighter. Dubois took a few steps toward the open patio door. "No! Didn't you hear me? There's a snake on the patio!" His eardrum should have burst wide open.

"I heard you. The door is open. Let me close it."

I held on like an eight-armed monkey, trembling as he walked to the door and slid it closed. "Aye, I see it." I clutched him tighter. "It's just a king snake. They are harmless. We have them on the island. In fact, I had a snake as a pet."

I leaned away from him and stared. In my world, normal people didn't own snakes. "You *did*?"

"Yes." He rubbed my back. "It was a big draw for the girls."

I bopped his shoulder and laughed. "Men."

"Well, I am honest." He kissed me. "Let me get rid of the snake, place the chicken on the pit, and then, how about we"—his finger traced my lips—"we try out your favorite place? It will relieve some of the tension I feel in your body." His hand roamed down my back to cup my hips. I felt his cock poking upward . . . into my hot center. Dubois slid me slowly down his front. I had ample opportunity to feel the length and breadth of him as the centimeters crept by. My clit jumped as the hardness brushed past it.

Damn, he looks good and feels like he's packing! "Sure. But *only* if you get rid of the snake first."

"Of course. I told you I planned to, so *everything* in correct order." A kiss to the forehead. "Your knight will return momentarily."

My feet were on the floor but I definitely felt like I was floating. *My knight.* Mine, all mine. I watched as Dubois retrieved the broom and advanced on the snake. The pointed black head lifted and I stifled the panicky scream bubbling up my throat. But Dubois kept his distance, curled the snake around the broom handle, and walked off the patio and toward the woods behind.

When he disappeared, I took my time, tiptoeing and peeking for any of the snake's friends or relatives before I turned on the spa, setting the temperature and velocity of the jets. Those jets weren't stand-ins for the real thing, but they weren't half bad. I continued searching the patio thoroughly before I placed the chicken on the grill. Dubois returned. He ran his fingers into the churning water. "Feels good." He let his fingers trail in the ripples. He rubbed the sweat from his forehead, then looked at me, smiled, and said, "Want to do this naked?"

My first thought was no. After all, I'd spent most of my life inhibited because of one reason or another, usually my feelings of inadequacy—weight, looks, attitude. But this was different. Dubois was my husband, so why not? "If you are game, I am."

Dubois crooked his finger at me. I dutifully walked over, tingles traveling all through my body. I stopped in front of him. His fingers brushed my hair off my shoulders. "You are such a beautiful woman." A girl never tired of hearing that. "Those other men were fools . . . and I am extremely glad they were."

His hands moved to the lower edge of my T-shirt. Warm fingers brushed against my skin. Butterflies swam and dove in my stomach. Dubois pulled it up slowly, inch by inch, and over my head. He smiled appreciatively. I felt some of my old fears return and my arms slid up to cover my chest. "Don't, you are truly so beautiful," he whispered. I let my arms drop to my sides.

He pulled me close, hands skimming my hips. I took this opportunity to unbutton the top button of his shirt. My lips lifted at the corners as I watched the vessel pulse on the side of his neck. I unbuttoned the next three buttons, allowing me to see the nice growth of hair lying on his chest. I loved a hairy man, so I slid my fingers beneath the fabric, ran them through the thick thatch. It was rough, prickly; my nipples rose in anticipation.

Dubois swallowed, and a pulse jumped in his neck. I unbuttoned the final two buttons and pulled his shirt from his pants and off his shoulders, getting my first full view of his upper body. This man was definitely a magnificent piece of manhood. I couldn't stop myself from walking around him and looking. From his broad chest to the delineated muscles in his back . . . pure perfection.

Further thoughts were erased because Dubois grabbed me and began unzipping my shorts. He held my eyes as he navigated them off my hips and let them drop to the ground.

Dubois's pants were a bit trickier. He wore a belt and his pants had double buttons before reaching the zipper. His bulge didn't make pulling the zipper down an easier task, but I persevered. Soon, we were both standing in our underwear.

"Your turn." I obliged and turned in a half-circle before hands stopped me. Dubois unhooked my bra and removed it, his tongue sliding down my arm in pursuit. My breasts puckered in the air. My breath held in my chest, unsure, as he dropped to his knees. A finger slid into either side of my waistband and my panties were gently tugged over the rise of my cheeks and off my hips. With a slight half-twist of my body, my bush ended up inches from his face. He licked his lips. My pussy pulsed, its fragrance wafting upward to my nose. My stomach flattened as his face moved closer, closer, closer. Dubois rubbed his face in my bush, his chin tenderly bumping, teasing my clit, eliciting a moan from me.

If he keeps this up, we're definitely going to go back on all that "Let's take it slow" stuff we said!

He rose. I saw smears of my juice on his face. I waited. Dubois lifted me, held me over the spa, and let me down easy into the warm water. He shucked off his boxers and climbed in beside me. Yes indeed, he was gorgeous from his head to his big-ass black cock to his big-ass feet. I was warm all over. Of course, it didn't help that the jets were shooting water directly at my pussy.

"You like?" I asked as he climbed in and submerged himself.

"Very much. I have only experienced one hot tub. It was at the hotel where I worked a few summers on the mainland."

I nodded. "Tell me more about you. The juicy stuff, like . . . what exactly does husbandship training include?" The husbandship referral had definitely piqued my curiosity. I'd Googled it, but came up with nothing but references to husbandry, and that was for animals.

He gave me a cautious look. "Are you sure you want to know?"

This further stoked my curiosity. "Sure. Why not?"

He thought a second before he spoke. "It can seem . . . *overwhelming* to some."

What the heck? "You start telling me and I'll stop you if I can't handle it. Deal?" I held out my pinkie finger.

"Deal." He wrapped his pinkie around mine. I guess some customs are worldwide. "It's very simple: I learned how to please a woman in every form and fashion."

"Etiquette and things like what we like, what to expect?" Sounded pretty basic.

"Yes, along with the art of making love." A smile teased at his lips.

Whoa! "The *art* of making . . . *love*?" In my world, it was learn as you go, not any formal training I'd ever heard about.

"Yes. Sex is more than just a meeting of bodies. A *good* lover has to develop skills to not only please his lover but to mix it up and continue to please her time after time."

This I could understand, after my few experiences and hearing so many married friends complain how sex was so hot in the beginning, then it began to fizzle out . . . until they either divorced and found a new partner or had an affair. "Yes, but you had . . . *classes*?"

"Definitely. Everyone who enters this program has at least three years in the lovemaking arts before they are allowed to be placed for consideration as a spouse."

Three years of sex classes? I swallowed hard. "What were some of these classes?"

Dubois showed me his pearly whites before answering, "There was The Art of Seduction, Mind Foreplay, Erogenous Zones and Pleasure Pain, Sexual Techniques and Positions, Oral Skills, Toys and Accessories, Fetishes and Role Playing." My pussy pulsed as he listed each class.

This information definitely blew my mind! I married a man who actually had classes to teach him all the various ways to satisfy me? I mean, we are talking about sex *à la carte* that he could deliver without the old third degree about why I wanted to do it, who I'd done it with previously, and not judge?

Hot damn! Mandingo with Advanced Sex Ed!

Am I a lucky heffa or what? I wished I'd invested the money years earlier. I could have avoided the fumbling about with the men around here.

"You are . . . quiet."

More like speechless. "I'm sorry. I'm just taking in everything you just told me."

He nodded. "Your reaction is actually milder than I had anticipated."

"I can imagine. You probably thought I would jump up and run screaming into the house or something, one hand speed-dialing for Simon."

"We have heard stories like that." He nodded in assent.

"Not me." I spread my arms wide around the edge of the tub and leaned back. "I'm thinking this is the best thing since light bread."

"Light bread?" Confusion twisted his features.

Dang me and my slang! "Light bread is what we call white bread. It just means it's better than a normal everyday thing like eating white bread."

"Oh."

A thought popped into my head and I had to ask. "So . . . I'm guessing these classes were . . . interactive?"

"Of course," he deadpanned. "There is no way to learn how to please a woman unless there is a woman present to please." Logical. "All of the males' instructors were women, and vice versa."

"So what, you guys just met, started having sex, and learned through on-the-job training?"

He shook his head at me. "No. Each prospect is assigned a specific teacher who stays with them for that year. The next year you receive a new instructor, to whom you must first *prove* you have mastered the previous year's studies before they will allow you to continue." His face was earnest, serious.

"Then you can enter the new set of classes."

"Yes. You can then add a new layer of knowledge on top of the old layer."

A thought niggled my mind and I had to ask. "These women . . . were they prostitutes?" I've always been health conscious, and even though we were each required to have a full STD screen, I still wanted to know.

"I suspect some of them were that or geishas in their former lives, but we were never told. I do know they seemed to enjoy their jobs very much." He grinned widely.

"Probably not as much as you men enjoyed being their pupils."

"Let's just say there was mutual admiration all around." His smile grew wider.

I was so . . . jealous. Actually taking classes to become a great lover was something I would definitely pay good money for. "And I'm guessing you passed all your classes with As?"

"It was pass/fail, but I never had to do any makeup work to pass. I aced it the first time—always." He winked seductively with hooded eyes.

Heat suffused my body that even the water couldn't cool. My legs widened, allowing the jets to again pulse fully onto my clit. I brushed against his leg. I gasped, gripped the edge of the tub as electricity shot through me. I started to remove my hand when his cock kissed my palm and . . . he moaned.

I liked the sound.

I slid my hand back and forth, allowing the head of his cock to circle inside my palm. His breathing increased; his eyes closed. I lightly moved my hand lower, allowing the eddy of the water to guide my journey down his shaft. His cock jumped, pulsed; my palm felt the precum release.

Oh, yes, I do like playing with fire.

I circled the head with my thumb and index finger and tugged. Dubois groaned, spread his legs wider. I definitely wanted a repeat of that sound. "Is this a class you enjoyed a lot?"

"They didn't have a class in th-this," he stuttered as I enclosed his rod in my fist.

Oh? I might be able to teach this learned dog a trick? Emboldened now, I stood, maneuvered until I was half floating between his legs. The water allowed my fingers ample lubrication as I stroked slowly at first, then firmer and faster, twisting in opposite directions. Dubois's response egged me on—his hips rose from the spa seat, began pushing into my closed fist, the head of his cock now surging above the water line.

I cupped his balls, massaged them slowly as I kept stroking, circling, and pumping. His cock puffed, stiffened into an unbendable steel rod. He bit his lips, but a cry escaped. I vised him, stroked him firmly while plucking at his head with my fingers. Though I didn't need to, I spat on his exposed head, earning a growl from him.

He was close.

I choked his head vigorously. He squirmed and I could see his toes curling, but I kept the pressure on. This must have been the right action because in seconds, his body clenched. He began blubbering in French, and a wad of cum spurted out of his head, hitting me squarely between my breasts. I continued to milk him until no more cum cascaded from his rod.

Dubois lay back, breathing heavily, as I resumed my place beside him. He pulled me to him, allowing his fingers to glide slowly up and down my arm. "Dina?"

"Yes?"

"Are you sure you haven't had classes in wifeship?"

A laugh burst from my throat. According to some of my lovers, I was as vanilla as they came. "I haven't. Why?"

Dubois held me tighter. "Your past lovers were arses."

The high compliment made me feel all warm and fuzzy. I snuggled closer to him. "Thank you, baby."

"I'm not a predictor of the future, but I do believe our sex life together will be one wild ride. I can tell about these things."

Same thing I was thinking.

We lay there in silent contentment as the shadows lengthened.

6

The butterflies danced and twittered in the soft breeze, their wings glinting in the sunlight. Delighted, I danced as they swirled around me, caught up in the beauty of the moment. They flew high then returned in a cloud, their feet alighting on my arms, my bare belly. I laughed as the brush of wings tickled my flesh until I was unable to stand it anymore. My hand moved downward to shoo them away and felt . . . skin?

My eyes flew open. Suddenly, I remembered. Dubois. My new husband. His lips touched my stomach again. I shifted as the tickling sensation returned. It intensified when his tongue poked out, swirling into my navel.

I groaned before clutching his head in my hands. "Stop. That tickles."

"Um." His head moved lower where he swirled his tongue just above the waistband of my bikini before nipping the tender flesh. His breath drifted over my exposed thighs in warm, rapid puffs. "What about here?"

My stomach was now doing flip-flops as his whiskers

scratched the sensitized flesh. I held his head firmly. "It definitely tickles."

Dubois grinned up at me. "That was my plan." He pushed downward. I stopped him. He made an unhappy face. "Still tickles? And here I was thinking all that thrashing about was because I was arousing you."

"Well, I'm sure in the classes they taught you the most likely positions to get someone aroused. However, I happen to be extremely ticklish all over. So I'm *tickled* right now, not aroused."

He nodded. His hands moved into the spot where his whiskers scratched, moving in slow circles. My stomach contracted, then released involuntarily as the circle widened. He watched the play of my abdomen, a smile creeping onto his face.

"Better?"

"Much."

Over and over his fingers dipped into my bush—just missing my clit—then back below my navel. I began a slow sizzle all over. His other hand rubbed up and down my thigh. My pussy began to leak; my legs shifted, widened slightly.

Dubois's long tongue snaked out and swirled into my belly button. My breath held in my chest, legs began to tremble. Dubois kept up the pace, fingers circling, hand kneading, tongue licking until I thought I would scream from all the sensations flowing through me. My clit needed his touch, my nipples cried for his lips, my mouth needed his kiss.

I couldn't take it anymore. I tugged him upward, slammed my mouth over his, tonguing him eagerly and vigorously. He met me twist for turn, indeed, pulled me atop him. I straddled him, knowing that my wet secrets would be revealed the moment my pussy touched his stomach. And I was correct. When my pussy connected with his flesh, he pulled back. "Well, well, well. Looks like you're no longer ticklish."

"I'm not," I assured him before I touched my lips back to his.

Dubois grasped my hip, mashed my pussy deeper into his stomach. I imagined the juices were pooling in his navel, sticky, the scent tantalizing, entrancing us both. He tugged at my camisole, pulled it over my head without really lifting from the bed. His hands stroked my breasts slowly, eyes darkening further in desire. When his nostrils flared, I cupped them, leaned them over for his lips to suck.

He did so willingly.

I sighed deep as his soft lips pulled at my stiff knobs. It felt *so* good, the tugging, the wetness, the pressure of his nips. My womb contracted, spewed more juice out of my body and onto him. I let my hips slide around, wanting my clit to touch his hot flesh. He shifted, allowing his cock to stab into the material of the panties just covering my lips.

"Mmm, baby. Oh, baby." His tongue probed and twirled faster as his hips pushed upward, searching. I opened wider, teased him unmercifully. Hands tangled in my hair, dragged my mouth to him. I ran a finger along the underside of his cock, felt him jerk, lurch from the touch.

I pushed the envelope further.

My fingers closed around his swollen head, began a slow stroke aided by my wetness. I let his cock head brush across my exposed bush hairs; knew *exactly* what I was doing. Wanted it, even.

Dubois stiffened, then surged, thrust his cock into the wet hairs; felt him growing, growing, hardening between my hand. "Sweet Jeeeees . . . oh, baby, oh baby."

His cock kept probing, seeking, wanting me to slide the panties to the side, welcome it into my hot pussy . . . and my pussy wanted him so badly. Wanted to clench around the thick muscle, slide up and down the stiff pole, releasing countless pints of juice in my wake. My mind warred with my pussy:

Just let him put it in a little, we don't have to go all the way. If he puts it in even a millimeter . . . I'm gonna fuck him senseless. *Girl, YOU control your pussy. He can't get what you don't give him.* I don't think I can stop right now. *You know you want it, get it!* No! I'm not that easy! *Easy? He's your husband, get it!* I don't know him well enough yet! *Wear protection and get yourself off, girl! Just think of all that virile cock stroking and fucking deep in your pussy . . . how long has it been again?*

It had been that long. As in six months without anyone other than my fingers stroking my kitty; only my mirror-reflected eyes seeing my bush, only my sheets receiving the wetness of my juices. It had been *too* long. . . .

With a sigh of pent-up need, a sense of diving into the deep bottomless end of the ocean without a wetsuit or oxygen tank, a mental shifting of accepting the gifts presented, I plunged ahead and . . . shifted the panties to the side. Felt Dubois's cock touch the sea of honey releasing between my lips. Heard him gasp, saw his face contort, felt the tremble ripple throughout his body. Knew he could not resist the invitation.

And after a few long moments of holding himself in check, he succumbed to my temptation. His cock eased past the fabric inch by inch, feeling the lips with his head; absorbing my moisture, tasting my nectar—readying himself for his entry. I aided him, opened wide, bunched the panties, pulled them farther to the side. Watched as the red fat head learned, memorized my anatomy. Saw its head rise, preparing to find its way home in its depths. I lifted, let my pussy lead as it positioned me over the head; began the descent toward the cock head, felt the tickle of my—

The doorbell chimed loudly.

It startled me; put me off center. I ignored the chime song, found my cock target, locked my pussy over the cockhead and descend—

The doorbell chimed again.

I rationalized the doorbell away; told myself it was probably UPS or FedEx and they'd leave the delivery on the porch when I didn't respond. For the third time, my pussy eagerly sought its denied mark, was pulsating in the wake of delayed gratification, was—

The doorbell . . . chimed . . . for . . . a . . . *third* . . . damn . . . time.

Dubois groaned loudly, let his hands drop. "I think someone is determined to see you today."

My groaned echoed his. "Damn." My body was on fire for this man! I hoped that the doorbell wouldn't ring again, would let us return to this luxurious interlude, but it was not to be. The doorbell chimed yet again—a persistent double ring this time—as if the doorbell pusher just *knew* I was inside and wasn't going away until I came out.

I slid—slowly—across his thick thighs, letting my now released panties trail over him before rolling out of the bed. Throwing on a robe, I made my way down to the irritating individual whose finger was now making me cuss, extending my list of transgressions long enough that I was in dire danger of being turned away at the Pearly Gates for this one moment alone. I flung open the door, scowl on my face, non-niceties on my lips, and stopped.

On my porch stood Michael . . . as in used-to-date-please-don't-call-me-again-this-lifetime Michael.

Shit.

7

Have you ever made a mistake and were glad when you realized it was a mistake and happier than hell when the situation ran its course and you got away unscathed? That was my relationship with Michael. Good looking, but that's as far as the goodness went—eyesight level. Beneath the skin he was Mr. Conniving to the Bone . . . Marrow.

"Heeeyyyyy! I called your job and they told me you were on vacation." His braces-straight teeth gleamed in the sunlight, illuminating his angelic-appearing golden face and curly hair, reminding those not yet disillusioned about his true character of a halo. A bouquet of multicolored flowers was encased in his flesh-covered claws.

I pulled my robe closer before folding my arms across my chest. "I am."

"I see. You're looking like it's been a good vacation, too. Girl, you . . . are . . . *glowing*!"

And you have nothing to do with it, buddy. "Thank you. What can I do for you?"

He didn't even blink at my terse attitude, instead forged

ahead. "Well, girl, I haven't seen you in a minute and I've left messages but can't seem to get a callback, so I thought since I couldn't catch you at work, I'd take the day off and see if I could catch you at home." He moved a step closer, held out his arm. "Here. These beautiful flowers are for my beautiful girl."

Michael was well aware of my one cardinal rule of dating: No dropping by unannounced. No telling what one would find, and I wasn't into participating in drama. But I guess he'd gotten amnesia, just like he was apparently an amnesiac about us no longer seeing each other.

I held up my hands but avoided taking the flowers. "Michael, we don't date anymore, remember?"

He flipped his eyes heavenward and dropped his arm before replying, "Girl, I know what we said, but I figured that I'd give you a moment to get your mind together, come to your senses, and so . . . here I am."

Did he say get my *mind together and come to* my *senses?* Time to set the record straight. I took a really deep breath. "Michael, for the last time—I hope—I will not, am not, planning on seeing you again romantically in this lifetime."

His lips slowly closed over his smile. Not surprising since he was a person used to getting his way. "Why not?" Petulance.

"Look, Michael, *we* didn't work. I'm not your type"—*'cause I won't put up with your bullshit and cheap-assed ways*—"and you're not mine. Simple. So, have a great life and thanks for the flowers, but you keep them." I moved back and pulled the door closed.

A foot stopped it.

This was not good. The hand that shoved the door open wider was even worse. Michael pulled himself up to his full height, dropped the flowers to the stoop, and said loudly, "What! Woman, I've invested time, energy, and money into you and you acting like you too good to give me the damn time of day?" He shook his head. "You tripping."

I kept my voice neutral, hoping to defuse the situation quickly. "Time for you to go, Michael." I pushed at the door to close it. He pushed back.

"I'm not going nowhere, girl, until we get this shit straight." His eyes were hard, serious.

Just as I was going to reply, a voice from behind me said, "Is there a problem, honey?"

I sighed in relief. Dubois. I turned to him. Michael took this opportunity to fling the door wide and step inside. His eyes bounced around as he took in the sight of Dubois—in underwear only—standing just at the foot of the staircase.

"Who the hell is *this*?" Michael's eyes vacillated between us.

"I'm Dubois Harrington, Dina's husband. And you are?"

Déjà vu, just swap Michael's face for Stacy's. "Husband? Dina . . . you . . . Let me get this straight." He shook his head as if to clear it. "You got *married*? Since the last time we dated?"

"Yes," I deadpanned. It *was* true.

"Uh-huh. I don't believe you." Michael vigorously shook his head, denying everything I'd stated.

"Sir, we don't care whether you choose to believe it or not. You just need to leave as Dina asked you to numerous times."

"Dude, I don't know who your funny-talking ass is, but I need to get my conversation finished with Dina."

I felt the pecs in Dubois's chest bunch up. He pulled me to him and gave me a peck on the lips. "Dina, if you would leave me and your friend alone for a moment, I believe we can get this entire thing cleared up."

This was definitely new territory for me, but my heart said to trust that whatever Dubois did, it would be the right thing. "Okay." I hugged him before walking up the stairway. This must have incensed Michael even further. "Dina! Dina! We're not finished talking! Don't you walk—" Michael's last words were drowned out by the slamming of the front door. I looked back to see that Dubois was outside with Michael. I'm guessing it was him who slammed the door shut. Since Michael was outmatched by at least five inches and fifty pounds, I figured Dubois didn't need my help.

The shrill ringing of the phone pulled me toward it. I lifted it wondering, as Bette Davis said in an old movie, "What fresh hell awaits?"

"Hello?"

"Dr. Charles?"

I recognized the voice of my graduate student Terrell. A serious young man, he was well aware I insisted that I never be contacted when I was on vacation unless it was an emergency. I tensed, waiting for the bad news. "Yes. What's happened?"

"I know you hate to be called when you're on vacation, but we received a fax from the Orion Group for the Egypt dig. There's a problem."

The Orion Group was the funding agency that had committed nearly two hundred thousand dollars for an excavation in Egypt's newly opened minor pyramid, the Tegreis. "What's the problem?"

"They're stating that the downturn in the stock market has severely affected their holdings and they're scaling back and terminating funding for many projects already committed to."

Big problem. "Did they say which we were? Scaled back or terminated?"

"They're asking for us to resubmit a revised budget by tomorrow at three for continued consideration. If we don't, we're definitely terminated."

I glanced up at the clock. "I'll be there in an hour or so. If you would pull the file and start thinking about areas we can scale back—number of students, equipment needs, time of stay, those types of things—I'd appreciate it."

"Will do. I'll have it laid out on your desk when you get here."

"Good. See you soon."

I clicked off the phone and turned, deep in thought. I was surprised to see Dubois sitting on a bar stool, a slight smile on his face. I hadn't heard him come in.

"Michael's gone?" I asked, suddenly remembering the mini-drama playing out on my front porch.

"Yes. He wasn't happy, but he now understands that life is . . . different . . . now."

"You sure?" Michael could be quite pigheaded at times.

"Absolutely. He will not bother you again." He stated this with confidence. "Sounds like you have some work to complete."

I let out an agonizing breath. "Unfortunately, I do." I explained what Terrell had told me.

He walked up to me, pulled me into his arms. "And I so wanted to finish what we'd started."

I looked up at him. "Me too."

"But it sounds like this is very important, so we'll just have to shelve our . . . *explorations* . . . until later tonight." He licked his lips, making me want to say damn the Egypt trip, the Orion Group, and the university—but I couldn't. My work was very important to me.

"Looks like we have to."

"Well, why don't we get dressed? The sooner we attack the problem, the sooner we can find a solution."

"Agreed." Unexpectedly, Dubois scooped me up into his chest.

"What's this?"

"Oh, I just like holding you close to me, sweetheart."

Mmm. Mmm. Mmm. I started humming Salt 'n Pepa's "Whatta Man": *What a man, what a man, what a mighty* good *man!*

8

I gave Dubois a quick tour around the campus as we rode to my office. The archeological building was on the back side of campus, near the agricultural building and farms. Dubois remarked on how lush everything was. We finally reached my building. I hated to admit it, but I did have a measure of trepidation welled up inside me. After all, today was the day I'd run into my colleagues and be forced to introduce them to my new husband—that they'd never heard me even mention.

I know. Sounds shallow, but it wasn't that I was ashamed of Dubois. It was more realizing that I was stepping outside of the box they'd put Dr. Dina Charles in. A side none of them suspected that I had. I imagined their reactions—dropped mouths, confusion, and disbelief—and, of course, that's what happened.

Dubois helped me out of the car and held the door open as we entered the cool air of the building. The halls were deserted. Summer school classes were infrequent and usually held first thing in the morning, so students didn't just hang around unless they had a job.

Terrell was the first person we met. "Dr. Charles!" He gave

me a warm hug like I'd been away for a month instead of a few days.

"Hey, Terrell, get everything together?"

"It's on your desk," he replied, not looking at me but at Dubois.

I turned to make the introduction. "Dubois, this is my graduate student, Terrell. Terrell, this is my husband, Dubois."

"Hus—husband?" Terrell's eyes grew wide, a frown etched his forehead. "Ah . . . I didn't realize . . ." He must have realized that his reaction wasn't the correct one and he changed up his expression, forced a smile onto his lips. "Hey, congratulations!"

"Well, thank you." I didn't add any more information. I was sure I'd be explaining it over and over as the news spread like wildfire.

"It's good to meet you," Dubois said, holding out his hand.

"Hey, great to meet you also, sir." It must be the accent, because Terrell stood straighter and became more formal as he held out his hand for the shake.

"Okay, let's get down to business."

Dubois gathered my hands in his and pulled one to his lips, where he kissed it. "Dina, you would not mind greatly if I just roamed around the building, would you?"

"Of course not, honey. We have some wonderful exhibits here. The new dinosaur one will keep you busy for a while. And of course we have the tomb excavation artifacts on display also. Some of their treasures are remarkable."

"Sounds like it. I will let you and Master Terrell get to work, then. How long do you think you shall be?"

"An hour, give or take."

Dubois glanced at his wristwatch. "I will return within an hour." He leaned over to give me a peck on the lips before leaving.

Both Terrell and I watched as Dubois left, my eyes glued on

how his gluteus muscles bunched and released as he walked. Terrell . . . I suspected for the same reason. He'd never said anything, but if I were a betting woman, I'd bet my money on Terrell being gay and reluctant to come out. But it didn't matter to me. As long as he did our work, his sex life was just that—his.

True to his previous form, all the information was laid out on my desk. I reviewed the initial proposal and cut money from a line here and slashed some things over there. Within forty minutes, I'd outlined the new proposal budget for submission. We quickly saved, then printed out the new budget as requested.

"Grab a fax cover slip and let's get this baby to them," I told Terrell, happy to have salvaged the upcoming excavation—I hoped. Of course, it was all in the Orion Group's hands to determine yea or nay. But my fingers were crossed that the budget was streamlined yet would still allow us to reasonably complete a project enough to write a paper or two from it.

"I'm on it, Doc," Terrell said. He then asked what I knew he'd been bursting to ask. "Doc, so when did all this . . . the marriage happen?"

I smiled. "Well, it was a short courtship, but we'd planned the marriage. I just kept it to myself."

Terrell laughed. "You can say that again. Last time you talked about a man, it was that Michael dude, the lawyer in the next town over."

"Ooh! Don't even remind me." I knew Terrell would love to hear the dish on what happened that morning, but I never broke my rule of not sharing my outside life with students.

"Guess he'll be heartbroken when he finds out about this."

"Oh, he'll be just fine. Just fine."

Suddenly, we heard voices in the hallway. Then the door to my office opened. In stepped one of the staff members, Mary Manor, assistant to the department chair and all-around busybody. Sixty, husband dead and children gone, her life was the department. If there was information to be had, she was the one who had it.

"Dr. Charles? Sorry to barge in like this." *No, she isn't. I'm sure she hoped to find me and Terrell locked in an intimate embrace.* "But I found this gentleman roaming around the department, and he says he is your . . . *husband*?" Age had been kind. Like the saying goes, "Black don't crack." She looked way younger than her years.

I smiled widely. "Oh, so you've met Dubois. I'm sorry I didn't get a chance to introduce you properly first."

Her eyes were curious; her hands rose to her throat in disbelief. This was juicier than hearing the basketball coach had impregnated two cheerleaders. "Well, that was . . . fast."

"Not really. As you've constantly told me, I can be very close-mouthed about some things."

"You certainly were about this one." She continued to stare at me. "Where, exactly, is he from?"

"Dubois is from a small isle off the coast of England. Extania."

"Extania?" I could see the cogs churning and whirling in her head. "I don't recall ever hearing about that isle. I was a history major in college, you know."

"I remember." *You've only told us a million and one times before.* "Where is Dubois now?"

"Dr. Chambers is talking to him outside the office."

I groaned a bit. Our department chair could be a bit stuffy at times, but then again, Dubois, with his impeccable manners and lovely accent, was the type of individual he craved to be associated with—exotic but educated. He'd shit a brick if he ever found out Dubois was a Mail Order Husband . . . *and* he'd had husbandship training. I giggled to myself deep within.

"Thanks, Mary. I'll go see what my *husband* is up to."

"Ah . . . Dina, I would have loved to have attended the wedding. When was it?"

This chick just will not quit. "It was yesterday."

"And you're here? Not on your honeymoon? Hmm . . ."

"Actually . . . with a man like Dubois"—I leaned so close she could count the pores on my nose—"*every day* is a honeymoon. Feel me?" Her mouth dropped open like a guppy gasping for air. Good. Nosy heffa.

I moved past her and out into the hallway. The cadence of excited voices led the way. I found Dubois one hallway down, his side to me while he held a Mayan artifact found by one of our archeologists nearly two decades before. Dr. Chambers's hands were animated as he delineated the finer points of the vase Dubois held.

"They think this is at least seven thousand years old, and the condition . . . surprisingly pristine for the location it was found in—a crumbled temple twenty feet below the ground surface."

Dubois turned it in his hand, then caught sight of me walking down the hallway. He turned. "Ah, here comes my lovely wife."

Dr. Chambers let a frown crease his forehead before turning my way. "Yes, Dr. Charles, it's good to see you again. It seems that your vacation has been"—he looked at Dubois—"fruitful."

"Indeed it has been." I walked into Dubois's outstretched arms. He hugged me lightly.

"Uh-huh." I felt his eyes peering into my brain but I maintained his eye contact. That stare-down thing got old after the first year on faculty. It only worked with the new hires. "Well, we would have loved to have given you a party or one of those, what do you women call them? A bridal shower, if we'd known."

"Oh, that's quite all right. I like my private life to be separated from my university life anyway."

Dr. Chambers's lips turned down. "I can see that."

Dubois saw the tense interplay and said, "Honey, are you all finished?"

"I am. I'm ready to leave when you are."

"Oh now, don't rush off. I've got plenty to show you, young man." The way Dr. Chambers stared, if I didn't know better, I'd say he fallen in love on first sight. Then I giggled to myself. Anal-retentive Dr. Chambers as a member of the gay coalition would be a sad and pitiful thing—for them.

Dubois handed the vase back. "I am sorry, but we have much to do to get settled in. Another time, perhaps?"

Dr. Chambers didn't want this fertile mind . . . and man . . . to leave, but too bad. It was my turn. He finally sighed before saying, "I'll hold you to it, young man. Have a great rest of your vacation, Dr. Charles."

"I will."

We both turned and walked outside in silence. We remained quiet until we had settled inside the car. Then Dubois spoke. "Is it just me, or is your Dr. Chambers an odd duck?"

I guffawed. "Baby, *odd* is one of the better adjectives I've heard used for him. The others are significantly unflattering."

"I believe you." Dubois intertwined his fingers in mine between the seats. "So . . . we on the way back to the house?" I saw the hopeful look in his eyes, but ignored it. That old apprehension rearing its ugly head and stuff. Instead, I said, "Not yet. I thought we'd tour the campus, then visit a place I think you'll enjoy."

He squeezed my hand in his. "Baby, I can't think of any place I would enjoy better than *my* favorite room of the house." He blew me a kiss, eyes hooded and making promises I sure hoped he kept.

My ovaries must have dumped a truckload of estrogen into my bloodstream because I was suddenly warm all over. *This man is* so *tempting! Damn! Look at his lips, his silky tongue . . .*

D-A-M-N! I took a few deep breaths before I could respond. "Just go with me . . . and then I'll let you take me *there*."

Dubois made a face, then said, "Spoilsport. I had some . . . things . . . I wanted to do to you, too."

My head almost popped, I was so horny. But I had to slow things down, keep things at *my* pace. "And I plan to let you do every . . . one . . . of . . . them."

He slid down lower on the seat, his free hand involuntarily rubbing over his cock. I understood. I wanted to rub my clit myself—but I resisted. Not having anything else I thought I could say, I put the car in drive.

9

I didn't half remember what I said as we drove through campus. My mind was definitely on Dubois—his lips, hands, and *especially* his cock. He didn't give me any strange looks like I'd let on or had spoken my thoughts aloud, so I guess I am as good at multitasking as I always tell folks I am.

At the back end of campus, we came upon the annual county fair. Dubois's eyes lit up. "A carnival! Can we stop?"

"Sure." I hadn't been to a fair since I left high school, but if he wanted to stop, what could it hurt?

The smells of the fair brought back memories, some fond, some not so good. The stand with Italian sausage with onions beckoned me and I quickly grabbed one along with a bag of cotton candy. Dubois laughed as the juice squirted out from my first bite.

"You really like those sausages, eh?"

I just nodded since my mouth was full. Dubois pulled me along and we strolled down the midway. His hand rested lightly in the dip in my lower back. It felt . . . right.

The midway was lined with games of chance. Carnies hawked

and enticed loudly for passersby to try to win one of the many prizes for their lady. I normally ignored them, but at the bottle toss, Dubois could no longer resist. We stopped.

"Dubois, you know this stuff is rigged, right?"

"Of course. But," he rolled up his sleeve, showing his bulging forearms, and leaned closer to my face, "I like a good challenge. Always." He sealed it with a kiss.

Did somebody just suck all the air out of the carnival?

"Oh, we have a contestant!" the ruddy-faced, grungy man proudly proclaimed to those passing by. Of course some stopped. "Step right up and knock down the rows of bottles and win a prize. One set, pick from the first shelf. Two sets, pick from the top shelf. All three, choose one of our huge stuffed animals!"

Dubois nodded, then glanced at me. "Which animal do you want?"

I thought he was being overly optimistic because like I said, these things are rigged. I imagined I'd probably leave with one of the small dogs at best, but since he asked, I told him the zebra.

"Zebra it is." Dubois took the first ball, bounced it in his hand, then looked up at the carnie. "Do I get a practice throw?"

"Why, sure! One practice throw. After that, they all count!" The carnie smiled a smile that showed chipped and rotten teeth. Why? I don't know. With a mouth like that, I'd keep my hand up in front of it.

Dubois bounced the ball again, then pulled his arm back and threw. I groaned quietly. He only managed to get three out of the six bottles in the pyramid to fall. Not a good sign.

The carnie must have thought it was a good sign for him because he quickly placed three balls in front of Dubois. "Not bad. Now keep that up and your lady can get something off the bottom shelf!"

Dubois pulled me closer. "I need a kiss for good luck." I

leaned in, planning for a peck, but he had other ideas. His tongue snaked in my mouth, hijacking my tongue and twirling it into submission. My hands crept up to curl around the back of his neck and pull him closer. Just as I felt my leg lifting from the ground, intent on wrapping it around Dubois's thigh, the carnie cleared his throat.

"There are children here, folks."

The redness crept up my neck and spread to my cheeks. A peek past Dubois showed we had indeed garnered an audience, including a kid who had dropped the top scoop of his ice cream cone as he stood with his mouth gaped open watching us. *Definitely the wrong place and time.*

Dubois seemed unfazed; in fact, a smile was perched on his lips. He lifted a ball, gave me a wink, and let it fly! The ball hit low on the pyramid and all the bottles tumbled over. Without a break, he threw the next two balls. The other pyramids collapsed just like the first. Hot damn! A smile broke out on my face and I clapped my hands in glee. The carnie looked like he'd just sucked on a lemon.

"The lady would like the zebra, please."

The carnie handed it over reluctantly. Dubois then passed it to me, and I hugged it to my chest like I was an excitable high school girl on her first date with a boy. Hell! I was on a first date with my husband, so I was entitled.

"I like to see you smiling like that at me." He ran a finger down the side of my face. If that zebra had been gunpowder, we would have exploded.

"Thank you. What else would you like to do?"

Dubois broke eye contact and looked at the rides. I groaned when his eyes landed on the Ferris wheel, my nemesis. "I have never ridden on the big wheel, but I always wanted to."

"They didn't have fairs in Extania?"

"No. Too small and besides," he looked away, "our . . . resources . . . were limited."

That sealed the deal for me. "Well, time to make up for what you've missed so far!" I said brightly and took his hand. "Let's go!" I tugged his arm, pulling him along beside me this time.

Dubois paid for the tickets, and in seconds, a slightly cleaner carnie was leading us into our car. The zebra was tucked between us like a child. My palms were sweating as I held on to the safety bar; my stomach fluttered since I'd failed to mention one important point: I really didn't like heights.

Dubois was chatty and I was good until the car stopped at the very top and began rocking. My stomach roiled then. I clutched the bar and the zebra and felt the sweat popping out on my forehead. All I wanted was to be on the ground.

Dubois recognized something was wrong. "You are afraid?"

"Very," I said between teeth clenched out of fear and to stop the vomit rapidly crawling up my throat.

He nodded and shifted over, squeezing me and the zebra tighter. "I will let them know we wish to exit when they swing us down."

I could only nod and hope the carnies were feeling like playing the let-it-turn-until-somebody-pukes game because I was gonna win that one pretty fast. As we neared the bottom, Dubois yelled out, "Emergency! Stop!" Not my methods, but the wheel came to a screeching halt.

"What's wrong, dude?" the carnie yelled as he came closer.

"Release us," Dubois ordered calmly. "My wife is ill."

The carnie gave me a "you're acting like a girl" look but I didn't care. I just needed to get off! He unlocked our seat and walked back to the controls, making no offer to help us out. Dubois lifted me out gently and set me on the ground. My legs were shaky and I stumbled. Dubois picked me up and carried me down the steps and to the car, where he promptly placed me on the passenger's side.

"You can drive?" I'd never asked and just assumed he could not.

"Of course. I just lived on an isle, not in the jungle." He chuckled. "You *will* have to keep reminding me to stay on the right, though."

Dubois took his time backing the car out and getting on the road. I navigated as he drove and had to remind him he could not turn left on red only once. I was feeling better, but not much, as we neared the house.

A flash of a yellow car in the distance caught my eye. *Stacy?* It was traveling in the opposite direction, so we never got close enough for me to tell for sure. I pushed the thought out of my mind as Dubois pulled into the driveway. Stacy wasn't the only person in the world with a yellow car, and I did live on a public road free to any who wanted to travel it. I thought about calling her to see for sure, but I wasn't up to an argument at that moment.

Dubois continued being the gentleman he was—he helped me out of the car, lifted me up and carried me into the house, and laid me gently on the bed. I wish I could say I still had that loving feeling from earlier, but honestly, my mood was shot. I just wanted some Pepto-Bismol and a nap.

While Dubois retrieved the Pepto and some hot tea, I listened to my messages. The first was from my father.

Daughter, if what Stacy says is true, I am past *disappointed in you. I expected better from an offspring of mine. I expect you to bring you and your friend over to your mother's and my house as soon as you receive this message. Don't disappoint me further.*

A headache started forming in the back of my skull. *Beep.*

Honey, ignore anything your dad might have said. You know how anal things get when he and Stacy get together. I'll see you and your husband on Saturday. Dress for dinner, sweetie. I'm so excited!

My sweet mother. How she put up with my father all these years has been a mystery. *Beep.*

Dr. Charles, this is Nancy Termis at University Relations. I just received an e-mail from your department announcing your recent marriage. I'd like to get further details and your permission before we print anything. If you would, please give me a call at 501-555-8787. Thanks. I'll wait to hear from you.

The headache became a skull tsunami. I knew Mary couldn't resist inserting her nosy butt into my business, but this took the cake. I'd give Nancy a call to let her know in very certain terms I didn't want my marriage announced to anyone unless I did it myself, thank you very much!

My head was pounding by the time Dubois returned with the Pepto. "You look worse."

"I feel even worser." Goodness, did I just use more slang? "I have messages from my mom and dad and a chick from University Relations wanting to announce our wedding." I reached for the Pepto and the tea he held out.

"You work fast."

I shook my head. "It wasn't me, it was the department secretary, with her nosy self." I grimaced as I swallowed the Pepto and the tea.

Dubois laughed. "There is one in every town. My grandmother was ours. If there was something to be told, she knew and was telling anyone and everyone who would listen."

"My grandmother was the same way! We couldn't do anything in the surrounding three counties without her knowing it by the next morning. One night, I spent the night at a hotel one town over. My grandmother called the house the next day talking about 'If I hear of your hot ass being up at that hotel again, I'm gonna drive up there and pull you out by your hair . . . with your hot ass.' She was a trip."

"Sounds like she was. Will I get to meet her Saturday?"

"Probably. Granny loves a good barbecue."

Dubois brightened. "I am glad to hear that." He lay down beside me on the bed. I scooted over to make room.

"Don't be too hasty. She's kept up plenty of hell and had the men—and their women—going with her antics. If I was hot, I got it from her."

"I sure hope so."

I turned to look at him. "You hope so about what?"

"That you are as hot as your grandmother." I laughed as I shook my head. "Really, I do. But despite hoping we could continue our morning session . . . we'll save that for another day." His hand began rubbing my scalp. "Want a massage to relax you and help you sleep?"

"That sounds like a great idea."

I remembered little else as I fell asleep beneath the strokes and glides of his very capable hands.

10

The good food smells woke me. I picked out the scents of bacon and coffee, but I couldn't quite associate the slightly cinnamon/orange smell with any of my typical breakfast fare. I stretched languidly, glad the monster headache was gone. After a quick brush through my hair and a trip to the bathroom, I ambled downstairs to find the source of the delicious smell.

Dubois was bent over, pulling a tray out of the oven when I entered the kitchen. "Hey you."

"Hello you back." I walked closer and we kissed lightly. "You look dashing this morn. Feeling better, eh?"

"Much." I looked down at the tray he'd placed on the stovetop. The smell was definitely coming from the buns on the tray. "Honey buns?"

He looked surprised. "Why yes. We call them honey bite buns. You have had them before?"

"Who hasn't? They sell them in every store down here." I picked up a hot bun, pleased that it easily came apart under my fingers, and took a small bite. The tangy sweet flavor had my taste buds singing—until that tangy sweetness suddenly morphed into *fire*! I fanned at my mouth, tried to grab a glass and turn on the faucet at the same time, fumbled and dropped the glass, and finally just put my lips under the faucet and scooped cool water into my burning mouth.

Dubois was bent over laughing. I didn't see anything funny, though. "What the hell did you put on those buns?"

"Cayenne pepper. I told you they were honey *bite* buns. Here," he pushed a glass of red juice toward me, "this is what we drink with them. It takes the sting out of your mouth."

I smelled the liquid. "Tomato juice?" He nodded and I took a sip. I have to admit, after the first sip, the burning lessened considerably. After the third, it was gone completely.

"Better?" Dubois stopped in front of me, hands moving up to rest on either side of my waist.

"Considerably."

He grabbed another bun, broke off a small portion, and held it to my lips. "Let me show you *my* way to eat one." I nodded in assent. "First, you slowly lick a small bit of icing off the top," I did so, noting that my tongue began heating up almost immediately, "then you spread that icing all through your mouth while I take a big swallow of the tomato juice." He did so and pulled me to him. His mouth quickly covered mine. My tongue slipped inside his mouth, felt the healing coolness of the tomato juice as it transferred between us before finally pulling back.

I tore off a piece of bun, held it up to his mouth. He opened wide as I pushed it inside. I sipped from the tomato juice before pulling him to me and covering his mouth. His tongue stabbed inside me, plundered me as his mouth organ scanned and memorized the valley, the ridges of my mouth. He bit my lips, sucked them inside to feel the lingering heat. I twirled and stabbed, intertwined and released, sucked him slow, then faster.

The strap of my nightgown was slid past my biceps, exposing a breast. Dubois pulled it away, smeared icing on his finger, met my eyes before rubbing the sticky concoction onto my nipple. The burning sensation was immediate and so intense I gasped. Dubois halted my hand as he placed his tomato juice–filled mouth over the stinging button. When his cold mouth met my sensitized berry, I moaned. His lips tugged and pulled, sucking me deep. His fingers cupped me, held me in place as his teeth nipped and tongue flicked over my point. My hands rubbed over his head, wanting him to never leave, never cease this feeling.

The other strap was lowered and Dubois pinched and stroked that nipple. I smeared sticky icing over my berry, wanting to feel the sensation in it also. Dubois didn't drink from the tomato juice; instead he pulled the sugary tit into his hot mouth. The heat radiated outward from my nipple, across my chest, upward and downward, waking up my cells. I pushed my breast farther into his mouth, wanting him to add pleasure to this pain. When he bit the tip, my pussy began to pulsate. I grabbed his ears and smashed his face into my tit.

The gown was tugged down over my stomach and past my hips to pool on the floor. Dubois lifted me onto the countertop, held my orbs, pushed them together, and sucked in earnest. I pushed my tits higher, wanting him to take more into his mouth. My pelvis began lifting, beckoning.

He pushed me onto my elbows, lifted a leg onto the counter, spread me wide. He grinned as he reached for the knife lying next to the tray. With two flicks of his wrist, my panties fell away. He then rolled his finger around in the honey bite icing before holding it up in front of my pube.

"Ready for this?"

I breathed heavily before nodding. His fingers were gentle as they parted my bush and exposed my clit. Dubois licked his lips before placing the icing on my clit. My body tensed, lurched as my clit caught on fire. I gasped and fanned at the pleasure pain, bucked my hips on the counter as the heat infused my pussy, made it leak more.

His lips covered my nub, his tongue my salvation and my hell. I gurgled my pleasure; my pussy pumped love juice onto his chin as he stroked and sucked my clit. A finger was inserted inside my pussy—not enough to satisfy but definitely enough to make me hotter. It moved slowly in and out, twisting and stroking, making me want more, need more.

Dubois stopped his clit assault, lifted his head. His eyes were dark, sensuous. "I want you now." A statement of need.

I responded by placing my other leg up on the counter, spreading even wider, my entire pussy on display now. A muscle jumped in Dubois's jaw as he surveyed my pussy peep show. Then he pulled the strings on his pajama pants and they dropped to the floor. His dark cock resembled a cylinder of onyx . . . and I hoped it was just as hard.

He captured both thighs, pulled me to the edge, threw my legs over his arms. And when his cock kissed my clit . . . I growled deep in my throat. We both watched as he rotated his cockhead over and over my pulsing tissue, making me gush, making me bite my lips in need. *Damn, this shit is erotic.* . . . He made his cock jump, pop the clit over and over until my clit stood at full attention.

His cock slid back and forth between my slick pussy lips, teasing the entryway but not entering. We both breathed like mutts in heat, watching the cock interplay, wanting and needing release. It finally came. . . .

Dubois pushed into me slowly, a millimeter at a time. I wanted to surge forward, slam him into me, but he'd read my mind and held my hips firm. The head was inserted inside my groping pussy, then pulled out—I grunted in pleasure/displeasure—before being pushed back inside. He took his time filling me slowly, retreating, entering, retreating . . . blowing my mind.

My hips struggled against his hand constraints, wanted to undulate, swirl . . . *feel all of him, dammit*! He held them still, wanting to run the show like he wanted to. *Not if I can help it . . .*

My legs wrapped around his neck, crossed at the ankles. I lifted my hips, surprising him as he surged deeper than he'd planned. I forced my hips down on his, deep as I could go. Dubois's head was strained back, face clenched, trying to regain control. *Give it up, baby. These thunder thighs ain't no joke.* I didn't relent or give an inch. I pumped, ground, and swirled in a frenzy. I hadn't had cock in forever and I was past needing release.

Dubois finally realized he could hold out no more. He locked eyes with me . . . and put his back into it. He bounced me into the air as he pistoned deep in my pussy. My pussy groped, Kegeled, and released honey all over his marbleized cock. I wanted to feel every damn inch he possessed.

The sound of the slaps of his balls on my ass took me to the brink. I stuck a finger in icing, smeared it all over my nipples. I heated up another ten degrees. I lifted higher, squeezed my thighs harder, and slammed my pussy as I felt the pinpricks begin in my feet, moving up my calves, my thighs, and screamed as they jackhammered into my clit. My pussy clenched, locked down on Dubois. His strokes stuttered . . . stopped . . . then he groaned—roared—as he pistoned like hell and I felt the molten lava spew up and into me.

11

"My mother is a sweetheart, but my dad is . . . different." I felt I needed to give Dubois some insight on my folks before we arrived for dinner.

"That is a very interesting statement about your parents."

"I know it is, but it's true. However, together, they do equal out and become a very convincing unit for the institution of marriage."

Dubois nodded, then said, "How do you really believe your father will act toward us tonight?"

I'd given this plenty of thought. Part of me—the little girl side—wanted to "play right"; give in to my father's pressures and act like he'd want me to act 24/7. The other part—the today's independent woman part—wanted to flat-out cuss him and tell *him* to grow up and see that I am grown also. So instead, I was at war with myself, and I hate being in that state. All I do is quiver in one spot, never moving forward.

"I imagine he'll bluster about, making veiled threats, and be aloof with you."

"Wow. You really are surprising them, aren't you?"

"Yes. This is probably the single biggest surprise I've ever given them."

Dubois nodded. "What about your sister? Do you think she is still miffed?"

"Yes indeed." I nodded vigorously. "Stacy doesn't like not getting her way, and her way would have been to stay around and try to seduce you."

Dubois frowned. "Your sister would try to seduce me?"

"Standard operating procedure for my sister." *Very standard.*

He shook his head. "That would be frowned upon very badly on my isle."

"It's frowned upon here, but that hasn't stopped Stacy yet."

He was silent a moment. "She's done this before?"

"Many times."

He stroked my hand in my lap. "Not ever again, okay?"

"Okay." *Looks like he might be a keeper, folks!*

There were cars lined up and down the street from my parents' home. I didn't know if the neighbors were having a cookout or what, but we had to park a block up and walk back. I spoke to my old neighbors as we strolled the sidewalk. We could hear music and people talking and laughing as I reached our walkway. *How many people did they invite for dinner?*

I rang the doorbell, and it was answered by my mother. She was dressed to the nines in a stunning pantsuit, diamonds flowing from her ears, neck, and wrists. "Hey, baby!" She pulled me into a heavily perfumed embrace before reaching for Dubois. "And you must be my new son!"

"Yes, ma'am, I am." She hugged him to her. Dubois grinned and gave her a hearty hug back.

"Y'all come on inside. Everyone is in the back waiting for you."

I hesitated. "How many people did you invite for dinner, Mom?"

She waved me away as she walked off. "Oh, just the usual—family and a few friends."

Dubois held on to my hand as we walked straight into hell in the backyard. I knew the folks would be asking all types of questions, and I'd hoped to have it out with my father in private. Not to be, though.

As soon as we walked into the backyard, my mother clapped her hands and had them shut off the music. "Everyone! The couple of the hour is here! Let me introduce to some and reintroduce to others my daughter Dina and her new husband, Dubois!"

There was plenty of clapping before they thronged all over us.

"Where'd you meet . . ."

"I love your accent . . ."

"I was shocked when I heard . . ."

"You're not from here, are you . . ."

"Damn, you're fine!"

I answered as succinctly as I could, really needing a drink to calm my rattled nerves from all the prying eyes looking my way. I definitely needed a drink when my father pushed through, grabbed me by the arm, and steered me inside the house. He closed the sliding glass door, locked it, and said, "Have a seat, young lady."

I seethed as I watched his high-handed manner.

"So, what do you think you are doing?"

I was tired of being the good daughter all the time. All my life I was the one having to conform, to toe the line, to be good. Well, no more. I straightened my spine and looked him dead in the eyes. "I'm living my life like I want to, Father."

"This? You think meeting some stud and marrying him—and let us not forget you didn't even *invite* your mother and me to the wedding, we had to hear about it secondhand—was a good choice?"

Once again, his tirade was about *his* feelings, *his* image, *his* wants. "Yes, I do. Dubois and I have hit it off quite nicely."

His face scrunched up. "Girl, that's just the sex talking. Good sex can cover up a multitude of sins . . . but what about next year, and the year after, and the year after? Who is he? What is his family like? Have you even met his folks?"

"Dad, I know all I need to know about Dubois, and the same for him. What's important to me is that he and I create a life *we* can live with . . . not anyone else."

My father grimaced. "Oh, it's okay for your mother and I to be laughingstocks, having folks saying you're so desperate that you married the first man asking you?"

My blood began to boil. "Father, for your information, I've had offers of marriage before. *I* chose not to take them for whatever reason. *I* chose to marry Dubois for a good reason—we were a great match."

"Match? This some Internet dating stuff?" His eyes were wide as saucers. "Please don't tell me you've had to resort to the Internet to get married."

I heard shoes tapping on the floor and we both looked up as Stacy entered the room. Of course, she was dressed like she had a strip show to perform later that night, but I guess that was fine because he said nothing about it. "Not only did she resort to the Internet, get this . . . she *paid* for him, too."

I was stunned into immobility. How the hell did Stacy know that? She looked at my surprised face and laughed. "Oh girl, I know everything—about the service, Extania, that he's a mail order groom." She gave a snort. "So hard up you had to buy you a husband." Her eyes narrowed. "Pitiful."

My father turned to me, face dark and furious. "Is . . . this . . . true? This can*not* be true. Please tell me she's lying, Dina."

I said nothing, just shot daggers, spears, and hand grenades at Stacy with my eyes as all of the puzzle pieces aligned themselves: It *was* her yellow car I saw the other day apparently leaving my house; Stacy had entered with her key and snooped through my personal stuff; and she'd probably encouraged my mother to invite all these other people to embarrass me and Dubois.

"Oh, I'm not lying, I've got proof," she continued, so sure of herself.

"Really? What did you do? Snoop through my stuff? That's so childish, Stacy!"

Stacy rolled her eyes. "Girl, when you get a man looking like that—all of a sudden—and nobody has heard a peep about him? Oh, it's time for me to find out. Hell, he might be a gigolo, using you and he's really after Daddy's money."

"You've got to be shitting—"

"You watch your mouth, young lady!" my father roared.

I closed the distance, got up in Stacy's face. "You lowdown, conniving, weasel of a sister. You just cannot accept the fact that I might, just *might* be happy, can you?"

She flipped her hair over her shoulder. "This has nothing to do with you and your happiness. This is about the good of the family."

Ah . . . the family trump card. The one thing that would always make my father side with her: keeping the good of the family. Dating my boyfriends . . . she was just showing us they really weren't any good for the family, and the list goes on and on. Stacy and Daddy versus me and Mama.

A tapping on the door got our attention. It was Dubois. My father reluctantly opened it a crack. "Yes?"

"I would like to see my wife."

My father didn't move, instead said, "We're having a family discussion right now. She'll be out in a bit," and closed the door.

"Open that door, Daddy." My face showed how furious I was.

"We're not finished talking. He can wait. This is family business."

"Here is a news update for you: He *is* family now." I moved around him and unlocked the door. Dubois read my face and pulled me close. "Things going all right?" he whispered in my ear.

I shook my head. "But it's time we all got on the same page," I said aloud. I then kissed him. My father cleared his throat. I finished the kiss—complete with tongue action for good damn measure—and turned to my father and Stacy. "Here is the man under discussion. Ask away."

Stacy was the first to respond. "So, what's it like being a mail order groom?" She laughed as she finished.

Dubois pulled himself up to his full height. "It is a most honorable thing indeed to be totally and completely prepared to love a woman such as Dina. She has much to offer and I am glad that my husbandship training has allowed me the opportunity to meet and marry a woman of her caliber. I am honored that she chose me to share her life with." He met my father's and Stacy's eyes. "Many people snort and laugh, thinking that these types of relationships mean one is desperate. Look at us," He waved his arms between us. "We are beautiful people. We have no need to be desperate . . . in any country. We just found a faster means," he took my hands in his, stared into my eyes, "to join our lives together and . . . create a *dynasty* together."

I felt the heat rising up my neck.

"Pretty speech, but, son, who are you? Who are your people?"

Dubois straightened. "I am Dubois Harrington, third son of Luckett and Maeve Harrington of Extania. My father is a carpenter, as I am also by trade. My mother is a housewife—by choice—who retired from teaching schoolchildren nearly one score years ago." I loved how his accent became more pronounced as he made his point. "Although I am a carpenter by trade, I also have a bachelor's degree in mathematics. I have four siblings, two brothers and two sisters, all living throughout the world. Is that sufficient?"

"Not really, but I guess it will have to do." My father refused to quit. "Do you have financial means? How will you support Dina? How do we know you aren't here just acting as a gigolo to bleed her—and us—dry?"

"Stop!" I'd had enough. This was ridiculous! None of them had to live a day with Dubois if they didn't want to. He was *my* husband and this was *our* life. "That is quite enough. Father, Stacy, this is my husband." I burned them with my stare. "Now . . . deal with it." With that, I took Dubois's hand and led him outside and straight over to where they were serving drinks. My grandmother, Louvenia, was already seated at the bar, two older gentlemen hovering close by. I recognized them as *very* married younger—well, in their sixties to Granny's seventies type of young—neighbors, but apparently that didn't matter to them. And they seemed to be arguing. Probably about her. Guess their wives had to stay home . . . or something.

"Well, well, well. It's so good of y'all to take time out from rutting"—she snickered this, her deep red lips quirked over her dentures—"to come to the barbecue." She burped, then patted dyed auburn hair that matched her lips.

I hugged her anyway. "Hey, Granny. Wish I could say I'm surprised to see you sitting over here . . . but I'm not."

"Aw, baby. You know I gots to have my toddy every day or I don't feel right." Johnnie Walker Black with a splash of tonic water and a slice of lime was her normal toddy of choice. She nodded, then looked past me. "Lawdy, Lawdy, Lawdy, I *wish* I was forty again!"

"Quit!" I swatted at her and pulled Dubois closer. "I know you've heard, so let me introduce you to Dubois, my new husband."

"Mmm, mmm, mmm, *mmm* good damned day!" She pushed

me aside and held out her arms. "Come on and give your new grandmother a hug." Dubois smiled and dutifully came into her arms. I had to smile a bit as I watched her veined hands press into his back, then rub slowly up and down—and down to his hips—then press again. I cleared my throat. She had the nerve to look past his arm and say, "Yes?"

"Could you possibly not molest him in public?"

She released him . . . reluctantly. "Girl, I was just welcoming him into the family." Her face turned serious. "I saw your daddy pull you away before you got here good, so go ahead and order a drink before you tell me what stick-in-the-butt had to say." She cackled loud and long. "You sucker punched his dry ass."

"You think?" The bartender was in front of us now. "A cosmopolitan, please."

"And refill this, please," Grannie said sweetly before winking and licking her lips. I swear the bartender blushed two shades darker . . . but he also grinned.

"You still got them going, don't you. He's kind of young, though, don't you think?"

"Well, I'm still going, so I gots to get somebody able to keep up with me." My grandmother actually leaned back, grabbed her boobs, and shifted them around, then straightened her skirt. "What?" she asked, looking at me standing there with my mouth open. "I needed to shift my underwire. You know I got a rack, and the girls don't like to be stuck."

"All . . . righty . . . then."

Dubois tried to cover his smile and looked at the bartender. "Do you have Glenfiddich?" I heard Dubois ask. The bartender nodded. "Great. I'd like a shot also."

My grandmother pulled me close to her and whispered, "Babygirl, now tell your granny . . . I see he got big feet, so is his—"

"Lou, baby! That's our song!" An arm mercifully tugged at

her arm, cutting her off. I looked up to see one of the gentlemen standing real close, an urgent smile on his face.

"Festus, I know you see me talking. I swear I'd cuss your ass out—if this wasn't our song." She turned to me. "Hold that thought. I got to cut this rug." She grabbed hold of a happy Festus's hand and he escorted her over to the dance area.

"Wonder if we'll still be acting like that when we get to be her age?" Dubois asked as he watched them wiggle and cha-cha away.

I looked at him and shook my head. "You better hope I'm not still that feisty three decades from now or you're gonna be walking around like a broke-down mule."

"I tell you what. You give it a shot . . . and let me worry about keeping up." He moved to stand behind me, cock rubbing across my hips in time to the music. His arms moved around my waist and he rested his chin on my head. "Baby, you were a tigress in there." He blew on my hair. "Who knew you could get that hot and bothered?" His tongue licked my ear, making my nipples stand at attention. "I got something in mind for when we get home."

I felt a slow burn start in my groin. Mercifully, the drinks arrived at that moment. He held my eyes before holding up his drink. "A toast to us." I held up my drink next to his. "That our love is long, deep, and satisfying for us both."

"Hear! Hear!" We clinked our glasses and downed our drinks in one sitting. "Another round, please!" I yelled to the bartender. When the drinks arrived, I said, "I want to make another toast. That Stacy and my father get a damn life!"

"Aye! Aye!" We clinked and downed our second round.

I should have stopped after that second round because I was well aware of the main reason I didn't drink publicly: I became a truthful drunk. Oh, not nasty or mean, just real truthful. That didn't go well because most people just can't stand to hear the truth about themselves. But Dubois wasn't aware, and so he innocently ordered another round. "Hell, we can call a cab, right?" That was correct, so I imbibed the next round only slightly slower but with much gusto.

We were onto the fourth round, and the world was now a hilarious place to be, when Stacy foolishly decided to grace us with her presence again. "Don't you think you've had enough? You are making a spectacle of yourself," she hissed.

Dubois and I looked at each other and broke out in laughter.

"Go away, Stacy. I just want to enjoy the night with my man." I waved her away with my hand.

"I am not going away." She grabbed my arm. "Let me call a cab. You guys are way too tipsy to drive."

I snatched my arm back. "We . . . are . . . fine. Go . . . away . . . now!" I really wanted her to get the message.

She didn't. Instead, she slapped the drink I held to the ground and got in my face. "You are so damn pitiful. You can't do anything right. Can't hold your liquor," she glanced at Dubois, "and can't get a man like a normal woman does. You had to *buy* yours." She shouted this last part; people stopped their conversations to watch our drama.

That—fueled by the liquor—did it for me. I grabbed her arm this time. "Look here, heffa. You may fool others, but I know you for who you really are." Since she decided to go there, I reached *way* down, like as in Bridezilla-acting-a-fool-on-one-of-those-keeping-up-shit-shows down. "You are just a jealous, mean-spirited girl who *obviously* likes the men I choose *and* is mad as hell since he didn't want you." The liquor was making me feel *real* good at this point. "Yeah, while you trying to tell all my business, let's tell yours. Hmm . . . how about telling the good folks how you spent so much time screwing my leftovers."

"Why, you—"

"What? Truthteller? It's true. If he wanted me, that made you want him all the more. Hell, I might have gotten married through *alternative* channels, so to speak, but know this one thing: He was worth every . . . damn . . . penny I spent." I turned to Dubois. "Come on, baby. Let's go find a cab. This party is done for me."

"I agree tot—tally." Dubois hiccupped, then smiled.

Without another look at Stacy or the gawkers, we intertwined our arms and stumbled across the backyard toward the street. My mother saw us leaving and stopped us briefly. "Gone so soon?"

"Yeah, Mama. We're still on our honeymoon." I let my hand roam up and down Dubois's back and over his hips.

My mother saw. Her eyes gleamed. "Well, I guess I understand . . ."

I kissed her on the cheek. "It was a great gesture. And have no fear, we'll be back often."

Dubois then captured my mother's hands, bringing one to his lips to kiss. "It was indeed a wonderful gathering. I look forward to seeing more of you."

It was just the right touch. My mother showed every one of her pearly whites and patted us on the arms before walking us to the sidewalk. "Don't be strangers, now!" she called after us as we walked away.

"Ah . . . honey, we didn't call that cab," Dubois reminded me as we neared the car.

I slowed my walk. "No problem." I whipped out the cell phone, got the number from the operator, and a cab arrived within a few minutes.

We snuggled on the ride home, Dubois blowing in my hair, lightly licking my earlobe. I was still fuming but I have to admit, that blowing and sucking redirected my heat to other areas. My breasts lifted, my nipples ripened as his tongue nibbled. The nosy cabdriver kept glancing back, I guess hoping we'd give him a show. I can't say that I didn't want to, but I wasn't that uninhibited . . . yet.

Dubois kept up the tantalizing tease—hands brushing across my sensitive breasts, over my thighs, teeth tugging my hair. I was on fire by the time we pulled into the driveway, the whole incident with Stacy the fuel.

Dubois paid the driver, then scooped me into his arms. I fumbled with the lock but finally got the door opened. He slid me to the floor before pushing me back into the door. Hot lips slammed over mine, biting, licking, sucking. My hands were all over him, rubbing, squeezing, tugging.

"Baby, we have on entirely too many clothes," Dubois stated before pulling my dress up and over my head. It was a strappy number that only needed bikini panties beneath it. "Mmm . . . much better." I cupped my breasts, displaying the distended areolas for him. He licked his lips before he nibbled on my chin, then moved down, nuzzling my neck. I loved how his bristles scratched at my flesh! My nipples wanted to scream as his lips tugged at them, pulled them taut. The liquor swirled around my brain, making me revel beneath his touch. But I needed a bit more . . .

I pulled his head up. "Bite," I urged.

He sucked in his breath. "My God, woman." His teeth nipped lightly at first, then applied more pressure. My clit lurched, jumped for joy; my pussy clenched, pushing juice out and downward to my now throbbing and tingling lips.

"Mmm . . . that's good, baby. Real good. Don't stop."

He pressed me farther into the wall, fingers sliding beneath the thin fabric of my panties. I spread, let my clit find his searching fingers. The fingers slipped beside . . . then down and across my pulsing nub. I sighed, let my head loll back in beneath his slow torture.

His breath was hot as it moved down over my stomach, his

tongue swirled in my navel. My muscles twitched, pelvis lifted, sought his searing mouth. Wanted release. Dubois tugged at my bush hairs; a frisson of electricity flitted up my spine. Made me cream even more.

His fingers diddled me, teased and stroked around, then on, around, then on my clit; used my moisture to ease his finger deeper into my sex. He pulled his fingers out, slowly slid them into his mouth. I moaned as he sucked my juice from his fingers. I wanted them back in me.

He stood, pulled me toward the living room. At the couch, he leaned me over the arm. I waited, not sure what was next. He slowly massaged my lower back, up my sides and to the front, fondling my breasts. The liquor and pheromones mixed; my hips began rocking, rubbing against the hard bulge seated against my hips.

My panties were suddenly yanked down. Dubois spread my cheeks and let those whiskers scratch across my rarely touched butt. His tongue followed, sucking my hips, tracing a hot pattern at the top of my cleft, and letting it trail lower . . . and lower still. My fingers clutched the arm of the couch, my knees buckled a bit as his tongue glided over my chocolate hole. My rocking became obscene rolling as he licked . . . pushed his tongue inside. I mewled, slapping the couch in ecstasy as his finger entered my pussy and began a staccato pistoning inside my slick walls.

I lifted, tried to turn. Dubois refused, held me still under his double hole *luxurious* assault. His tongue increased the pace. Damn! This was some good shit! I capitulated and grabbed my cheeks, held them open wider. Dubois slid in tighter, melding his mouth to my hole. My thighs quaked; my muscles felt like butter as his tongue snaked inside me over and over again.

I wanted more than fingers in me. "Baby . . . I need you in me now."

Dubois lifted from my hips, letting his whiskers scratch over my cheeks, up my back. "You sure you're ready?" His teeth pulled at my lobe; his tongue flicked inside my canal, making goose bumps rise on my skin.

"Mmm . . ." was all I could eke out.

His cock rubbed back and forth between my leaking lips, kissing my clit, then sliding back to my anus. I leaned over farther, needing to hit the spot, dammit! He teased me further, pushing his head into my sopping hole, pulling it back out.

I wanted to cry in frustration, scream my need to the heavens. Dubois kept torturing me; punishing me deliciously. Finally, he pushed inside and . . . stayed. My hips pushed back, wanting to feel all of him at once. He slid half of his cock inside; I felt it pulse, grow. Then he pulled it all the way out. In . . . then out.

The teasing finally got the best of him. He grabbed a thigh in each hand and *surged* into my heat. My back arched, hips lifted, wanting him to touch my deepest recesses. He did.

His cock kissed my womb, made it kiss him back, tongue him, suck him deeper still. He groaned in my hair before giving in, pumping with the gusto I craved. I loved the sound of *slap! slap! slap!* as the front of his thighs contacted with the back of mine.

Dubois bit my shoulder. I growled through clenched teeth as the sensations zigzagged up my calves, over my thighs, and shot to my clit. I howled as my pussy sprayed its release. Dubois's pumping increased, breath sounding like a mad bull before he spread my cheeks, surged deep, and tensed as his cock pulsed and pulsed and pulsed his cum into my cavern of love. . . .

We slumped to the floor in an alcohol/sex stupor.

12

The following weeks zipped by. Dubois settled easily into his new job and I fielded questions from all directions concerning my marriage. They were divided into two very distinct groups: Those clucking their tongues, and those wanting more information.

I ignored the sad looks sent my way from the folks thinking that "buying a man" was pathetic indeed. If they'd been getting the sex I'd been getting, they just might rethink that thought. Those on the other end of the spectrum kept me so busy answering questions, I considered doing a blog on alternative marriages.

We'd had dinner with my parents on two more occasions. Surprisingly, my father and Dubois seemed to have reached a truce. I wouldn't admit it to my father, but I was glad. I guess deep down, I still wanted his approval.

I pushed all thoughts aside as I stopped in front of the Leather and Lace Emporium. Tonight was day thirty—Do or Die Day. After tonight, there was no turning back, no annulment, no refund. I cut the car off and sat there.

I have to admit, we'd both been a bit antsy as the day moved closer. Nothing real obvious, but we both seemed to have a level of insecurity, unsureness in the air. I could see it in his eyes as I caught him staring at me; I saw it in myself as I hesitated to initiate sex that I craved—even when it was obvious he was more than willing.

Honestly, I think all the negative energy had infiltrated my mind a bit; made me believe that I wasn't deserving of a man as great as Dubois. Maybe he *was* only staying around to "get his green card," as Stacy had nastily screamed on the answering machine. Try as I might, it was hard to get the ugly words out of my head.

Then I smiled as I thought about how happy Dubois had been when we'd found an old Toyota truck so he could drive back and forth to work. How we'd talked about the differences between our families—well, some differences. His family seemed just as close as mine, minus the domineering father figure. And then there was the sex. Every man needed to have the husbandship class. I'd never felt so loved, admired, worshipped by a man like Dubois acted toward me. The sweet words in so many languages, the deep massages, the awesome sex. I truly had made a great choice.

I shivered as I wondered whether the great times were coming to an end. Surely he'd have hinted at something if it was . . . wouldn't he? But then again, many times men shocked the women who loved them out of thin blue air, right?

I opened the door, trying my best to dismiss the nagging thoughts swirling in my head when my mind took over.

Girl, what the hell is wrong with you! Dubois is not *that type of guy. You know this!*

Right. I nodded, suddenly feeling surer than I'd felt in days. Dammit! I just might lose . . . but I wasn't going down without a fight. I grabbed my purse and stomped into Leather and Lace determined that if I lost my man, his last look at me would be one to remember.

The day dragged as I ran through all the things I needed to do for our Last or New Beginning Night. I kept glancing at the clock, half listening to Terrell banter on about this or that. At four-thirty, when I was just gathering up my things to leave, my cell phone rang. It was an unfamiliar number.

I took a deep sigh before answering. "Hello?"

"Hello, daughter." It was my father, and he sounded . . . strange. Whose number was he calling from?

"Hello, Father."

He sighed before continuing. "You need to come to the hospital."

My mother? Dubois? My heart started pounding. "What's happened?"

He waited a long, torturous moment before answering. "I'm at the hospital with your mother."

I clutched at my chest. "What's wrong?" *Please don't let it be anything bad*, I silently prayed.

"Just . . . just come to the hospital." He clicked off after that.

I threw my purse over my shoulder and said something I don't remember to Terrell before rushing out the door. I broke all the speeding laws and ran a few stop signs in my haste to get to the hospital. I swerved into the emergency room entrance and parked haphazardly, ignoring the security guard telling me I would be towed if I didn't move, and ran through the double doors.

"What room is Matilda Charles in?" I asked a harried-looking nurse who was talking on the phone.

She held up one hand and continued her discussion of insurance with whoever was on the other end. I fanned my hand in front of her face. She placed a hand over the receiver, a frown on her face, and said, "Yes?"

"I'm trying to find my mother, Matilda Charles. She just came in."

"Please hold . . . Yes, I know it's important, but this shouldn't take but a moment." She hit the Hold button, shifted to the computer screen, and clicked some buttons. "What was the name again?"

"Matilda Charles."

She leaned closer to the screen, pushed some more buttons, then looked up at me. "I'm sorry. I don't see a Matilda Charles listed as having come in in the past few hours."

"What? My father just called and said they were here. Please check again."

The nurse clicked a few more buttons, took her time scrolling the screen, and repeated again, "I'm sorry. No Matilda Charles has come in."

"Are you sure? Do you think you could have overlooked her?"

"No. Anyone that comes in that door, especially if someone is with her, would have been entered into our computer." She shook her head. "I'm sorry. I don't see your mother here."

What the hell is going on? I pulled out my cell phone and called my parents' house. Surprisingly, my father answered.

"Daddy! I'm at the hospital. What are you doing there?"

"Oh, I brought your mother on home. She's resting now."

My fears deflated, but I felt my anger rising. It hadn't been fifteen minutes since he'd called, and he'd managed to get her checked out and back home? "So she's at home resting?"

"Yes. You need to come on over."

I'd already walked out the doors to my car. "So what was wrong?" I asked as I snatched the parking ticket off the windshield.

"I'll tell you when you get here." With that cryptic sentence, he hung up.

I sat in the car and took some deep breaths. My father was

acting way too hinky for me. And what was wrong with Mama? I cranked up and pulled out like I had some sense, worried as hell at what I'd find when I arrived at my parents.

My father met me at the door. "Keep your voice down. She's sleeping." He sounded exhausted. I then noticed he had circles under his eyes, and he suddenly looked his sixty years. I nodded, wanting to find out what was wrong and to see my mother for myself. "Have a seat."

I sat and waited. Suddenly, I remembered Dubois. He'd be worried if I didn't arrive home soon. After all, we had plans. I rose.

"Where are you going?" my father asked, rising from his seat and walking in front of me.

I halted. "To the car. I need my phone to call Dubois. He'll be worried if I'm late."

I moved around him, wondering at his actions, my hand on the door when what he said next stopped me cold. "No, he won't."

I turned to look at him. "He won't?"

"No . . . he . . . won't." I swear a smirk was on his lips.

Suddenly, I had the feeling that I'd been hoodwinked. "Why won't he?"

He laughed loud, his head thrown back. "Because right now, Dubois should be boarding a ship back to Extania or wherever the hell he's from."

The blood congealed in my veins. "What have you done, Father?"

"What needed to be done." With that, he lifted a sheaf of papers from the foyer table. "Here."

I took the offered papers, wondering and hoping he'd not done anything foolish . . . but that was not to be. My breath stuttered in my chest as I read the NOTICE OF ANNULMENT AND RETRACTION OF CONTRACT and the check for seventeen thousand four hundred and twenty-three dollars. My deposit minus traveling fees.

With accusing eyes, I looked at him. "Please tell me this isn't what I think it is."

"If you are thinking you're no longer married to that . . . gigolo, then it's true." He laughed again. "I'm sure his lawyer has given him his copy by now, along with your sad letter explaining why you needed to end it."

"What? Have you lost your mind!" I was incensed that my father could be this devious. My God, what Dubois must be going through right now.

"No, you lost yours, and I'm helping you find it." He snorted then. "Why the heck you wanted to marry some man you know nothing about . . . His bloodlines could be full of murderers and rapists, for all you know."

Well, mine was obviously full of liars and charlatans, so I was thinking it was definitely tit for tat in my book. I got right in his face. "You had no right! None! To interfere in my life!"

He stuck a finger under my nose. "I have every right, girl! It was my blood, sweat, and tears that got you as far in life as you've gotten!"

I was so done with him. I moved around him. He grabbed my arm. I slapped at it, trying to get him off me. I knew it was disrespectful, but respect be damned! "Let me go!"

"Why? So you can show the world what a slut you have become!"

"What is going on?" my mother said from the hallway. She moved quickly toward us, her eyes growing wider the closer she got. "What are you guys arguing about?"

I'd forgotten about my mother with all the father drama. "Mother." I went to her and hugged her close. She didn't appear the worse for wear. "How are you feeling?"

She gave me a strange look. "Fine. I was just taking my

afternoon nap when I heard loud voices and came to see what was happening."

"So you haven't been to the hospital?"

She scrunched up her face. "No. I'm fine. Why?"

It had been one big lie. I gave my father an ugly eye. "Nothing."

"So what's got you and your father so riled up?"

I didn't even wait for him to explain. "Father has gone behind my back, rescinded my contract with Dubois, and apparently, he's on his way home."

My mother's mouth dropped open, then closed as her face flushed, then frowned. "Harrison Charles, please tell me this is *not* true."

"Matilda . . . I did what was best for—"

"—you." Her eyes burned hot as coals. "I cannot believe you would be this low down simply because you don't like a decision your grown daughter made. And yes, Dina is a g-r-o-w-n woman, capable and able to make *her* choices for *her* life, none of which you have to live with or be a part of."

My father, wisely for once, remained silent beneath my mother's harrowing gaze. "You should be ashamed of yourself, because I'm definitely ashamed of you." She turned to me. "Baby, go see if you can catch him." She hugged me and patted me on the back. "Tell him I love him when you find him."

I totally ignored my father as I rushed out the door. "Now for you, mister. You've got a hell of a lot of explaining—" I missed the rest of what my mother said as the door slammed behind me.

13

I drove like a demon, with my first stop being the house. It was vacant and Dubois's clothes were gone. My gut clutched as I saw the empty side of the closet. But I turned right around, jumped in my car, and headed for Pensacola. I was betting he was going home the same way he came, by ship.

I stopped only once to fill up and drove way past the speed limit, praying that the highway patrol officers were all tied up elsewhere as I sped toward the dock. So many thoughts and memories swirled in my head. At one point, I could barely see through the tears as the thought of no more Dubois reached my soul.

Finally, I saw the WELCOME TO PENSACOLA sign. I cursed as I sat in the heavy traffic as it crawled toward my exit. I had no idea how far ahead he and Simon were and when the ship left the dock. I beat the steering wheel, then blew the horn in frustration. Some blew horns back, adding to my irritation.

After crawling for what seemed like eternity, I finally reached my exit. I zoomed down the off-ramp, ignoring the yield sign, cutting off an eighteen-wheeler as I journeyed to the dock. I could see a huge ocean liner in the distance. I just knew this was the ship.

I found an open space, threw my car in Park, and jumped out in a flat-out run. My heel broke off before I'd gone a good ten feet, but I limped onward. The ship's horn let out a long, keeling Baaaaahhhhhhhhhhhhhhhhhhh! calling those riding to its deck for departure.

I jumped over a baby stroller, jostled an elderly woman with a cane, and accidentally knocked a hot dog from a teenager's mouth—earning me an ugly curse word—as I ran. My eyes strained, my heart pumped overtime, as I searched for some sight of Dubois and Simon. I couldn't discern who was who as the people walked up the long ramp. When it looked like they were about to pull up the gangplank, I saw them near the top, about to disappear out of sight.

I screamed, "Dubois!"

He didn't turn or appear to hear me. Tears streamed down my face; my heart hurt. *So close, yet so far.* I screamed again, louder this time. *"Dubois!"*

I saw when he turned, looked down. I waved and jumped up in the air, trying to get his attention. He saw me and started down the gangplank, first walking then running. He jumped to the dock and continued running towards me, arms wide open. It was déjà vu all over again.

I ran into his arms. He squeezed me tight. "Dubois! Dubois. I thought I'd lost you." He kissed my hair, said things in many languages as we twirled around. I kept blubbering, trying to explain what had happened, that it was my father, but I knew he couldn't half understand through my tears. Finally, we both just stood there crying and holding each other.

Simon cleared his throat. "Did I miss something, miss?"

Dubois and I broke apart and he offered me a handkerchief. "Yes. There's been a horrible mistake."

Simon's eyes narrowed. "I'm sorry. I don't understand. I received your letter and the rescission of your contract . . . is that not correct?"

"No, it's not correct." I turned to Dubois, needing him to understand. "Dubois, my father did this. He is the one who wrote the letter. I guess he got the information from Stacy . . . not me."

Dubois smiled and brushed a finger along my cheek. "I was so devastated. I did not understand what I had done. We seemed so happy—true, I think we were both nervous about this day, but we were happy."

"We still are."

"When Simon came to my place of employment, I was stunned." His eyes darkened, saddened. "I felt very low when I read the letter. I did not know where I had gone lacking."

Lacking? Many things he might be, but lacking ain't one of them. Bet that.

"Only in my father's mind. But I think he's got his mind back on straight."

Simon asked, "So this whole thing was just a farce?"

I nodded. "Yes. Of my father's making."

Simon vacillated between Dubois and me. Then he asked, "Well, this is the thirtieth day, so I must formally ask the both of you . . . do you wish to remain married?"

"Yes!" we said simultaneously.

A huge grin broke onto Simon's face. "The day has gotten better all around."

The ship's horn blew again. Simon looked up at the ocean liner. "Well, it appears that you will be staying after all, Dubois."

Dubois held my eyes. "Yes, sir, I will."

I handed him the check. "With pleasure."

A mate yelled, "Last call!"

"God be with you both, Mr. and Mrs. Harrington, and may your lives be long and happy." Simon then gave us a small salute and walked back up the gangplank.

Dubois and I hugged again. "Must we go back tonight?"

"No indeed! I'm fixing to find a hotel and . . . rock your world, baby!"

"One of the best things I have heard all day."

"For sure." Sometimes, slang is just . . . *right*.

We checked into the exact same hotel, and miracle among miracles, they had the bridal suite available. Dubois lifted me into his arms after we registered and held me close as we rode the elevator to the top floor, littering my face and neck with sloppy, wet kisses that I just loved.

With no luggage, but thankfully my bag from Leather and Lace, he carried me across the threshold. He kicked the door closed with his foot. "So you want me, eh?" he asked before sliding me down his body. His cock was already hard as metal.

"Just like you want me, baby. The feeling is mutual." I squeezed the piece of metal as my body sizzled. He lurched beneath my touch. "I almost died when I realized what my father had done."

"Do not be so hard. A father does what he thinks is best for his children." Despite being mistreated by my father, he still had a good word for him. My eyes softened. *God, what a man. Thank you.*

"Let's not talk about him. Let's do some talking," I rubbed my pelvis over his hardness, "about us." I left him and turned the water on in the Jacuzzi. Dubois punched on the stereo. Maxwell's silky voice floated out onto the air.

As Maxwell crooned, Dubois unbuttoned my shirt, then my pants, and let them drop from my body. I returned the favor, fingers not nearly as sure, so some buttons were sacrificed in the process. When we were both nude, we stood looking, admiring each other.

"If I have not said it today, you are beautiful and I love you,

Mrs. Harrington." Dubois stroked the indentation in my throat and let his finger trail down between my breasts.

"I know I haven't told you this today, but, Mr. Harrington, you are gorgeous as hell and I'm proud to be your wife." I let my finger tiptoe along the top of his long cock—then squeezed the head.

"Mmm. You do not play fair," Dubois whispered as my lips closed around a hairy nipple and sucked.

"You know the saying, 'All's fair in war and . . . love.'" I dropped to my knees and let my mouth close around his dark head. I sucked the tangy lollipop, pulling it deep to the back of my throat.

Dubois's fingers tangled in my hair and his toes curled as I bobbed and swirled my mouth over and around his cock. When I sucked a ball into my mouth, Dubois jumped and yelped, "My! My!"

I gurgled on his cock, let my tongue tease his piss slit. The hands in my hair moved under my arms, lifted me from my kneeling position. Dubois slanted his mouth over mine, tongue moving at rotary speed, making my body cry for release. He backed me into the wall, lifted a leg, and while his mouth was still fused to mine, surged into my slippery hole.

I ground against him, loving the friction on my clit. Dubois picked me up, slung my free leg over his arm, and put his back into it! I held on to his neck as I rode my bronco with everything I was worth. I let all the angst, the doubts, the love pour out of my sex and into Dubois. My pussy gripped, released, clutched, and Kegeled like this was my last time getting a piece of cock this lifetime.

Sweat dripped between our bodies. Still we fucked. Juice slid down my leg. Still we fucked. Nails scratched and welted flesh. Still we fucked—harder. I had a steam engine in my pussy and it was about to blow. Dubois held on, met me stroke for stroke as we pumped into Sex Heaven.

I twisted his nipple. He twisted mine. We both arrived at nirvana at the same time, howling loud as coyotes to the moon as the feeling rocked us, quaked us, finally brought us to our knees, bodies still undulating, dragging out the climactic release and finally dissolving into a pool of wet, sticky satisfaction.

My cell phone ringing woke us the next morning. I stretched and smiled as I looked at *my* man lying there beside me. I extracted myself and fished my phone out of my purse. Clothes lay everywhere. I'd never had the opportunity to wear the outfit, but no worry. I'd get my chance.

I answered without paying attention to the number. "Hello?" I really didn't give a damn about who was calling. Nobody could mess up my day.

"Dr. Charles?"

"Yes, Terrell."

"I know you didn't come in today, and I wasn't sure if your mom was all right, but I took a chance and called because we just got an express package from the Orion Group."

My ears perked up. "Well, open it and tell me what it says!"

I heard the package tearing, then paper crackling. After a few seconds, Terrell returned, excitement in his voice. "Dr. Charles, you aren't going to believe this!"

"What is it!"

"The Orion Group has decided to fund us!"

"Yes!" I yelled and began doing my booty dance.

"What has happened, baby?" Dubois sat up in the bed, rubbing at his eyes.

"We got the grant!"

"Dr. Charles! It says here that not only did we get it, they have decided to not fund some other grants and award us with, get this, three million dollars!"

My voice dropped to a whisper. "Did you just say three million?" That was twice what I'd asked for.

"Yes. They think your idea is so good, they want to fund us a million dollars a year for the next three years . . . in Egypt!"

I sank to my knees in the bed. This was way better than I could have hoped. Not only funded but funded for more than I'd asked for, for longer than I'd expected. *Thank you, God!*

"But they do have one stipulation. We need to get started in one month and have a translator in our employ, one who can read and write Egyptian Arabic."

I groaned. "Always some catch." I shook my head. "What's the likelihood of us finding someone who can read and write Egyptian Arabic and wants to stay in Egypt for three years, in one month?"

"Pretty slim. I know some guys from Iran and Iraq, but I don't know how that whole going to another country thing will play out. They are over here for an education and I don't think they'd want to be put on hold."

"Yeah. Dang!" I slapped my forehead.

Dubois took that moment to clear his throat. I looked at him and he made a face. I waved at the face and focused back on Terrell. Dubois then cleared his throat again. "Hold on, Terrell. Yes, Dubois?"

"You are looking for someone who can read and write Egyptian Arabic?"

"Yes. You know someone?"

He then pointed at himself. "Me."

"You?" I then remembered he was fluent in at least five languages. "You read and write Arabic?"

"Fluently. We never know who in the world will *request* us."

I narrowed my eyes. "Are you serious?" *Please! Please! Please be!*

"As you American say, 'As a heart attack.' "

I then stood and did another booty dance. "Terrell, we're in business! It seems that my hubby can read and write Arabic!"

"Great! Give me his full name and I'll fax the information

back to them. Oh, I forgot to tell you—they enclosed a check for a cool half a million dollars!"

"You have got to be shitting me!"

"Nope. It's made out to the university, but I'd say we need to get our behinds in gear, Dr. Charles!"

"Start setting up the account and I'll be in tomorrow to finish things out and start ordering."

"Will do. Bye."

I clicked off and dove onto Dubois. "My wonderful, gorgeous, amazing husband. You know this means we'll be gone for three years, right?"

"Yes."

"And you're okay with that?"

"Yes."

"You won't miss my father, Stacy, and the rest of my family?"

He looked to the ceiling for a moment, then back at me. "It will be hard, but somehow . . . I'll survive."

I looked at him tenderly. "Will you ever stop surprising me?"

"I surely hope not." He pulled me down and under the covers. His hands began skimming over my thigh. "In fact, I have got a surprise—or two—I would like to try out right now."

"Whatchu say."

"Feel this." I felt . . . and felt . . . and he felt . . . and *we* felt some more as the sun rose, sealing our love.

Creating *our* life . . .

Together.

FIENDING FOR IT

1

"Honey, either we spice up our love life or I'm getting a boyfriend."

Helluva way to start a conversation, I know—and definitely not one you ought to spring on your spouse over dinner, as evidenced by the Heimlich maneuver I just had to perform when he choked on his chicken teriyaki. But I'd begun, so I planned to finish.

Chaz gasped air into his lungs, probably a combination of a near-death experience and my profound statement. "Wha . . . what did you just say?"

I sat back down, putting a little distance between us, before I replied. "I said, we either spice up our love life, or I want to have a boy toy."

There, I'd said it.

Twice.

I imagined the thoughts zipping through his mind: *Did she say she wanted a boyfriend? She has lost her mind. She can't be serious. I want to wring her neck!*

I don't know why. Let's face it, the bloom falls off every rose if you don't keep watering it, adding fertilizer, and giving it the sunlight it needs. Relationships were the same way. We'd been married eight years, no kids, and we were both very, very successful. You'd think we'd be vacationing on the Riviera, Paris, or Rio on the regular. Well, guess what? All I get is a "Maybe next year, honey." Well, baby, next year is gonna start today, one way or the other.

Chaz took a sip of water and cleared his throat, all the while staring wide-eyed at me. He cleared his throat again, then said, "I think that's just foul."

I was expecting something like that, so I responded, "No, foul is actually *getting* a boy toy, screwing him every which way to Sunday, and you not having a clue—ever."

Well, it *was* the truth. Infidelity creeps into any relationship you don't nurture. It wasn't that hard to cheat. But I didn't want to cheat. I wanted to get some gasoline on these smoldering embers to make them flame up. And what better thing to get the flames rising than the possibility of another love interest?

Chaz stared a moment before swallowing hard. "So . . . you think inserting other people into this relationship is a good alternative?"

"Actually, I *know* it's a bad alternative. However, you need to realize that I am a vibrant, sexy woman whom you are constantly putting on the back burner to something else. If you don't want to 'make my day' or 'rock my world' anymore, then there is the likelihood I'll be looking for the attention I should be getting from you from other sources."

He shook his head. "I don't want that. Hell, I've never even considered it, so I definitely don't see it for you."

That was good to know, but still, I wanted a commitment to change. I didn't want to just exist; I wanted to live life to the fullest. I nodded and stayed silent.

"Baby . . . okay, I'll confess, I may not have been as attentive as I should have been lately, but . . ."

"Uh-uh. This lack of real attention and time has been going on much longer than just lately. Chaz, when was the last time you initiated a date night with me?" I sat back in my chair and watched as he frowned, trying his damnedest to prove me wrong. "Don't worry, I'll wait." After a minute of silence, he finally spoke.

"Okay, it's been longer than just lately, but," his eyebrows raised and his fingers began speaking with him, "this goes both ways. When was the last time you wore some sexy lingerie and seduced your husband?"

"Wait a minute. I give you sex any way you want it, don't I?"

"That's not the point. The point is yes, we've gotten routine, our sex has gotten routine, but it's not all me that's not doing anything about it." He scratched at his head before continuing. "Why haven't you slid on a G-string and stripped? Ambushed me in my sleep, handcuffed me to the bed, and had your way with me? What, exactly, am I doing that has prevented you from showing me how wrong I am? That there is more out there . . . to our relationship than what we've been doing?"

No, he didn't want to flip the script! This was my conversation to go as I pleased. Not one that he hijacked to work for him. "Oh, so now it's my fault?"

"Calm down." He waved me down. "I didn't say it was all your fault, but I don't think it's all mine, either." He leaned back. "I'm just saying you come out with this boy . . . *toy* idea"—insert classic eyeroll here—"and spring it on me, like I'm supposed to say 'All right, it's all my fault our love life isn't up to snuff.' Come on. It takes two to tango and to screw us up."

I can't stand when he gets logical. Yes, I knew all that, but my point was to jump-start us. Not talk about the jump start. I swallowed my cutting words and sighed—dramatically deep—before answering. "Yes, it does take two to mess up any relationship, and yes, maybe I could have done things differently, but you don't make me *want* to do anything different, although I want something else. More. More you."

"Okay, so we're together on *us* messing us up. Now, what's on your mind to change it?"

I wanted him to lead this charge—that's what men want to do, right?—but looks like he wants to be led, so it's time for Queenie to step to the plate. "I have a proposition to make."

"Apparently you've been thinking about this . . . a while . . . so I'm all ears."

"Well, I've toyed with many ideas. Of course the boy toy," that earned me a frown, "but in lieu of that, there are the sex toys."

Chaz nodded. "True. We've never gotten into the realm of sex toys—and actually, I was thinking some playacting would be pretty cool, too."

"Ah . . . you want me in the French maid outfit with my booty hanging out as I clean?"

Chaz stood up and walked behind my chair, leaned over, and whispered, "Damn the outfit, I think you in an apron and high heels, cooking dinner, would be all I'd need."

Something so simple, yet we'd never gotten there. "Done."

"And what about a belly chain . . . and nipple pinchers as . . . accessories?" His hands began massaging my shoulders.

"Uh-huh. You bring the bling and I'll surely wear it. But that toy stuff is just the preliminaries. I think we ought to push the envelope just a bit." The hands stopped massaging.

"What do you mean?"

I twisted to look up at him. "How about we take off a few weeks and give us our own personal Sexolympics?"

Chaz leaned down and got in my face, a hint of a smirk on his lips. "Sexolympics?"

"Yes. We spend the one—no, two—weeks traveling to different places, watching other people sex each other down in various ways and then experimenting with them ourselves, incorporating them into our sex life."

The hands began massaging again as Chaz stared out into space. "Two weeks . . . of sexing one another in new and different ways . . . in foreign locations . . . I don't know . . ."

"Uh-uh. We *need* this." I huffed in frustration. "We are so routine right now, I'm about to scream!" I pulled at my hair. "I want"—I stood and got all up in his face—"I want my pussy to start to leak when I see you, knowing whatever we do together will take me to nirvana. I want you to be swimming in my head, pushing out all that mundane shit that won't matter anymore a day after we walk away from it. I want you to know you make me cream, scream your name, and I mean every . . . damn . . . word . . . and . . . action."

Chaz breathed heavy, his pants front tenting. "When you put it like that, that's what I want, too."

"So, the Chaz and Elena Sexolympics . . ."

". . . need to start today?"

"Music to my ears." I moved in real close, let his cock throb on my thigh. "We clear our calendars for two weeks starting in, let's say two weeks, and we forget who we were, what we already know, and let new things enter our lives."

"Damn, baby, this sounds amazing, but I do have one question."

I rubbed my thigh over his cock, creating friction with his pants. "What's that?"

"What are the limits?"

I hadn't given that any real thought, but I winged it. "Just don't be no fool and I won't be, either. Let's not do anything that would negatively change our opinions of each other or that we can't live with in the morning."

He nodded. "So no other people . . . for either of us?"

"Oh, we can use them to get the motor running, but," I cupped his sac, "you and me gonna be the *only ones* to seal *our* deal." Squeezed. "Feel me?"

"Yes and yes." Chaz suddenly grabbed a handful of my hair and slammed his mouth over mine. "Damn, baby, you got me hot as hell."

Understatement. "That's good but—and this is a big but—since we've agreed to do this, I believe," I moved in closer, let my breath caress his lips, "we should . . . wait."

"Wa . . . wait? What the hell?"

I pushed my point home. "Yes, wait. Now imagine the level of sexual tension we'd build up if we"—my voice dropped to a whisper—"waited . . . watched . . . learned the techniques . . . *then* experimented on each other."

His eyes were hooded and horny.

A groan. "Baby . . . baby, I don't think I can wait." A hand slid down my thigh and squeezed.

"I know it sounds hard. Shit, it's just as hard for me." I grabbed his stroking hand, placed it over my pube. "Feel me." His fingers roamed, stopping as they encountered my fatty mound. "My pussy leaks like hell even though I'm suggesting to wait, but I'm willing to forgo this helluva screw I know you want to give me if we can take it to the next level, not be satisfied with where we are—together."

His fingers swirled, knuckles brushed my clit . . . before abruptly pulling back. He backed to the wall, breathing heavy. "This is one of the hardest things you've ever asked of me." Chaz ran a hand down his face. "How can we talk about something this . . . *erotic*, fucking with my head"—his teeth snapped together, jaw clenched tight—"and then say, 'Let's wait until we actually start the trip?' "—his nostrils flared—"Honestly, all I want to do is throw you over the table and bury my dick so . . . *deep—so damn deep*—in your pussy right . . . now . . . I could just scream." His cock jumped, twitched.

My body tensed, tingled for release, but I remained silent. I'd long ago learned you always had to delay quick gratification if you wanted to move farther, deeper than you were presently. But I won't lie. I needed that cock in me like I needed another sip of air right now. My pussy was pleading, *begging*, COMMANDING that I succumb, slip my panties off and slide its slippery walls over Chaz's twitching cock and ride like he was my own personal unbroken bronco. Instead . . . I shifted, squeezed my thighs together, pushed down the unbidden impulses, held the scent—the titillating scent of fresh pussy wanting to be fucked—in its deep, boiling recesses, because sex at this moment would be only a battle victory. I wanted to win the entire war.

Chaz's eyes finally opened, held mine; his rapid breaths became slower, deeper. A finger traced across my jaw, under my double chin, and lightly over my full lips. "Elena, I don't know what we're doing. Do *you* even know?" I shook my head. "But I want you and me to take this relationship to the mountaintop in every way and shape feasible. So"—deep breath—"I guess . . . let's give it our best shot." His smile and mine lit up the room.

I jumped into his arms, momentarily forgot as I wrapped my legs around his waist—felt the cock rising, searching like a heat-seeking missile for its hot target—knew I needed to get off and calm him down, pronto. His arms held me tight, were reluctant to release me as I pushed against them. "Baby, let go." He seemed to deflate, and his chest unstuck from mine. I pushed again, and this time he let me down . . . grudgingly.

I stared into his eyes, held his face in my hand. "Trust me on this, baby. We can only get better . . . *together*."

His eyes told the story of his thoughts: *Yes! No! HELL no!*

Okay, I can do this. This is ludicrous! Fuck that, I wanna fuck now! Maybe! Shit! If I don't, will she get a boyfriend anyway? This is hard, so damn hard! Grow the fugg up, man! DAMN! She's right.

"Okay, baby, we'll do it your way."

I had to smile. Who wouldn't? After all, we were planning to fuck our way around the world.

2

Elena

New Orleans

Sin City.

The Big Easy.

Nasty Nawlins.

The first leg of our trip. My body was humming with anticipation, with the need to allow my inner voyeur to rise to the surface. Earlier, we'd walked the street, imbibing various liquors, and eaten the world-class seafood and joined the uninhibited revelers as they danced in the streets. New Orleans always lived up to its name, in my book.

It was now nighttime. We'd dressed to impress in our quest for some after-hours entertainment . . . and I knew just where to find it. We'd walked past the building twice without seeing it before finally breaking down and asking a parking lot attendant for the location. He apparently got this question often, since he voiced our destination before it fully left Chaz's mouth and then smoothly pointed across the street at the nondescript white building with only a number and a clock as adornment. If it were a snake, we'd have been on the way to the ER. But here we were.

Coquette's. The sex den in our backyard we'd never experienced. But amazingly, quiet queries revealed a regular traveling patronage by my contemporaries. Their stories fueled my desire, made me toss and turn in bed, skin sizzling as the regular contact of sleeping with a spouse—without sex—became an erotic, torturous journey . . . 'cause that's what I wanted, right? But the day of reckoning, of sexual revival had come—and I planned to enjoy the reentry.

I took a deep breath as Chaz opened the door. The entry was upscale; the receptionist was filing her nails while popping gum. She gave us a lazy look before asking, "May I help you?"

"This is Coquette's, right?"

"Huh?" The frown she gave me made me wonder if we were indeed in Coquette's or if we'd just stumbled onto another private club.

"This *is* Coquette's, right?" I repeated.

"Let me get you some help." She vanished behind a door near us. Music drifted out before it closed. In seconds, a young guy entered, shades over his eyes. The room was already at dim light, so I was definitely thinking he couldn't see a thing.

"Can I help you folks?"

Chaz stepped up to the plate. "Yes, we'd like to buy a membership."

"You been here before?" The shades were removed and he eyed us up and down.

"No. First time."

He eyed us another few seconds before walking behind the desk and handing Chaz a clipboard. "Fill this out."

Chaz handed the paperwork over to me, and I strained to read the ten-point-font application while Chaz negotiated the money side. I filled in the names and addresses quickly. The rest of the bylaws I read with growing amusement, but they weren't extreme, just sensible: Safe sex, leave if you have a closed mind, and definitively no cameras or camera phones. I could live with that. We both signed off, showed our licenses, and promptly became the newest members of Coquette's.

"Want a tour?"

"Sure." I definitely wanted a lay of the land before getting my body immersed.

"Follow me." Shades replaced as he opened the door.

The inside of Coquette's reminded me of a loft apartment: brick walls, open spaces. There weren't many people mingling around: a couple hugged up on a chaise, five patrons at the bar—BYOB only—and a few in the sitting areas. All eyes were on us as we entered, though. I had a good idea of their thoughts: Fresh fish on the line.

I was surprised to learn that no sex was allowed in the common area. "*Next* we go to the sexing level." Our guide led us up a steep staircase to the second floor, the action floor. More people were upstairs. I carefully avoided the eyes perusing me as we followed our guide to the private rooms. When he pulled back the curtains, I became rooted to the spot, watching two couples, one female riding a male and the other getting ridden. I was hesitant to draw my eyes away from the wide, loose hips pumping over the cock, but the guide dropped the curtain, explaining that in these rooms you watched—or participated—by invitation only.

The rest of the tour was fast: the orgy room featuring a huge round bed—empty tonight, though—with an even larger picture window facing the hallway; the common rooms, where you could watch the sex going on inside and partake if invited; and finally the separate shower and locker room areas.

He walked us back downstairs, then left us. Ravenous eyes watched us. I chose to go to the bathroom, get my mind together before partaking of . . . anything. The bathroom downstairs was full of women in full dominatrix regalia repairing makeup and straightening up their outfits. I kind of wished we had done some playacting, but no way was I leaving just for an outfit.

I met Chaz back in the common room and we decided to sit a moment, scope out the scene. Many couples watched us, but I have to admit, both of us tensed up when a large woman and small man made their way over to us. His eyes stalked us. I kept a neutral face, not wanting any action to be taken as an enticement. We spoke; I was glad when they moved on past.

"He wanted you. I could see it in his eyes."

"You must have X-ray vision 'cause you can't see much of shit up in here, and definitely not an eye." I laughed, but I *was* relieved.

"Girl, he licked his lips before he got to us."

"I missed that . . . thank goodness." The short man was not my idea of attractive and definitely not even close to the first image to pop in my mind to get me horny, so add a tongue sticking out in a provocative manner, and I just might have vomited and been asked to leave. "While you are joking, do you think you could have handled big girl?"

Chaz leaned back, a smirk on his face. "We'll never know, will we?"

"Hey." I halfway leaned up off the couch. "I can catch them if you want . . . and I'll just watch," I jested.

"Quit tripping." He nodded toward the bar. "Check out that interracial couple on the stools." Marine dude and stripper girl—in my mind, anyway. The chick seemed . . . tense as she sipped from her drink; the man's eyes darted back and forth to every woman in the room, survey—no, hunting. I won't lie and say he didn't meet my eyes more times than you would consider casual, because he did. I wasn't feeling them, though.

Time for a change of scenery. "Let's go upstairs."

"Sure you're ready?" Surprise in his eyes.

I got bold with my man. "Can't be no Sexolympics if we ain't getting no sex."

"Now who's horny?"

"Only for you, baby. Only for you." I patted his hand.

"I'll bet. You just remember what we agreed upon."

"Always."

I was excited but nervous as we reclimbed the steep staircase. We immediately felt the change in the air—the second floor had heated up considerably since we'd left. A crowd was gathered around a couple in the hallway. We edged closer to see what the action was. A brunette was laid back on a bar stool, legs spread-eagle in the air as an ebony haired older man ate her pussy. The man had both hands spreading her, while his head rotated around and around on her pussy lips. The woman moaned; made my nipples point in response.

Chaz moved behind me; I could feel his cock growing, lifting, thickening between the thin material covering my ass cheeks. I rubbed against his cock, felt his precum soak into, then through the fabric. He grabbed my orbs, squeezed them together.

I watched as the brunette let her legs clench the man's ears; she rocked on ebony hair's face. In my mind, I changed places, had his wet pink mouth licking and tugging at my clit. I swayed, feeling their groove. Chaz read my body; let his hand slide beneath my short dress and into my panties, covered my clit. I moaned, spread my legs, let the feeling, the emotions wash over me.

Chaz moved over to an empty chair, sat, and pulled me down onto his lap. I spread my legs over his and entwined them beneath. His tongue licked my exposed back, making my pussy cry. The brunette gasped and uttered something unintelligible—however, the backward bowing of her spine told the whole story: she was about to cum. Unwillingly, I began rolling on the hard cock beneath me.

"How you feeling?"

"Mellow." And I was. The music got me in the mood, the people weren't the overbearing, sex-crazed maniacs clawing at us liked I'd half envisioned . . . it was a really cool, sexy scene.

Our chair sat in front of a public room. Scanning through the sheer curtains, I could just make out a couple fucking in my favorite position—doggy style. The woman's head was pressed into the bed. Her partner's face was just out of my line of vision; she lurched each time he pumped into her. Her eyes held mine, watched me watching them through the sheers as she pitched forward with each thrust. Sexy, indeed.

The woman's eyes closed and she screamed. I moaned as her body bobbed from the force of her partner's impaling cock. My hips ground into Chaz, my pussy weeping copious tears of lust.

A shadow stopped in front of us. An attractive older redhead. Alone, from the looks of it. She watched our foreplay, a smile tugging at her lips. Her dark eyes held mine. I felt suddenly unreserved as she stared at us; it made me grind my pussy harder on the cock. Wondered what she'd do next.

I didn't have to wait long. Red—as I'd nicknamed her—moved to stand directly in front of me. "You look"—her eyes roamed to my breasts, then back to my face—"hot." Her voice was husky, sexual. Her fingers moved to my neck, tugged at the strings of my halter dress, pulled. In my mind, I knew I should stop her—she was a stranger, could have any one of a hundred diseases—but I didn't. Deep down I wanted to see where she was going with this.

Chaz bit my neck as the strings were dragged down to waist level, exposing my breasts to anyone wanting to see. "Much better." She stood back, looked at my girls, her eyes gleaming in the dim light. Chaz plucked and mashed my clit, taking me higher, making my nipples tighter. No surprise. Girl-on-girl action always made men horny. I became his complicit accomplice—arched my back, lifted my breasts into the air.

The woman said nothing, just let a finger trail between my breasts and onto a stiff point. I flinched at her touch. "You okay with this?" Chaz whispered, voice heavy with want, anticipation, lust. I nodded, slightly ashamed . . . but also very much wanting to see where else she would go with this. He cupped my heavy breasts, pushed them together . . . offered them to the redhead. She licked her lips; green eyes narrowed, browned.

Chaz's cock fattened, begged to be released from the fabric prison formed by his boxer shorts. I reached behind me, unbuckled him, let him free. In the dim hallway, while others watched the cunnilingus exhibition, he slowly slid his hot meat between my thighs, his precum lubricating the way, cock sliding amid my wet folds and finally touching my clit.

She opened her blouse. It was obvious she was no novice; she'd left the bra at home. Her tits were naturally larger, fuller than mine, with distended nipples. She licked her fingers and pulled at her own nipples until moisture beaded up on the tips.

"Ever had titty milk before?" She squeezed her nipple again, let a thin stream of milk squirt into the air.

I hadn't, but I wanted to.

The liquid drop clinging to her nipple mesmerized me, taunted me, tempted me; my tongue slid around my dry lips. Chaz lifted my hips, shoved me closer to those engorged tits. He encircled my nipples with two fingers, pulled like he was milking a cow's teat. She moved closer, brought her tits eye level.

She lifted those pointy-eyed twins, got in my personal space, was close enough for me to smell the scent of her expensive perfume. "Wanna suck?" My pussy juices released as I leaned down and my tongue flicked out to capture the drop of milk on her nipple. I let the milk roll across my taste buds. Mixed reviews—sweet, tangy but not unpleasant. My mouth covered the nipple, pulled it into my mouth, sucked deep. A stream of milk squirted and hit the back of my throat, watery, sweet. She squeezed her breast, shot more milk into my mouth. My pussy clenched, produced more honey.

I tugged and pulled at the nipple; bit and chewed on the tight tissue. Red held the back of my head, pushed more of her tit into my sucking mouth, indeed seemed to *need* this suckling of her. When the stream slowed, she unlatched my mouth, slid her other breast over and between my waiting lips.

Chaz raised me slightly, let his cock knock at pussy's door, slid inside. I pumped on him slowly as I sucked the milk-laden tits, maintaining the vital contact with both places.

"Damn, baby, that looks so good."

Men and that girl-on-girl action . . . you already know.

My tongue lapped around the nipple before slipping it back inside my mouth. Red pushed at my forehead, lifted my head. She slid to her knees, let her mouth cover my throbbing nipple.

People watched us now, got ignited by our loveplay, stroking, kissing. I didn't care one bit.

In fact, it fueled me. I growled, began a soft bounce on Chaz's cock. He held me around the waist, Red's arm holding me around the back as I bounced. Her mouth was hot, wet, teeth just the right level of sharpness when she sank her teeth into my nipples. Firecrackers exploded in my ears as Red tried to suck all of me inside, pushing the nipples together and alternating between them. Oh, this was heaven.

Chaz pumped, Red sucked, and then she *pinched* my nipples. The pleasure pain shot through me, made me grab the back of her head, mash her face into my chest; made my pussy vise Chaz's cock; made him knock deep in the back of my pussy.

"Baby, I can't wait!" he gasped in my ear.

I couldn't either. "Bite harder."

Red did my bidding; made the pain shoot from my nipples, radiate up and down my spine. I mewled as the cock mushroomed, became flesh-covered steel before liquid heat splashed against my slick vaginal walls. The goose bumps spread from my calves to my upper legs over my back and down to my nub before honey shot from me, commingled with Chaz's moisture.

As we came down, Red lifted herself from the floor, straightened her clothes, and moved farther down the hallway. The crowd dispersed, moved away with her.

Chaz, still lodged deep in my pussy, blew in my ear. "That was incredible. I'm still cumming." His cock pulsed.

"It was definitely a new experience."

"Level with me. You've never had any girl-girl action? Some drunk chick sucking your tits?"

Secretly, sucking tits always turned me on, especially girls sucking girls, but I'd never admitted it before now. "No . . . but I always wanted to suck some." He had no idea how hard it was for me to admit that. This was my one deep-down shameful craving I'd only discussed at Me, Myself and I conferences held inside the comfort of my head.

"And you hadn't before because of what?"

I shrugged. "I guess because I didn't want the *whole* lesbian experience. I just wanted the tit sucking."

"You mean no licking pussy, just tit sucking."

"Yeah. But if a woman is willing to suck tits, usually she's into the whole 'girl-girl' thing, and I'm not. I like dick, but I like watching girls sucking tits." Suddenly my bladder claimed my attention. "Honey, I've got to take a potty break."

He looked down. "Me too."

We rejoined one another minutes later. By this time, there were three couples on the orgy bed. We stood near the back and watched as the three couples swapped, fucked, sucked in numerous positions. I wasn't surprised to see the woman who'd sucked my tits as one of the participants. I had to say, she fucked with the same relish she'd sucked my tits. After another hour, we left.

One a scale of one to ten, I'd give Collette's a six—what I'd expected but not over the top.

3

Chaz

Honolulu, Hawaii

The plane hit another patch of turbulence, making my stomach lurch, but Elena slept away. I guess she should. Last night—wow, my wife was a tiger in the flesh. God, how sexy she was as she had her tits sucked. It was an effort . . . a *great* effort for me not to shoot my jism the moment she slid down my rod. And then watching that orgy. What man wouldn't want to be a part of all those tits, pussies, asses licking, sucking, biting, nibbling, cumming . . . I bit my lip as I felt my balls tighten up, ready to spew my cum everywhere.

I have to be honest and say the whole way she presented this idea—starting with the whole wanting a boy toy because she was unhappy with our sex life—wasn't the best way to get me on her side. I mean, what guy is cool with having his wife even *talk* about getting with another dude and he's fine with it? Not a real man. Tell that to the wrong guy and somebody would end up at the ER. But I'm not that guy.

Sure, I get approached all the time by women hinting, flirting, and many, nowadays, who are just blunt about what they want, hoping I'll be wanting it, too. She does, too. But I let that stuff pass over my head; act like I don't have a clue. Since I saw busty Elena almost a decade ago, she's had me, hook, line, and bait. I mean really. I *might* flirt back every purple moon when a random chick catches me in a great mood, but that's all I'll do, and not too much of it. I've seen enough situations to know it doesn't take much to go from innocent banter like that woman in Beyoncé's movie, *Obsessed*. Now that chick got caught up in Beyoncé's husband, but they weren't having an affair . . . except in stalker chick's head. Uh-uh. Elena is *not* that calm about anything. That chick and I would already be somewhere pushing up wildflower roots.

I pulled Elena's head up on my shoulder, as it had dropped a bit, and blew on her hair. She shifted, making her breasts peek over the top of her blouse; it made my mouth water. I liked how she always had that lady/whore thing going on when she dressed. Yeah, she'd be all ladylike in public, but once she got behind closed doors—as she always told me, she was *my* personal whore.

Men complained all the time how the sex was great at the beginning and then you had to beg your wife to give you some as time went by. Not us. I had to work out just to keep up with Elena. Her appetite was fierce! Yes, I was truly blessed . . . and the one dropping the ball.

With how fast the business took off, I took my eyes off my prize and started slacking. News flash to women: Men do get tired, stressed, and lose their sex drive just like you do. I know women don't see it since we aren't running behind the kids, cleaning up the house, and so on . . . but it's stress, just of a different kind. We don't have kids, but some of my clients act like a kid . . . or two, and that would stress the hell out of the pope.

I tried to forget my last call from the office. I represented Barney Phiffe—yeah, pronounced just like that deputy from Mayberry, acts like him, too, I must add—once a top National Hockey League draft pick who couldn't leave his troubles, and troublesome friends, behind and move up to the big leagues. DUIs, failed drug tests, and yesterday, photographed in a compromising position with a teenybopper young enough to be his daughter. The man had no moral compass in a league that placed decency and morality high on its list. We'd gotten him bailed out, a hearing set for after I returned, and I'd told him to stay put. I was sure that piece of advice would go in one ear and out the other and any moment the cell would ring with another crisis to ruin my holiday. Typical.

The ocean was blue, blue, blue as far as my eyes could see. This was my leg of the trip to plan, and I hoped it would be as exciting as I'd mapped it out in my head. Anyway, I wanted it to be simply because, as Elena said, we *needed* it.

Elena lifted, stretched. Her sleepy face and tousled hair gave her that bedroom sexy vibe. She glanced out the window, then at me. "How much longer?"

I looked at my watch. "We've been in the air for three hours, so I'd say another hour or so before we hit the island."

A smile played across her lips. "Are you going to tell me what we'll be doing? Where we're going? I mean, I Googled Hawaii, and didn't find any public sex clubs online." I gave her a noncommittal shrug. Elena grabbed my forearm. "We *are* going to a sex club, right?"

"Woman! Unhand me and calm down." I laughed at her expression. "You gonna get sexed, have no fear." I nodded.

She let go of my arm, a smile now on her face. "Oh. The way you've been acting, I wondered."

"You know curiosity will get a cat's ass spanked, right?"

She shook her head. "I'm not feeling like getting spanked right now—but you can *pop* it anytime, Daddy," she purred, running a finger over the front of my pants. *Now I love when she calls me Daddy!* Lil One-eyed Chaz responded just like she knew he would, tenting the front of my pants, making my balls ache.

"Keep it up and we're gonna become the newest members of the Mile High Club."

Elena vigorously shook her head. "You know I can barely pee in a public bathroom, so no way will we *ever* be bumping and pumping in a nasty airplane bathroom. Yuck." She shook her head again for good measure. "However, if you decide to *charter* a plane . . . you just *might* get lucky." She pressed her palm over Lil Chaz this time; he jumped in response. "Understand?"

Boy, oh boy, did I indeed.

4

"Honey, where are we going again?" Elena asked as she stumbled up yet another step. She was blindfolded.

"You'll see. Just wait."

I gave a slight push to her lower back and her feet gingerly moved up to the next step. Her hand groped and slid all over the walls of the stairwell but thankfully, the stairwell of the Hyatt Konoko Beachfront was clean and smelled of fresh paint. I feverently hoped she wouldn't by accident encounter a hard booger. She'd be washing her hands for an hour before we could move another inch.

Finally, we reached the top. I opened the door to the roof and led her outside. The wind from the rotor blades hit us in the face.

"Whoa! Where the hell are we? What's going on?" Her hands lifted to pull at the blindfold.

I grabbed her hands. "Just be patient, honey!" I yelled over the rising whir of the blades. "You'll see!"

The pilot of the helicopter spotted us and ran over. "Hey, I'm Max!"

"Uh-uh." Elena pulled her head back and the blindfold down. Her mouth dropped open. "What . . . the . . . hell?"

Max, a short guy with a big afro reminiscent of Lenny Kravitz back in the day, repeated, unfazed, "I'm Max! Your pilot for today! Follow me!" He then turned and trotted off back to the helicopter.

Elena looked at his retreating back then at me, a question in her eyes, a bit of a smirk starting at the corner of her mouth. I squelched it quick, having a good idea what she was thinking. "No, it's not the kidnap and get sexed by a bunch of hunky hung men fantasy come true!" I tugged her along as her hair flew about her head.

Her face fell; lips poked out a bit. "Then what is it?"

"Just what you see. A helicopter ride!" The engine was louder here and I coughed as a bug flew in my mouth. I spat the insect out.

Elena paused before stepping into the helicopter. She stuck her head inside and looked around before turning to me. "There's no doors!"

"I noticed." I pressed my hand into her back, ready for her to get in the helicopter. She didn't budge, instead took a step back.

"How do we stay inside?"

I grabbed a harness off the seat and held it up. "This will keep us safe!" She eyed the harness with narrowed eyes. "It will! I promise!"

She looked back at the door we'd exited. My hand rose slightly, ready to stop her if she broke into a run for it . . . but she didn't. She gave me a peck to the lips and stepped into the helicopter.

One hurdle down . . . probably fifty . . . thousand more to go.

"This is the most active volcano we've got on the islands, folks! Kilauea," Max said. The headphones were multidirectional. We could converse with each another and Max. "It's been active for the past twenty-five years."

We looked in the distance at the tall peak with gray smoke curling from the top. Suddenly, fire shot from the top and a sea of red lava flowed over the lip. "There she blows!" Max yelled.

Max steered the helicopter closer. The temperature was in the nineties but the air heated up to over a hundred the closer we got. We flew through the smoke, both of us coughing as the acrid ash flew into the cabin.

"Yes, folks, this is God at his finest!" Max was pumped up! It was obvious he loved his job. "Let's get a bit closer."

The helicopter tilted sharply as he turned. We grabbed on to each other, the sudden reality of potential danger filling our minds. Max dipped low as another puff of smoke belched out. The heat was intensifying. Even the soles of my sandals were heating up.

"Four hundred and fifty degrees is what scientists say this baby cranks up to. That's enough to make any of us toast real quick like." Max cackled at his own joke. He hovered over the lip, letting us enjoy the beauty—and fright—of the fire red color of the lava. It was definitely nature at its finest. The smoke puffs accelerated.

"Gotta go, folks!" The engine whined and we lifted quickly. It wasn't but a few seconds before fire shot up into the air again.

Close damn call.

Max kept going straight before slowing down and hovering over the mouth of another volcano. "I wanted you guys to see what's it's like down in the belly of this beast."

Elena pulled the headphone away from her mouth, covered the receiver, and yelled, "I sure as hell hope he knows what he's doing!"

"Yes, ma'am, I do!" Max responded.

Oops.

"Been doing this for ten years and have yet to lose a passenger or a bird. I know the last one was kinda hairy but you hold on to your britches. You'll enjoy this one here, for sure."

Elena rolled her eyes, but wisely kept any new comments about Max to herself. Max whirred us in a circle, then descended. We went lower . . . lower . . . lower until we were actually inside the mouth of the volcano. My body tensed. I didn't see any smoke, but I also knew volcanoes were like people—unpredictable at times.

He set the helicopter down and cut the engine back. He turned in his seat. "This is Mauna Loa, once thought to be one of the most active volcanoes on the islands. She's been out of commission with nary a peep for at least twenty years, though." He pointed to the walls. "See how the walls were carved by the lava that flowed?" We nodded as we looked at the splendor in front of us. The walls were a gorgeous mosaic of colors and textures layered on top of each other.

"If you want, you guys can get out and grab a souvenir rock."

Elena didn't hesitate. She unstrapped her harness and jumped out before I could get unlatched. The first thing I did when I exited was feel the ground with my palm. Not too warm. I was hoping it was a great sign that Mauna Loa wanted to stay asleep for another twenty years . . . or at least until we were safely out of her.

"Grab one for me too, honey," I said as Elena grabbed free rock after free rock, stuffing them inside her purse suitcase. It was only a few minutes before Max summoned us back.

"No need to tempt the gods, you know?" I didn't, but decided to take his advice. I hustled Elena back to the helicopter and we strapped ourselves back in. Max took his time rising up out the mouth. I snapped some great shots of Elena against the backdrop of the volcano.

We were back on the heliport within fifteen minutes. I

shook Max's hand and Elena gave him a peck to the cheek before dancing her way over to the stairwell door.

"I think your missus enjoyed herself." Max nodded.

"I believe you are correct. Thanks again."

"Tell everybody you know about me. I could always use more business."

"Will do." We shook hands again before I left to find my happy bride.

5

Elena wanted to visit the mall. I wasn't up to it, but as they say, happy wife, happy life, so I trudged along behind her. We were now into hour two and Elena had tried on plenty of things and bought exactly nothing. When we rounded the merry-go-round, Elena became rooted to the spot. In front of us was a Leather and Lace Emporium, and its windows were in full regalia. Whips, chain, clothing made of only leather and chains, feather boas—all beckoned the adventuresome. If we'd found this an hour ago, I'd have been ready to see what the hoopla was about. But that was an hour ago.

"Looking for anything in particular?" I hoped the irritation didn't show in my voice, but it must have.

"Um . . . I don't know." Elena then patted my arm. "Go to the Rolex store while I stop in here. I'll find you when I finish."

Music to my ears. I didn't wait for her to change her mind as I turned on my heels, spotted the store mentioned, and headed for the double doors. The store was cool and *manly.* A pretty woman came up to me before I'd taken ten steps inside.

"May I help you? I'm Isis." Her eyes screamed boredom.

"Yes. I'd like to see your tank watches." I watched in amusement as her eyes morphed from boredom to potential sale brightness.

"Right this way, sir." Even her voice perked up. "We have a wide selection, and I'm sure," her hands gave my upper arms a squeeze, "we'll find something you like."

I followed her to the counter and allowed her to pull the watches out of the case. "See anything that sparks your"—she reached for the lower shelf, allowing her cleavage to be on display—"interest?"

Once upon a time, I would have met her double entendre with one of my own, but that was then. I kept my eyes on the watches displayed in front on me. Honestly, I already had three Rolexes and wasn't in the market for another, but she didn't know that. I let my finger linger over a black tank with a large face surrounded by a double row of diamonds.

"That's a new one, isn't it? I haven't seen that style before."

"It was made for some guy in a band called Drunk Donkeys, but he changed his mind." She made a face. Guess she'd missed that commission and wasn't too happy about it. "Try it on."

"Sure." My clients wore plenty of bling, so why couldn't I?

She lifted and pulled my right wrist to her and slid the watch on. "Looks like it belongs."

I had to agree with her. "How much?"

A smile wide enough for me to see her molars was on her face as she recited the price. I had to swallow since it was twice what I'd paid for the others. Even if I had been in the market, I didn't want it *that* bad, but I teased her anyway and reached for my wallet. I slid out my American Express Black. I swear she licked her lips.

"Want it gift wrapped?" Her hands moved toward the card.

I pulled the card back, tickled at how her eyes were mesmerized by the piece of black plastic. "No. On second thought, I really need to get my wife's input before I buy it."

Her head snapped up, lips started to curl at the edges, eyes sparking fire. "I understand," she said tightly.

"Thanks anyway." I turned and headed for the exit but not before I heard her mumbling something that sounded like *asshole* as she all but threw the watches back in the display case.

Elena, thankfully, was walking toward me as I exited. "Ready to go?" she asked, all bubbly.

"Sure." I looked at my watch. "We have just a few hours until we go see more sights. Want dinner now?"

"Yes. Let's get it out of the way. I don't like to sex you . . . hard . . . on a full stomach."

Elena had on a skintight dress that would make a ninety-year-old man get an erection. Her boobs were front and center, her ass succulent and stuck way the hell out, her cheeks rising and falling as she walked around the room. Part of me wanted to rip the dress off and bury Lil Chaz deep into her pussy. She stopped that thought before I could even voice it.

"No. I'm not getting redressed." She then applied a layer of lipstick and grabbed her purse. "I'm ready when you are."

I patted my cock's straining head and followed her out into the hallway.

"Where are we going?" Elena asked for the thousandth time.

"Just something I want you to see."

"Okay. Something I'll enjoy, right?" Elena bantered.

"I believe so. You said you'd keep your mind open, right?"

"That I did."

"So just sit back and go with the flow. I think you will get a kick out of it."

"I sure hope so."

Elena leaned back and watched the buildings go past the window of the cab. It took twenty minutes before we pulled in front of a long structure on a busy street. The sign in front said Expressions.

"Are we eating again?" It had been fewer than two hours since we'd had dinner.

"If you want, but they have some . . . amusement, too."

Elena nodded as we exited the cab. We entered through maroon double doors. Inside was a whole 'nother universe. The music was foreign, for lack of a better word, and there were low tables with pillows placed all around on the floor. The room was full of laughter, smells, and people of all nationalities.

"Interesting."

Before I replied, a turban-draped man walked to us and bowed. "Welcome. Table?" he asked, eyes lowered.

"No. We'd like to go upstairs."

The man's expression was neutral as he turned. "This way."

He led us to a narrow stairway and waved us up. I let Elena go in front of me as we navigated the steep stairs.

"Do all sex clubs have these steep stairs?" Elena whispered. As I watched her hips rise and fall, I sure hoped so.

Music reached us halfway up. It was different from the sound downstairs, more pulsing, and the smell of incense was heavy. A door suddenly opened and a man with a woman draped over him stumbled out. Their lips were fused and they seemed oblivious to our presence. We watched as the man grabbed the woman's breast and squeezed. He looked our way then. He said nothing as he shifted the woman and allowed us to pass. Elena looked back as we walked past, but I propelled her forward. We stopped in front of an indigo blue door.

I didn't wait, just turned the knob and pushed the door open. The room was dark, smoky from incense, and a blue light hung overhead. Elena hesitated. I placed a hand around her waist and pushed her inside, shutting the door behind us.

My eyes soon adjusted. I saw there were around ten other people in the room, lounging, sitting, talking amongst themselves. I guided Elena to a love seat. "Want something to drink?"

"Sure. Something fruity but not too powerful." Ah, my baby was being tame tonight.

"Wine?"

"Yes. White if they have it."

Elena watched the other patrons as I went to retrieve our drinks. No faces were visible, but even in this light I could make out couples and singles sipping drinks, eating food, and conversing. I had to wonder if this was a place to just hang out and chill, instead of the *Eclectic sexual experience* promised by the brochure. I was getting my damn money back if it was.

The music changed from thumping to sensuous. Fans were turned on and the material behind me wisped onto my shoulder. I returned with the drinks just as a figure strode from behind some curtains. No lights were switched on, but the figure was outlined since it was covered in luminous paint. Obviously a woman, and she was naked.

Alrighty then! This is what I'm talking about!

The silver woman undulated to the music, a pink neon fluorescing scarf drifting into the air and wrapping about her body. She bent and twirled to the beat, her breasts bobbing. A strobe light was suddenly turned on, making her appear ethereal.

Elena looked entranced. I sipped from the wine and watched the play of emotions across her face. The woman squatted low and twirled the scarf between her legs as she rose. She rolled and swung her hips to the music before she walked over to various people, rolling and grinding in front of them, in their faces, on them. Hands rubbed all over the woman's body—her breasts, her legs, between them. Her undulations never stopped.

She walked toward us. I could now see she was older but definitely well preserved. No bulging fat was evident on her lithe body. She was not self-conscious in the least as she wrapped her scarf around my neck. Her fingers diddled my lips and she leaned in close as if to kiss me before pulling back.

Tease. The woman's eyes bored into mine as she turned sideways, shimmied her hips in Elena's face. Her hands beckoned me, called me forward.

If you dare me, I will meet the challenge head-on.

The scarf was now around my neck, my waist, my butt as she continued to sway her hips, her pelvis brushing over the front of my hard cock . . . teasing again. She smiled, her eyes watching me; reading my thoughts. I snatched her around the waist, stood, and fused her to my groin. The woman showed no surprise, instead continued to hold my eyes captive as she snaked on my rod. I tried to hide my grin—glanced at Elena, hoping that she didn't think I'd crossed the line—but I was truly enjoying myself. When Elena's hands slid between our fused pelvises and unzipped my pants, it was confirmation she was fine.

As my cock was pulled free, I sensed the change in the room. Gone was the talking, now it was groan layered upon groan layered upon groan. Bodies were naked, entangled, humping, pumping. Tongues licked, hands squeezed, fingers pulled.

Elena held my cock as the woman undulated and rolled on it. The scarves tickled, teased my sensitive head, made it blossom further. The woman pulled back, looped a scarf over my dick, turned slowly. A string of precum trailed along her side, her cheek before resting at the top of her ass. She backed up, let my cock roll back and forth along the cleft between her ass cheeks. The friction, the slipperiness of the scarves made me leak, made my nipples pebble, made my sac rise. Her ass rolled on, taunting, promising.

My staff needed the heat of a hot hole! My hips pushed forward, ignoring my conscious mind, searching for that needed burn. Elena touched my shoulder then. I looked at her; knew I was pushing the limit. Saw it in her eyes. I stopped.

The woman lifted her head, took my hand and Elena's, and pulled us behind her. We walked behind the curtains and I was surprised to see a lighted hallway with doors on each side. The air smelled cleaner. I heard the pulsing beat behind us, but there were no obvious sounds here.

The woman stopped in front of one room, two doors down. My face was flushed from the need to fuck. She turned to Elena then. "I am Suona." Her voice was husky and she seemed oblivious that she was naked. "This is your first time here, no?"

Elena nodded.

"I can tell." She held Elena's face, caressed her cheeks before her small hands gathered Elena's hands within them. "I meant no disrespect." She then pierced me with her eyes. "When we are dead, we are dead and cannot recoup what we missed. You must live for now." Her eyes scanned me before returning to Elena. "Take this man and enjoy what you have been blessed with." She reached onto a table and pressed a jar into Elena's hand. "Show him he is special also." She nodded at the door before walking back toward the room we'd just left, her firm hips resuming a sway with the beat.

Elena looked at the jar in my hand, then me. "What the hell was that?"

I searched her face, then cleared my throat. "I have no idea . . . but we don't have to do this. We can just go back to the room and do something else if you want." *If she does, I swear somebody gonna give me money back tonight!*

Elena took a deep breath, grabbed my hand, and opened the door. The room was furnished completely in bright satins. A gold satin spread covered the bed, pale green satin curtains hung over the window, and a red iridescent satin formed the canopy. My first impression: cathouse.

"This is something else, isn't it?" I asked, scanning the room again.

Elena smiled and replied, "Have you been here before? A business trip or something?"

I am nobody's fool. I didn't even hesitate when I answered, "No. Never." That was my story and I was sticking with it.

Elena looked at the jar she'd been given. "Wonder what's in here?" The jar was opaque, lead-bead decorated, and as she shook it, fluid sloshed inside.

"Open it up and let's see." Elena twisted the metal top off. It was filled to the brim with silver paint.

"It's paint." Obvious.

"Probably iridescent body paint like she wore." I walked close enough for my breath to blow on her ear.

"And I'm guessing that we should . . . *explore* one another with this paint?"

My nine o'clock shadow scratched her cheek. I licked her earlobe. "I believe that's the idea."

Elena swallowed when my tongue dipped into her ear. "Is there a script we should follow, or just . . . freestyle it?" My hands crept downward, caressed her thick thighs.

"Spontaneity is always good, so freestyle." My tongue swirled around her ear.

I turned her to face me. My mouth captured hers, plundering, taking what I wanted from her. She reciprocated, sucked my tongue into her hot cavity. I felt her unbuttoning my shirt, felt her plucking my nipples, squeezing them. I let a finger flick across a covered nipple; Elena sighed around my tongue. My hands roamed her back, her neck rubbing, grasping her close. Her body felt liquid, melting under my magic tongue.

I opened her bra clasp. Her babes fell into my hands, nipples stabbed my palms. I gingerly removed my lips from hers, placed them around the aroused tips. I sucked and nibbled at the sensitive flesh, felt them swell as I tugged harder. She arched her back to give me more room to engulf her now-throbbing orbs. My fingers moved lower, my thumb pressed into her belly button. I felt her hands on my cock, stroking. I closed my eyes, clutched her head as she fisted my cock. Her mouth left my flesh then, teeth closing around the material of my pants as she mouth-tugged them lower—

An alarm clanged! We jumped apart, not sure what was happening. Running footsteps, then pounding on the door. "Fire! Get out! Fire!"

We scrambled then, shifted our clothes over our bodies. We flung open the door and the smell of smoke was obvious.

"Follow me!"

I didn't have to tell Elena twice. I heard screams, voices, the sounds of panic. The warmth of the floor seeped through my sandals, and that worried me greatly. Just as we reentered the main room where we'd previously sat, smoke rushed at us.

Panicked, Elena screamed, "We can't go that way!" The heat from the floor felt way too hot to risk it anyway.

People were scrambling everywhere as we entered the hallway, pushing us, jostling us to get to safety. Elena's hand was torn from mine. A woman stumbled and fell. Those behind her pushed forward, ignoring her screams as they ran for the stairwell. I was propelled with the mass, Elena no longer visible to me.

Screams from below! Smoke was coming thick now. My heart thundered as the crowd tried to turn, go back the way it had come while the ones behind continued to push forward. This was a nightmare. *Where is Elena!* With this fear taking hold of my mind, I turned into a raging madman. I elbowed, clawed, pushed, trying to make room, make them understand we had to get out!

The smoke made me cough; made my tears flow. Hands grabbed my shirt, pulled me back. "This way!" I recognized Elena's voice. I grabbed her hand as she yanked me behind her, going back where we'd just left. The room was devoid of people as we trotted back behind the curtain. We ran into the room we'd recently left, tore the curtain from the window, sighed as we saw the plate glass window, no bars present. Elena moved to the side as I sent a chair through the glass.

We need to tie the sheets together.

She read my mind and we worked in concert. I stripped the bed, my fingers nimble as I tied quick knots to create a long fabric rope; Elena tied the curtains together. We hooked one end to the heavy bed and flung the other end through the window.

I pulled Elena in front of me to the window. She hesitated, swaying as she looked at the distance to the ground. It was no more than twenty feet, but it probably looked like a hundred to her. Either way, it was of no importance. It was jump or die—and I wasn't ready to die yet.

"Take your time and go slow," I urged quietly, trying to keep the impatience out of my voice.

"I . . . I'm a-fraid. I feel d-dizzy," she stuttered, fear lacing her voice.

I took a deep breath before speaking. "Elena, I know you're scared, but when you go down, just keep looking up at me. I'll guide you."

"But what if the rope breaks and I fall to the ground?" Tears were threatening now.

"Elena, the building is on fire. It can't be more than fifteen feet to the ground. No more than a regular house roof. You might hurt yourself, but kill yourself, no," I assured her.

Just then, a tremendous scream reached our ears as the building shook and shifted. We were thrown backwards, Elena landing on her knees. She screamed as the hot floor made contact with her flesh. I said nothing, just lifted her, pushed her backwards out the window, and yelled, "Slide!"

Her legs flailed in the air, she screamed with all her might as the material slid between her hands.

"Keep moving!" I yelled as Elena reached the first knot and held on, unable to bring herself to move her hands below it.

I slid out, stared upward, watched smoke belch into the air. Water suddenly sprayed over the top of the building, sluicing down my head and body. I choked, gasping as the gallons poured from the roof. My fingers became slick and I grappled to hold on to the satin material and breathe. That's when the knot came loose. I yelled mightily as I felt myself falling . . . but the ground met me in milliseconds where I thumped soundly onto my butt, cutting off my voice.

Elena had already navigated out the sheet and stood. "Are you okay?"

My butt hurt, heart thundered in my chest, but as I flexed my arms and legs, I realized I was fine. "I'm good. You?"

"No sweat." All fear was gone now.

I nodded. I saw a closed privacy fence separating us from the sidewalk. "This way. We can scale the fence if it's locked."

No sooner had we made it to the fence than it was opened. A fireman rushed forward, his yellow jacket bulky on his body. "Anybody hurt? We have paramedics out front! Anybody else coming behind you?" he yelled.

"Just us!" I supplied over the clanging fire bells.

"Thanks!"

Other firemen rushed behind him, hoses clasped in their hands. We moved aside as they passed us. Water sprayed in seconds.

"Let's get out of here." My adrenaline rush was thinning and I felt weak. I guess Elena was feeling the same effect, because her knees buckled and she slumped.

Out cold.

6

Elena

The thunder pealed again, signaling impending rain. I ran the bottle of Diet Coke over my forehead, thankful for the temporary coolness.

What a night it had been! Three hours and twenty minutes ago, we'd almost died in a horrible fire. Three hours and about eighteen minutes ago, I'd blacked out . . . cold. I hadn't done that since I'd been overheated in cheerleading camp a few decades ago. We'd been lucky, lucky, lucky to have beaten death—this time. I shuddered to think how many people actually had been hurt. I glanced at the silent television but didn't move to turn it on. I'm sure it would be on every bellboy, maid, and concierge's tongue in the morning. I'd let them fill me in.

I shifted my mind to what had been nagging at me. The whole club thing Chaz had set up . . . kind of weird to see a woman coming on to your man. I admitted to myself while in the hallway, I'd been a bit jealous. Chick was confident in her sexuality, not that I'm not. Hey, I did let that unknown woman suck my tits at the other club. But this time, I felt . . . disrespected. Yes, slighted—made me wonder how I measured up.

And the look on Chaz's face . . . the desire was so obvious. I couldn't help but speculate on how many other women he'd looked at like that. He's off on "business trips" all the time. He had the opportunity . . . by the truckload.

My mind intruded. *Focus. Focus. Focus, girl!*

Yes, focus. The whole point of our Sexolympics was to reconnect and expand our sexuality out of the box we'd been living in. I just thought it would be a bit easier—you know, fun times between Elena and Chaz. A club here, a sex game there . . . I just didn't factor in how I would feel about the temptation to Chaz. How actually seeing women flirt with him . . . try to fuck him . . . how his reactions would affect me.

Had my Sexolympics in reality backfired? Did I just open Pandora's illicit box? Was I walking down a wild side that was about to get out of control? My mind churned with a million and one thoughts.

The rain came down in sheets, moisture misting over my outspread legs. I heard a footstep, then, "I wondered where you were." Chaz stood next to me, eyes still sleepy.

"Just enjoying the fine weather." I ran a finger up the firm thigh near my shoulder. I may feel a bit insecure, but he's still mine.

"Only you would call this fine weather." He snorted as warm rain drifted over us and he shielded his face. Chaz lifted my legs, sat on the chaise, and draped my limbs across his lap. Lightning flashed across the sky. We both watched the intense electric light show. "Think we should head inside?" Chaz flinched slightly as thunder boomed and reverberated across the terrace.

We were sitting on a metal chaise, out in the open with iron grillwork not five feet from us. Prime lightning rods. But after the fire fiasco, I'd decided to throw all that caution stuff to the wind; live again for as long as I could. I shook my head, pushing away my insecurity as a naughty thought popped into my head. "Naw. In fact, why don't we join in, do a rain dance or something."

"Huh?" Chaz squinted at me.

I pulled on the neck of his wifebeater, bringing his face close to mine. "Grab the paint, let's smear ourselves and dance in the rain."

"O . . . kay." His eyes widened as he fully understood my meaning. "Oh!"

Who was it that said big men moved slow? Chaz shot off that chaise like an errant bolt had actually hit him, trotting across the floor in eagerness.

Lightning flashed again. The electricity in the air lifted the hairs on my body. I ran my hands over my hair, smiled at the mini-shocks I received in response. Something in those shocks triggered my nipples, which sprang to life. I rubbed my skin, smiling as more sparks were emitted.

Music with a heavy bass beat suddenly pulsed from the living room. The tune was unknown to me but it reminded me of Suona, her movements. I wanted to recapture some of Suona's essence, some of that energy, the sexual tension she'd created by her dance. My mind tugged me down that other road, but I stopped it.

I eased from the chaise, smiling as rain splattered my feet and legs. I let the robe slide from my body, not caring that a million and one eyes might be able to glimpse me in all my glory on this terrace. I stepped willingly into the rain, turning my face up as drops pelted my body. I opened my mouth, tasted the flavor of the city, the volcanoes in the cloud water.

The bass beat claimed my body. I moved in a slow, languorous mambo, my hip sway exaggerated as my legs moved front and back. My hands skimmed my body, massaging heaven's dew into my pores.

Lightning flashed again. I leaned back, gyrating in place as I held my breasts up as if in offering. The tempo quickened. I jiggled my hips, slapping the flesh together as I'd seen numerous women do in music videos. The cheek slapping ignited my pubis. I felt my labia swell, my clit engorge.

Chaz silently pressed against my back, hunched in concert with my movements. A hand slid down my front, leaving a silver trail behind. The tempo suddenly slowed. I slowed my body as well, held on to the metal railing and settled into a dangerous, deep, outward rock that allowed my hips to rhythmically brush against the hardening front of Chaz's pants.

Hands caressed my back as the liquid coursed lower. Flecks of silver glittered on the terrace floor like navigational bread crumbs in the dark night. Paint was poured over my shoulder, rubbed into my breasts and abdomen before it trailed into my bush. I felt the cool moisture as it coated my clit, slid between my lips, ran down my legs.

Thunder rumbled across the terrace. The air crackled in response. The rain pounded in fury.

Chaz's hands were everywhere—my back, my nipples, my clit. I was strung taut with need. He milked my tits with hot, luminescent fingers, teeth nipping my neck. My pussy juice factory surged into overproduction. I sighed as he kneaded my hips into liquid submission. Whimpered as he parted my globes. Stifled a scream as I felt his tongue roam where tongues rarely roam.

He took his time flicking over my puckered opening, lapping at the skin around it. I felt my body relaxing, opening, yearning for . . . more. He drew me backwards. His breath tickled me, made goose bumps break along my skin before his tongue probed, then stabbed inside the orifice. *Oh, the sensations!* My body bucked involuntarily as his goatee scratched the virginal tissue. My pussy wept, cried viscous tears of envy.

His fingers spread me wider, tongue delved deeper. My legs trembled violently against the cement wall; steam rose from my flesh. I leaned over to anchor myself. My nipples grazed the rough concrete, sending sparks throughout my body.

Chaz forced his tongue deeper, looped his biceps around my thighs, captured my hips between them. He lifted me then. My legs herky-jerked in the air as his head rotated between my cheeks. His tongue darted lower, parted my labial lips. My pussy welcomed the attention; honey showered him in adoration.

He settled into a nice rhythm, lapping among both holes. I undulated midair as his tongue spoke volumes to my womanhood. Magic fingers searched until they slid along my slippery highway and inside my folds. I almost cried as the digits stroked my core.

I was too close, too quick. I needed to slow down, get control. I turned, slid down his chest, nuzzled my face into his crotch, inhaling his fragrance. I couldn't resist as I pulled his pajama pants button free and pulled them slowly down. The tip of his cock pushed past the top of his BVDs waistband, red, pulsing. I pulled him to me and my lips tugged his shorts lower as I inhaled the musky scent of manliness. I let my face and hair trail over his heavy loins while drawing the material downward. He gasped as I breathed on his bulging sac, stepped out of the shorts as I passed his knees.

Strong fingers massaged my hair as I kissed up his thigh. My hands enclosed his stiff pole, stroked as I sucked and bit his tender flesh. He moaned as I enclosed one ball in my hot mouth. He emitted precum into my hand as I engulfed the entire scrotum. Just as I poised his cock to enter my mouth, his hands tugged my hair roots and drew me upright.

"First we paint, *then* we finish what you have started."

I remained silent, dipped my tips into the cool liquid before skimming them across his cheeks. My tongue flicked his lips as I coated his entire face and neck. He returned the favor, lingering as the color coated my lips.

This paint love play was taking too long for my overheated body. I brazenly tilted the jar, allowing the paint to flow across his chest and belly. My eager fingers spread the silver, covering every visible inch of his torso before I moved lower still. I left his cock untouched as I kneeled and kneaded the shimmer into his thighs, knees, and calves.

"Turn around." It was a command.

He held his arms open as I repeated the procedure along his back, his hips, and below. When I finished, he resembled a silver statue with a red-tipped cock as a focal point. I smiled at my handiwork.

"Your turn."

I stood, nipples peaked, showing my arousal. I'd expected him to just pour it over the areas he'd missed before, but he surprised me as he drew me into a kiss. The silver commingled between our mashed bodies as he rubbed me slowly across his chest. Fingers lifted my hair from my face as silver paint was drawn around my eyes, my mouth, my nose. Two silver statues embracing on a hotel terrace.

"In our new world, there are few rules and even fewer boundaries," Chaz whispered around my lips. "Inhibitions are negated by the promises of pleasure."

He was getting with the program! I nipped his top lip in affirmation. His tongue flicked into my ear. "Pleasure is accepted in whatever form or fashion is needed to achieve nirvana. There will be no censure, no shows of displeasure, no repercussions. Tell me what you need and I will fulfill your desire. Whatever it is . . . let go and let *me*."

I held his eyes. "I need to be fucked . . . hard . . . deep, like we'll never get another fuck again."

His nostrils flared, eyes darkened. He lifted my leg; his cock surged into me. My pussy groped, grasped the hard pole; wanted him to love every inch of my love hole. He grabbed my hair, twisted my head to the side as he sucked my neck. I scratched his back, pulled his ass to me, making him go deeper. Our bodies slid across each other, the paint creating a wild mosaic on our skin.

I slapped his hips, impaled myself on him, craving his dick like it was my favorite chocolate. He growled, tried to see if his cock could cut off my breath as he pistoned into me. Chaz's granite arms forced my legs wider still, shifted me higher. His cock suddenly brushed against my clit. Sparks zipped from my breasts, my fingers, my feet, triangulating at my nub. I added my voice to the thunder and yelled to the heavens as my womb clenched and geysered honey that mingled with the paint streaming down Chaz's legs.

7

Chaz

"Honey, wake up."

An elbow was nudged into my back. "Huh?" Elena had interrupted a very erotic dream in which two mermaids were about to defin themselves and spread wide before their god—me. Damn. I opened my eyes, stretched, and yawned widely. "What time is it?"

Elena was sitting up on her side of the bed, pulling at the skin of her big toe. She glanced at me. "After noon."

"Really? Wow, we really slept in today." The sky outside was still dark. "Rain?"

"Yes. According to CNN, they're expecting rain for most of today and tomorrow."

Well, that screwed up my sunset bonfire, reciting love poems, then sexing her down on the beach. I stretched again. "What do you want to do today?"

Elena looked up from scrutinizing her big toe and said, "We have an appointment at three."

I squinted at her. "Appointment? With whom?"

Elena gave me a lopsided smile. "You'll see." Then she resumed the whole big toe perusal.

She was definitely acting . . . different. I could see fine lines around the corners and a hint of darkness beneath her eyes. Jet lag? I tilted her face to look at me. "You feeling okay?"

Elena pulled out of my grasp. "I'm fine. Really. I am." She gave me a better, more normal smile, but I remained skeptical. I slipped an arm around her hips, laid my head in her lap. Her thigh muscles were tight, tense as I lay there. Something definitely wasn't right.

"What's up, babe? You don't look right."

She let out a deep sigh. "It's nothing. Probably my hormones."

I'd known Elena a long time, and never before had she used hormones as an excuse for any of her actions. "PMS?"

She made a face and shook her head. "No."

I suddenly grinned, rubbed my cheek into her belly. "Pregnant?" We'd been hinting at the whole baby thing but never gotten serious. Maybe it had caught up with us?

"Not that I know about."

Okay. It was time to give up and accept that this was one of those "things about girls men just don't get" moments. I shifted back to the original topic. "So, we've got an appointment at three."

"Yes, we do, so why don't we get dressed, grab some lunch, and get to where we are going. Time's a-wasting."

"What the wifey wants . . ."

". . . this wifey *surely* gets."

"Right."

Lunch was a lazy affair. There was no crowd in the dining room, so the service seemed exceptionally good. After lunch, we pulled up the collars on our borrowed slicks and jumped into a cab. Elena gave the cabbie the address. His eyes bucked and he glanced back and forth between us before finally turning around and putting the car in gear, a half-smile on his lips.

"What was that about?" I asked in her ear.

Elena feigned innocence. "What do you mean?"

"You know what I mean. The cab driver's reaction to the address."

She shrugged her shoulders. "I have no idea." My eyes bored into the back of her head as she stared out the window.

"I'll just bet you don't but I'll go with your flow."

She smiled and pecked my lips. "Thank you, baby."

The terrain changed from urban to suburban to finally rural. Through the rivulets of rain, I was surprised to see dairy cattle grazing on a wide pasture. "You have a dairy here?"

"Yes. The only one left on the islands."

The cattle looked like Holsteins but I couldn't be certain. "Are those Holsteins or a breed native to the islands?"

The cabbie looked in the mirror as he answered. "They are Holsteins. We don't have native cattle. Every one was imported here from somewhere else."

The cab sputtered, the transmission jerked then caught as it pulled up a hill. The engine sounds leveled off as we reached the top, then crested into a lush valley of palms and bougainvillea plants. The trees and plants were large, encroaching, diminishing the available light to near dusk. The cab driver stopped in front of a small, well-kept white house with a picket fence around the yard.

"This is it?" Elena asked.

"Yes'm. This is Ms. Beret's place."

"We'll need you to return in two hours. Let me give you my cell phone number."

The driver held up his hand. "I already know Ms. Beret's number by heart. Just tell her to ask for Harvey when she calls."

Elena nodded before opening the door. I paid the driver, then got out and stood beside her. The foliage was heavy, fragrant; the water just dripped here. I was no longer sure if it was still raining or if the plants were a shield, deflecting the rainwater elsewhere. Pulling Elena to me, I asked again, "Baby, what are we doing here?"

"Chaz, I want—no, I *need* to do this."

I quirked my head. "And what's that?"

"You . . . will . . . see. Trust me." Elena slid her palm into mine and squeezed. I squeezed back. She then pulled me along to the front door.

The doorbell had not finished its chime when it was opened by somebody's grandmother. No lie. The woman was at least seventy, wore thick glasses, had gray hair, was short, dumpy, and dressed in a caftan. My curiosity meter was on high alert.

"Elena?" she asked, showing off two rows of dentures.

"I am and this is my husband, Chaz." Her eyes gave me a quick once-over that left me feeling . . . exposed.

"I'm Beret. Come in."

"I'm glad you had a time to fit us in." *For what?* I wanted to ask for the umpteenth time.

"Oh, I always allow time for visitors to the island."

The inside of the house was just as tidy as the outside. We followed her through the foyer into her living room. "Let me have those slicks, and make yourselves comfy. The air isn't too low, is it?"

"It feels good in here," Elena supplied as we pulled off the rain slicks and handed them to Beret. She left the room and returned bearing a tray.

"Fresh cookies and tea." I declined the offer, but Elena picked up two of the chocolate variety. Beret sat in a dainty chair across from us and sipped from her cup. "Let's get the preliminaries out of the way. Welcome to my home. I am Beret, as in Green Beret. Not my birth name, of course, but what people of the island call me." She looked at Elena. "Does he know?"

Know what?

Elena shook her head. Beret nodded and continued. "Today will be a wonderful experience in the world of . . . fellatio." I glanced at Elena, puzzled. She was all pearly whites now.

"The art of fellatio is just that, an art form. The penis, as you well know, is not only an instrument of pleasure, it also loves being pleasured. But not everyone can pleasure it in the manner you want. Sometimes, a partner can be too rough, not rough enough, mouth too shallow, not enough spit to lubricate, teeth get in the way—all of these can decrease the pleasure fellatio was meant to be." This speech was so not right coming from some kid's granny—but I was more than down with allowing Elena to perfect her technique.

"But it's not totally about the male. Oh no. Good fellatio affects the woman, too. The taste, the feel of sucking and nibbling a ripe penis"—*Did she say ripe?*—"will make a woman's nipples tighten into small balls, make her womb leak, make her nostrils flare and her asshole pucker." Passion infused her speech; no shame evident—Sue Johanson in a decade still dispensing advice. I chuckled in my mind. "That's right, good head will make your hips quake, your stomach quiver, and your toes curl. A good blow job ought to make you sweat, make you cry, make you howl like a werewolf on a full-moon night." She clasped her hands to her bosom, eyes closed, an expression of awe on her face.

The exterior might be Granny . . . but the interior is definitely *Superhead.* I was sold!

She let her neck roll, then opened her eyes and smiled. "My goal is that by the end of this session, you both will have the tools to figure out what you need . . . and know how to get what you need from fellatio. Questions?" She looked at us.

"Yep. When do we start?" I asked. Elena laughed and swatted my arm. "I'm just saying, time's wasting, right?" Hell, my cock was on G just waiting for the O.

Beret stood. "It starts right now. If you will enter the room behind you and put on the robes hanging inside, I'll be with you in ten minutes." She gathered up the tray and left the room.

I tapped Elena on the ass as she crossed in front of me. She hit me back, giggling before dashing inside the room. I closed the door, grabbed her, and pushed her against the wall. "Girl, you are a trip! A blow-job class . . ."

"You know your kinky ass will enjoy it."

"Damn right! Shoot, I'm ready to cum right now." I rubbed my cock against her pelvis. "Just touch it, baby."

"Uh-uh. I know you. I get to touching you and before you know it, you'll have popped."

I had to admit it was true. "True . . . but I can get it back hard."

"Yeah, in a few hours." She snorted and gave me a quick eye roll. "Let's just wait and do it right the first time."

"I guess so." I dry-humped her a couple of times for good measure.

"Boy, if you don't get off me!" She hit me on the shoulder and pushed me back, blowing kisses at the sad face I'd put on. "Now let's get these robes on!"

8

The room we entered was obviously made for sex. A full-sized canopy bed took center stage, a sheet its only bedding. Candles had been placed around the perimeter and lit. The smell of incense was strong; the music, New Age—a pulsing bass or drums.

Beret entered through a door across the room. She had changed from her flowered caftan into a red one of similar cut, the glasses were now pince-nez, and a red wig sat on her head, matching her red lipstick. "If you would disrobe and lie on the bed."

The robes slid to the floor and we positioned ourselves facing each other on the bed. Beret smiled, then began. "The widely held practice of making a cunt of your mouth and bobbing up and down until a man climaxes does *not* make you a decent cocksucker. To become a good cocksucker, you have to study your subject, the penis, as well as what's attached to it, the man. And I hate to say this, but it's true: Know the penis, know the man." Elena nodded vigorously. I kept silent, not planning to give up *any* Man Laws.

"Now, before you jump into fellatio, you must set the mood, allow the biggest sex organ—your brain—to catch up to the changes in your body. Like they say, 'Screw the mind and the ass will follow.' Let's start with a warm oil massage." She handed me a small vial of oil. "Begin at the neck, move down the shoulders to the breasts, then back to the neck. The neck is the key. It needs to be as limber as possible."

I squirted a copious amount of oil into my palm and began spreading it lightly. "Knead it. Work it in. Let her feel you." I followed the directions, applying additional pressure as my hands rubbed and swirled, swirled and rubbed around the neck, over the shoulders, slipping the nipples through my fingers, then back up and repeating.

Elena felt pliant, relaxed. "Ooh. That's getting hot." My palms were pretty warm also.

"It's working, then. Swap."

We shifted. "Elena, now, your job is a bit larger. You need to focus on the lower part of Chaz. Start at his abdomen and move downward, but at no time do you touch his cock, okay?"

Elena had never been the massager; instead, her normal role was massagee. She kneeled between my thighs and began by dribbling oil into my belly button. It was nice to feel her hands slowly rubbing all over my body, pushing in, squeezing, massaging, her hands feeling like silk as they moved around. I felt the heat radiating from her on my cock but, true to the directions, she never let the flesh make contact. Over and under my thighs she stroked, rubbed, moving slowly, torturously down my appendages.

"Blow."

Elena blew lightly on my skin. My flesh heated, tingled, reached the point of burn . . . but not quite. She blew again; I sizzled—the hair stood up on my legs, my arms. She leaned her face down, let the raised hairs brush against her, let them telegraph the sensations back down to me. My cock thickened;

rose slowly. Elena watched my cock as she moved to my ankles, sucking, licking the inner bone, letting her tongue trail over the tops of my feet to my toes.

She met my eyes. "This little piggy . . ." She laughed before engulfing my big toe between her lips, letting her wet tongue slather spit over and around it. Her hot mouth moved to the bottom of my feet, lapped up and down slowly, tickling and making me twitch. My feet flexed, curled, wanted to escape her harrowing tongue. I clenched and unclenched my fists; wanted to slide her back up my body and onto my cock.

Elena sensed this. She snapped her teeth at me, nipped my pinky toe before letting hot fingers trail back up my leg . . . over my knee . . . over my thigh . . . inside my thigh. Her hair brushed my sac. My cum juice pushed up my duct, readied itself for release at the first opportune moment.

"Elena, tongue all around his pubic area, avoiding his cock at *all* costs," Beret urged.

Elena's heat, her breath on my pubic hairs . . . blood thickened my cock further. Her tongue traced circles, swirls, diagonals, rectangles, alphabets, and numbers in my bush; she pulled at the coarse strands with her teeth, making my pube sting, hurt—please repeat. I wanted to wrap my fingers in her hair, drag her mouth onto me, let her wet heat soothe my cum-bloated cock. My toes splayed, curled, splayed, curled as she got close, retreated, got close again, retreated.

Sweat popped up on my brow, over my lips, around my neck, across my chest, inside my navel, between my thighs, beneath my knees, and coated my calves—and on played Elena's tongue. She licked, lapped, dipped and dappled here and there, tracing my body creases, catching a rivulet of sweat that she just lapped back, commingling it with the other sweat on my flesh.

I tensed my pelvis, lifted my cock's head; tried to sneak onto some mouth action. Watching her tongue had my nipples tight;

wanting her tongue made my balls tight. My sac pulsed, pushed, tested my sphincters, looking for a weakness, a breach in the muscle that would allow release. Elena let her breath flow over my cock, let her tongue extend farther, closer to my red head . . . closer . . . *Got*damn! Touch it, baby! . . . then pulled back at the last possible moment. Cum pushed harder, made it halfway up my cum highway . . .

This was too much!

I slid back from her mouth, my breath rapid and heavy. "Give me a sec."

Beret handed Elena a cock ring. "Slide this on in a minute." She then passed her a lozenge. "Suck on this while you wait."

Now I'd seen cock rings, but had never worn one. Never needed it before.

"Now we get into the touch aspect," Beret said quietly. "Cocksucking is to be savored. Time should be of no meaning to you. You should start by letting your tongue trail around and over the cock, avoiding the head." She looked at me. "Whenever you're ready."

I took a deep breath, knowing that when I shot this load, it would be a doozy. Like not since I first got married or was in college climax doozy. The kind that makes me feel like I'd shot a plug from my dick; like it was a mini-volcano, happy for the release of pressure.

I knew it . . . because I smelled it.

Elena's fresh pussy was ripe for the taking. Her fragrance drifted up to me, was a fuck-the-sucking-just-let-me-bury-my-dick-deep-in-your-snatch temptation. Ain't much sexier to me than when I know that *my* woman is ripe for *my* cock. And boy, was she ready. Her fingers rubbed, rolled the cock ring between them, anxious to slide it down my pole, keep me in the game a bit longer. A light sheen of sweat glinted off her chest. Her eyes stayed on the prize. Oh yes indeed, she wanted me.

"Let's do this." I slid back to her, let my thighs spread

around her kneeling form. Her hands were cool; I lurched as the ring slid slowly down my shaft to the base. Elena slid her hands up over my belly, then grasped my rod, let her tongue slide up the side, a rope of saliva trailing behind its path. She nibbled, licked around to the other side, never touching the head.

I felt the skin tightening, swelling. The nerve endings in my head were tingling, anticipating, filled with anxiety to feel the hot wetness of her mouth.

"Now lick the underside of the head. That's where most of the nerve endings are."

Elena complied, tongue flicking beneath my meaty bulb. My hands bunched the sheets; the constant slapping and flicking of the tongue twisting my feet in unnatural positions. I shifted, tried to stick it between her lips; my head wanted to find its warm hole. Cum leaked from my head—more to follow soon.

"Now slide down to his balls. Suck them."

Her tongue burned a trail past the cock ring to the sac. My spongy head protested, but not for long. She captured a ball in her mouth, rolled it around, sucked it lightly. My pelvis lifted as she commandeered the other nut, slid it beside the first in her warm mouth. The double nut suck made my asshole clench and release; made me bite my lip to stop the groan just behind my teeth; made me dig holes in the sheet to stop slamming my cock into her mouth.

"Go back to the head, but this time, put it in your mouth."

Elena lapped my lollipop back up to the tip, taking her slow sweet time, tongue finding, investigating every nook, cranny, and crevice along the way. She circled the skin beneath the head with her fingers before—finally, thankfully—letting her mouth cover my head.

I yelped, the shit felt so good! Her mouth tingled as she closed her lips around it lightly. Then she started circling with her head. Clockwise, counterclockwise, slow then fast. She nibbled along my ridge, let her tongue diddle my cum slit. My head swelled, tried to expand to reach every side of her mouth. I felt cum dribbling from me, not in climax but uncontrollable nonetheless.

Elena rose higher on her knees, positioned herself directly over me.

"Bob on it."

Her teeth purposely raked slowly, delectably across the head. "Ooh shit." Then she opened her mouth wider, let my head touch the top of her mouth. She rolled her lips over her teeth, slid me farther inside. The tingling intensified as she sucked and pulled at my rod. A hand cupped my balls, the other fisting at my base. Her head bobbed up, down, fast then slow . . . as . . . hell while one hand massaged my balls, helping the cum farther up the cum highway, and the other twisted and massaged my rod. My heart pounded, eyelids twitched, toenails pulsed, and hair throbbed as Elena let her mouth engulf more and more of me.

Her lozenge-enhanced cavity was an inferno. And my cum wanted to quench the fire!

"Hum on him."

Her vocal cords emitted a vibration I could feel to the base of my balls. My cock lengthened, searched for the source of vibrating pleasure deep within her mouth. Saliva poured from between her lips, her fisted hand gripped, released; made the bulbocavernous tissue expand, then harden with blood.

I . . . am . . . going . . . to . . . *cum*!

"You ever had a deep throat?" Beret whispered in my ear. My breath stuttered, and cum began a rapid march up the highway to the head. "If you can hold out, I can show Elena how to give you one."

My eyes rolled in my head as I tensed, clenched, strained to stop my soldier from shooting its load. My temples throbbed with the effort. I tried to shift my mind anywhere but the thought of being buried to the hilt in my wife's mouth as I came. Sperm pushed, shoved at my sphincter; pounded at the flesh, determined to see daylight since there was not an available egg to attach to. My face morphed into uber-ugly mode, the exertion of not cumming turning me into a monster. Elena squeezed the cock ring, aiding my efforts. It was touch or go for a few seconds until I felt the cum receding; felt the soldiers retreat . . . but only a few steps.

"Lie on your back and let your head hang over the side." Elena turned over and complied. "Now, Chaz, Elena won't have much of a gag reflex because of the lozenge I gave her, so you must be extra careful. Take your time, pump slow, and above all else, watch your partner's face."

I positioned myself in front of her mouth and angled downward. Elena wrapped her arms around my hips and opened her mouth. I slid inside. The different position made it very obvious to me I would be going deeper. I took my time pushing in a bit, then pulling back; being careful. Elena began licking me then. Her tongue wrapped and curled around my pole with each thrust inward. She let her teeth scrape my head as I pulled back.

I watched how my cock slid between her lips, the saliva pooling, her throat working. It was when I saw the impression of my cock in her throat that my soldiers snapped to attention and began their march home. I plucked Elena's stiff nipples. Her fingers dug into my ass, pulled me closer. I held back, not wanting to injure her. She started to bob her mouth on me. *Bad move.* My head mushroomed; my cock became a piece of steel in her mouth. She pulled my thighs, threw me off balance, made me lean over, pushing me deeper . . .

"Relax the throat!" Beret yelled.

Elena's muscles relaxed. She rotated her head beneath me, made me slide the length and breadth of my cock into her throat. Her mouth felt too damn good, like a slick glove hugging me close. The sucking, the wetness, the depth—I didn't stop the cum rising, running, rushing up my tubules, telegraphing to the rest of the sperm it was get the hell out of Dodge day as my sphincter finally gave way, the tissue trampled in the wave of sperm crashing, shooting, catapulting from my head. My volcano had erupted.

We dressed and joined Beret back in the living room. "Sit, please." We complied. "So, what did you think?"

I spoke first. "I've had blow jobs, but today"—I looked at Elena—"today, baby, you outdid yourself." It was true.

Elena smiled. "You know, when I first saw the sign in the store, something scratched at me, my soul, made me admit that this was an area where I needed some help."

"What do you mean, baby? I never complained about the way you . . . performed head before."

"I know you didn't say anything. It was something I just . . . felt; an area where I knew I wasn't up to snuff." She made a face and looked away. "So when this chance came along, I jumped on it."

I turned her face back to me. "And it was worth it."

"Well, that's a good start." Beret clapped her hands. She passed Elena a bag. "Just a souvenir from me." Inside were more of the lozenges and a small book. "Now, your driver is waiting." She rose, walked us to the door. "Have a great trip home!"

"We will, and thank you for everything." Elena gave her a hug.

"Bye." I hugged her also, still not able to reconcile her looks with her true nature. Her eyes twinkled, hinted at a wild life. In her ear, I whispered, "I'll bet you were a handful when you were younger."

She pulled back, showing her double row of dentures as she winked before replying, "Honey, I still am."

I chuckled low. "I'm sure every bit of that is true."

"Oh, it is. Y'all come back and try my playacting next time."

"If we ever get back, it's a done deal."

Harvey, the cab driver, held the door open, a cracked-tooth smile on his face. "Had a good time?"

"Pretty good," I responded as Elena ducked into the cab.

"That's what most folks say when they come out."

"You haven't tried Beret?"

He frowned and vigorously shook his head. "I'm only a poor cab driver. Ms. Beret's stuff's too rich for my blood."

I scrunched up my face. "Yeah, right. Sounds like a hint to get a big tip."

"Now, would I do something like that?" He broke into a smile again.

The ride back seemed faster. Harvey and I chatted back and forth while Elena stayed pretty quiet. He dropped us back in front of the hotel with an admonishment to look him up if we ever came back. I paid him—plus a very large tip—and escorted Elena to the room.

Though sex was on my mind—like it was twenty-four seven—Elena had reverted to her previous slightly strange behavior. Gone were the smiles and the giggling. Now she sat mute, silent. Our flight left tomorrow morning, so we just showered and lounged around, watching television. The coverage of the fire continued to be the top story. Yes, after seeing the footage, I knew we'd been given a heaping dose of grace.

Thanks, God.

9

Elena

Mexico City

When the plane sat down on the tarmac in Mexico City, my mood suddenly changed. I was feeling f-r-e-a-k-y!

Customs took a long minute to get through. Chaz and I conversed about mundane things—the people we saw, the terminal, even the workers' uniforms. I was fidgeting inside, ready to see whatever there was to see in this wild and crazy city. Finally we were through. We grabbed our suitcases and stepped outside into a wilting heat, like the sky had zipped down and wrapped us in a sweltering cocoon. Chaz pulled at his shirt, sweat rings under his armpits. I felt a bit cooler. After all, I loved the heat.

We stood around with two other couples, waiting for the hotel bus to arrive. From the easy exchange they were having, I'd say they appeared to be traveling together. The bus arrived in a cloud of exhaust. It was a double-decker affair, needing a paint job and, from the squeal as it stopped, some brake pads.

We shuffled up the metal stairs and claimed a seat. The couples sat around us.

"You guys down on vacation?" a short pert blonde leaned

over the back of the seat and asked. Her partner was a taller, blonder man with a prominent Adam's apple and bad acne.

I turned to get her into my view. "Yes." I held up my hand. "I'm Elena and this is my husband, Chaz."

She shook our hands. "Nice to meet ya. I'm Pokey and this is my sweetie, David." David nodded but didn't offer his hand.

The man across the aisle got into the discussion. "I'm Steve and this is my wife, Dana." Dana smiled and gave a wiggle wave. "We're from Scottsdale, down at a conference."

"Really. What's the conference about?" Chaz asked.

"Engineering. We work for the Department of Defense, and they sent us down here," Steve supplied. "What about you guys?"

Chaz looked at me, a smirk forming on his lips before he spoke. "We're down on vacation—kind of."

"Ooh, I smell a secret!" Pokey squealed. "What's a 'kind of' vacation? Share!"

I couldn't wait to see how Chaz answered this question. He quirked an eyebrow at me. I gave him a shrug back. "Well, my wife and I have embarked on a . . . Sexolympics adventure."

"What!" Pokey screamed. Chick definitely had been a cheerleader—the squeal, the hyperactivity about anything—cheerleader recognized cheerleader. "That is so . . . wild!" She turned to David. "Why can't you ever come up with something delicious like that!" She bopped him on the arm. David rubbed his arm and looked out the window.

We all laughed at her. "For real, man? You guys aren't just pulling our legs, are you?" Steve asked.

"For real," Chaz replied, nodding. "It was Elena's idea."

"No shit." Dana finally spoke, her eyes wavering between me and Chaz. I could see the deep interest in her baby blues. "So, what . . . how do you do this? Swingers clubs? Swaps? What?"

"Yeah, what!" Pokey squealed again.

"So far, we've gone to sex clubs, did some body painting . . ." Chaz looked at me.

"And we took a class in fellatio," I finished.

"Whoa!" Dana yelped.

Steve slid to the edge of his seat and leaned over, his head rotating back and forth between us. "Seriously. They have blow-job classes? And you guys participated in one?"

"They do and we did." I felt Chaz's chest swell. Guess he'd scored some Man Points or something with these guys.

"Do you know if they have one here?" Dana asked.

"Yeah! We wanna go!" Pokey jumped up and down in her seat.

I held up my hand. "Actually, we were in Hawaii and it was a fluke that I found out about it. I was shopping in Leather and Lace—"

"Don't you just *love* that store?" Pokey clapped her hands. "The thongs are to *die* for!"

"Yes, I do. I ran across the ad in the store and decided to surprise Chaz with it." I patted his thigh. "I didn't look for anything like that online here, though."

"Was it worth it?" Dana asked, looking at Chaz.

His head shook like a bobble head doll. "Every dime she spent."

"Shit." Steve sat back in his seat, a faraway expression on his face.

"So what do you guys have up while you are here?" Dana asked.

"I found a place call Juanita's. It's supposed to be upscale, anonymous, and wild as hell. The site said whatever you think you want, you can find at Juanita's."

"And when are you guys going?" Dana obviously was interested in seeing Juanita's for herself.

"I don't know, today or tomorrow. We figured we'd chill, hang out in a bar or two tonight, see how we feel and go from there."

"Can we tag along?" Pokey asked.

"No!" David responded, then turned and looked back out the window. Pokey huffed and slammed back into her seat, a frown on her face.

Okay, they won't be there.

"Is it hard to get in?" Steve asked.

"I don't think so. I paid for everything online and they said to bring ID, but otherwise, it didn't seem too complex."

"Cool." He turned to Dana. "You down for this, baby?"

"You already know I am. Hell, I'm getting hot just talking about it." She pulled Steve to her and slammed her lips over his. Chick tongued him deep and thorough, making Steve's hands pull at her waist.

Damn! They're going to screw right in front of us!

The bus stuttering and shuddering to a stop in front of the hotel was what finally jostled them apart. Not that I was complaining. I was a voyeur first, partaker second.

We disembarked the bus and entered the crisp air of the lobby. The wonderful architecture impressed me—stucco walls, brick floors, multiple archways. We women lounged on the sofas and continued to chat while the men checked in.

"Was it really your idea?" Dana asked. "You know men can be anal about their women and sex."

"Yes, it was all my idea. We'd gotten dull, and it was either this or get a boyfriend." We all chuckled at this.

"Boyfriend! You actually said that?" Pokey whispered. I nodded. "Girl, you are crazy! David would have shit a brick . . . *after* he punched a hole in the wall . . . just above my head."

The image was a bit disturbing to me. From what I'd seen so far, I could see him reacting like that. I had to ask. "So what's your story? You guys seem so . . . different from each other. Y'all really soul mates?"

Pokey glanced over to where the guys stood, still at the counter, then gestured for us to lean in. "I don't ever tell everybody, but since we're talking about your Sexolympics, I feel the need to share. You know, bond and all—"

Dana yanked Pokey's hair, cutting her off. "Girl! Cut the chatter and get to the point! Damn!"

"Okay." She took a deep breath. "He is my . . . master."

"What!" Two sets of astonished eyes peered at her.

She scrunched up her face. "Yeah, you know, S and M, sub and dom? He's my Dom and I'm his Sub, Fem."

Shut my mouth, folks!

"And you had the nerve to be excited about my Sexolympics?" I laughed. "We're taking baby steps and you're already in the big leagues."

"Steve and I have played at S and M, but I can't see it as a lifestyle," Dana added.

Pokey shrugged. "Well, it is one, and there are plenty of people into it, too. It's not a hobby we indulge in a few days a month. We are 'on' twenty-four seven, three sixty-five."

"So I saw," I said recalling how David had snapped on the bus.

"What are you ladies whispering about?" Chaz asked. Six startled eyes whipped around to look at him. "What?" He took a step back.

I stood, went over to him. "Nothing, honey. We were just getting acquainted a bit more. That's all."

"Sure you were." He chucked me under the chin, one of those I-don't-believe-you-but-I'll-get-the-info-from-you-later chucks. "The guys want to meet around four-ish and maybe we can see the sights a bit."

"Sounds good." I turned back to the girls. "We're going to go up and take a nap, then catch you around four."

"See you guys then," Dana and Pokey replied.

We went to our room and fell into bed, sleep claiming us almost instantly.

The bar they chose wasn't too far from the hotel, a five-minute walk that probably took fifteen since I had to stop and pick up stuff at the market booths along the way. When we arrived, the place was moderately packed, the music thumping, but we were led to a table quickly. I was sorry that Pokey and David had reneged on the invite after initially agreeing, but after what she'd shared, I thought I understood. David was flexing his Master muscles, probably punishing an eager Pokey with hard, rapid slaps to the ass right this second.

We chatted as we ate, swapping more information on our lives. Drinks were ordered and more and more people drifted in. As the daylight became dusk, we noticed the place was now packed to the hinges. Many nationalities were represented, not all in good taste. The air was electric, like the people who were waiting. We soon found out what for . . .

A spotlight was switched on at a stage at the end of the bar. A dark, mustachioed man stood there, a microphone in his hands. He hit the head of the mic twice; the feedback made us all wince. He cleared his throat, then leaned back and said, "Ladies and Gents! Jews and Gentiles . . . along with a few Muslims, welcome to Mucho Mucho! Tonight is Ladies' Night, and you know what happens when it's Ladies' Night . . ."

A raucous roar rose from the crowd. "Show your girls!"

"That's correct! It's Show Your Girls Night! For those uninformed, the girls are those two things on a woman's chest. And how do we like them?"

"Firm! Front and center!" the crowd yelled.

That explained the crowd. This obviously was a normal event for the establishment, and the folks were salivating for some tits!

"This ought to be good!" Steve rubbed his hands together. Chaz had the good sense to act unfazed.

"So, Laaaa-dddiiieeesss! Don't be shy. Just step right up and show us your girls! And remember, the most memorable pair gets what?"

"A place on the Show Your Girls Hall of Shame!"

"Correct! We have a trophy wall specially designed to let the winning girls be shown off for eternity—or until we go out of business. So step right up, ladies! Now, DJ, rock the house!"

The place got rowdy after that. The music thumped, the people danced and swayed, ground and rolled, and woman after woman was helped onto the bar. The breasts were typical—some large, some small, firm, droopy, and one grandmother who obviously was young at heart . . . only in *her* head.

I saw the man with the mic walking through the crowd. He stopped at our table and looked at Dana, then me before speaking. "Hello, everyone, enjoying yourselves?"

We all nodded.

"Great. If you hadn't noticed, the pickings are kind of slim tonight. How about you two ladies go up and give those chicks a run for their money? Hmmm?" He glanced at Chaz, then Steve. "Think of how great of a story it would be when you got home, right, fellas?"

Steve, too many shots of Jack Daniel's under his belt, yelled, "Damn right! Go on, Dana! Show your girls!" He gave Dana a push to the arm.

"Naw, they ain't ready for what I'm packing." She pulled her T-shirt taut, letting her pointed nipples press through the shirt.

"Wow! That's an impressive rack you've got there, lady." The announcer man licked his lips. I'm sure if Steve hadn't been half drunk, he would have slugged the guy. "I think you should." He turned to me. "What about you? You game?"

Now, I was a "thickum," as the old folks called us healthy

chicks. My girls were thirty-eight double-Ds and firm as they came. Doctors hated them; said they were "too firm." I looked down at them, then at Chaz. He smirked. "Scared you'll start a riot?"

"Actually, I was worried about what you would think."

"Hell, this journey is about pushing the limits, so . . ." He waved toward the bar.

I looked across the table. "Dana, you in?"

She looked at Steve, who gave her another light push. "Yes. Let's show them how the USA does it."

The announcer couldn't wait to pull the mic to his mouth. "Looks like we've got some new blood joining us straight from the US of A!" The spotlight scanned the room and held on us as we walked to the end of the bar. Bodies pressed into us, copped a stolen feel here and there under the guise of making room and helping us to navigate the crowd. We were lifted onto the bar behind the already waiting women.

"Last call! Going! Going! Gone! Now, gentlemen, you know the drill. We'll cue the music and the women can *expose* their girls—and anything else they think we need to see—for you to judge. We determine the winner by the noise you make! And please, fellas, don't get carried away or a bouncer *will* carry you away."

The crowd laughed.

The music began, and I have to say, the song selection was on point. It was the song from the movie *Shall We Dance?* where Jennifer Lopez is teaching Richard Gere how to tango in a near-dark studio. It always turned me on, and tonight was no different. At the first chords, I felt my body come alive.

My hands started at my thighs, drifted up and over my butt, squeezed and moved around to my stomach, where I pulled my T-shirt free. Every fourth beat, the song hit a hard note. My body started to "vogue" on each hard note. First the shirt was pulled over my head. There was appreciative clapping as my bra-covered boobs were revealed. I lifted a hip, paused, swung the opposite direction, paused, dipped low, paused. A man in the crowd suddenly tugged my arm, pulled me off balance. I went down on a knee, hands flattening on the bar to steady myself.

The men surged, held me in place. My eyes were wild as thick fingers fumbled at my bra clasp. I struggled, yelled out as the clasp opened and the bra was pulled from my chest. A loud yell went over the group of men nearest me. I watched as my bra was swung in the air, then flew across the crowd. The hands released me then.

I stood, now naked from the waist up. Whistles and catcalls rang out. The other women were also naked from the waist up and posing, smiles all around. Dana was seated on her knees, holding her tits just out of reach of a man who was trying his damnedest to pull one into his mouth. Just as he got close, she laughed and pushed his head away.

"Swing them!" someone yelled. I leaned forward, let the girls fall, then swung them back and forth, picking up tempo. I cupped them, pulled at the nipples before placing a stiff button in my mouth and sucking.

Hands tried to grab my feet, pull me close as I sucked my own breast. I sidestepped them, enjoying the tease show I was putting on. I mimicked Dana, slid onto my knees, pushing my tits toward the crowd. I let unknown, barely seen hands stroke and rub but pulled back before a mouth made contact.

The lioness in me rose to the surface. I got on all fours, crawled, allowing my tits to jiggle before I touched them to the bar surface, pumping my ass in the air. I felt something hit my butt. I turned, saw a twenty dollar bill sliding down between my legs. I nodded at the crowd. More money followed as I dry-humped on the bar. I had to confess, I liked the anonymity, the attention from the unknown men. I licked my lips at the crowd.

A hand suddenly grabbed the leg of my jeans and slid me

across the bar toward the crowd. My hands found no purchase on the slippery surface. I was pulled to the edge and flipped over. My hands were trapped above my head and a mouth clamped on to my nipple. I yelped, struggled . . . at first . . .

The mouth on my tit was warm and practiced. The tongue swirled around and around before the head was lifted, pushed aside. A new tongue lapped at my distended nipple, pulled at the areola; my pussy was on fire. "Bite," I urged, wanting more pressure, a touch of pleasure pain. He did. My pelvis rose into the air. Hands were on my crotch, pulling, mashing over my clit—igniting my body.

Just when a hand began fumbling with the button of my pants, the music ended. The hands stopped. The crowd clapped. I was released. The overhead lights were turned on. I smiled as I saw Chaz just below my waist, hands still on my jeans. I guessed he was the one trying to unbutton my pants. His eyes gleamed, sweat was on his forehead. He licked his lips.

"Was that a show or what, fellas?" the announcer yelled, gaining everyone's attention again.

The crowd screamed its approval.

"Now, the hard job. Just who was the winner or, possibly, in this case, winners?"

There were whistles and catcalls.

"Show your appreciation if you think number one is the winner!" The spotlight shone on a young lady with a surgery-enhanced rack. The surgical lines were evident but the boobs were large enough to make a man not notice. The applause was loud and long. Competition indeed.

The announcer followed down the row of women, the applause not as loud as the first woman. He finally reached Dana. When the spotlight fell on her, the applause and noise was immediate. It continued for a few minutes. Dana gave a modest curtsy when the noise died down.

Next was my turn. When the heat of the spotlight hit me,

the men yelled, screamed, began hitting the tables, and jumping up and down. I wasn't sure if it was more than Dana, but it made me feel pretty good. I cupped my breasts, gave them a squeeze for the crowd.

"It was a tight contest, but looks like we have a winner!" The spotlight shone on *me*! I bowed, letting my twins bob about. The announcer walked over and said, "Pose for the camera, honey." I stood in a saucy pose that had my tits pushed way out. "Congratulations to our newest winner . . ." He placed a hand over the microphone. "What's your name, honey?" I gave it to him. "Elena from the good old US of A!"

Chaz, wisely, had scooped up the money that had been thrown my way. He'd also retrieved my T-shirt. I glanced around, saw my bra being worn over some guy's head. He didn't look like he was trying to give it back, so I decided to let him keep it. A souvenir.

"Who the hell were you, up there?" Chaz asked, pulling me into a deep, wet kiss.

"Just me," I said as I pulled the shirt over my head. "You liked?"

"Very much so." He pushed his pelvis against me. "Feel that?" His cock was hard as a boulder.

I ran a hand across it, squeezed. "Want me to take care of it for you?" I let my tongue circle my lips.

"Hell yeah!"

Dana had dressed and Steve had joined her. After a complimentary Polaroid was given to me, we exited. Dana and Steve headed out to another bar while we headed back to the hotel. After all, I had to help Chaz with his little problem . . . didn't I?

10

Chaz

Elena bumped and twirled, backed up and ground on me as we walked back to the hotel. Her mood had definitely shifted to happy . . . or maybe I should say it was more happy-daredevil mode. What else could explain her taking up the dare, getting into the bare-breast contest, and by damn if she hadn't won. Confirmation of what I already knew: Elena was *smoking*!

Now, I wasn't real calm when those dudes pulled her to the edge and took off her bra. Nosiree. I slung dudes left and right trying to get to her. But once I was barside, it was obvious my girl was having the time of her life—shaking her tits, jiggling them in their faces, and finally, letting those hungry jokers get a suck.

Elena stopped, backed into me, pumped her ass on my hard cock.

"Girl, you are just looking for trouble, aren't you?"

"Nope, just a long . . . hard . . . *fuck*."

My cock expanded another centimeter in my pants. "You keep teasing and you're gonna get what you want."

She tweaked my nose, pulled away, and did that exaggerated hip sway thing she knew I loved: her fuck-me strut. Her round ass swung from side to side in her jeans. I wished they were tight enough to make a camel toe, but I had to be satisfied with the bouncing ball effect since they weren't.

She switched back into conservative businesswoman mode as we strode through the crowded lobby, but once we hit the walkway to our room, fuck mode returned stronger than before. She dropped her key, bent over, looked at me from between her legs, her hips gyrating slowly. She patted her ass and began singing Janet Jackson's "You Want This": "Early in the morning . . . you want this!" Her ass lifted with each pat, the healthy globes jiggling obscenely.

Be careful who you tease . . .

I stepped up behind her before she could lift upright. She yelped midsong, tried to straighten up.

Uh-uh, baby.

I wrapped a hand in her hair and placed the other on the small of her back, holding her in the bent-over position she had chosen. She fidgeted, tried to shake me.

Thought you wanted to play the tease game, sweetie.

I squatted a bit, fit the head of my throbbing cock into the crook of her pussy, humped her hard and fast. She gasped, putting her hand out to steady herself as I slammed into her. Elena's knees buckled and her hips trampolined in the air from the force of my dry fuck.

I heard voices coming closer. I stopped, released her hair, let her stand just as a family turned the corner. They nodded and walked past, no break in their conversation. Elena's chest rose and fell from the unexpected exertion. Her eyes were glazed, her face vacant. Sexual shock?

I leaned closer, a smirk on my face. "Now . . . what were you saying again?"

Her eyes jumped around my face but she said nothing. I

took a hand in mine and pulled her close. Elena was quiet and compliant as we walked through the double doors leading to the sidewalk to our house suite.

Now, our house suite was at the back of the main structure. These house suites were really duplexes with shared terraces. I wasn't crazy about the whole be on the first floor with an outside entrance into our room, but so far I'd seen nothing to make me too concerned. Security guards were visible, and other than an elderly couple power-walking around the perimeter wall, I had no clue who the other neighbors were or even if there were other neighbors.

I unlocked the door, planning on ambushing Elena the second it closed. Fate, however, intervened—let the key stick in the lock. I cursed as I pulled and jiggled, tried to twist and turn the stuck key. *Damn, they need to get keycards!* Elena, unaware of my licentious intentions, walked to the sliding doors and out onto the terrace, where she stood looking up at the sky.

It took a few more vigorous shakes before the damn key finally slid out. I tossed the key on the foyer table. Elena leaned her head in. "Psst!" Her finger twirled in the air, beckoning me.

"What?" I asked as I joined her. She pointed across the terrace. I saw . . . something . . . but I wasn't exactly sure what, since a street lamp glared in my periphery, interfering with my sight. I moved out farther onto the terrace, got the street lamp behind me, and looked again. This time I definitely knew what I was seeing—a dude was screwing the hell out of some chick.

Elena tugged at my sleeve. "Don't let them see you. Let's walk around the edge of the bushes and get as close as we can."

Damn watching them! *My* cock was hard and ready to screw the hell out of my *own* chick.

She pulled me into the shadows, tiptoeing around the terrace furniture, making our way closer. She stopped suddenly; making me bump into her. "Shhhh," she whispered, a finger held to her lips.

A guttural moan hung in the air before *Thwack!* My cock jumped. There was a *clank!* The moan cut off, then resumed. I leaned around her head to see what the action was. Long blond hair was what I saw first, hanging over the terrace rail, obscuring the woman's—or man's?—face. From my angle, all I saw were slim hips backed against the paleness of a standing body. Another *clank!* My eyes were drawn downward, searching for the source of the noise.

Handcuffs.

Metal cuffs were closed around the railing, clanking as the person's arms moved. Huffs from the male as he pistoned into the woman. The hair was grabbed, hand twisting the long strands into a cord, pulling. The head lifted . . . Pokey, the chick from the bus. I guessed the man was her dude, David.

This is getting interesting.

Her eyes were closed, mouth opened, gasping. David said something low I couldn't understand. Pokey's response must have been too slow since David yanked the hair, leaned closer, said something in her ear.

"Yes, Master," was what I heard then. The David dude went ballistic—slapping the hell out of her ass. Pokey moaned louder, her body twisting.

"I need to stop this," I said, stepping around Elena. She grabbed my arm, pulled me back into the shadows, shook her head.

"No, you don't. This is normal for them."

I was confused. How the hell did Elena know what was normal for some folks we'd just met on a quick bus ride? "What? How do you know?"

"I'll tell you later," she eked out, head ducking around me as Pokey yelped.

"You tell me now or I'm going over there." I was down with rough sex, but if any chick was being hurt and I didn't do something . . .

She sucked her teeth, her irritation evident even in the dark. "Will you keep your voice down?" she whisper-shouted. "This is what us girls were talking about earlier. They're into S and M."

"S and M?"

"Yeah, bondage, spanking, tying each other up and having sex for the hell of it. She says she's a Fem and he is her Master, or Sub or something."

"You are shitting me." I'd heard about it but never done it.

"I'm not." From the look of her face, I believed her. "It weirded me out when she first said it, too. But it's a lifestyle. A bunch of people are into it."

"Getting the hell spanked out of you is a lifestyle?"

"Yep. Pokey said they are 'on' twenty-four seven, three sixty-five."

"Damn." I looked back at the terrace where David now had Pokey bent completely over the railing, hand still twisted in her long hair. He'd stopped spanking her like a fiend; now he was rubbing the must-be-red-as-hell terrain. He did this for a minute or so before releasing the hair, which cascaded to the ground. He stepped back into the light—where I could see his cock standing at attention—and kneeled down and unlocked the cuffs.

Guess the party's over.

Pokey leaned upright, stretched, then . . . slapped the head out of David!

"Oh *shit*!" Elena elbowed me in the stomach. "If he's the Master, why is she slapping him?"

"I don't know. Hell, maybe they trade places or something. Now *hush*!"

David rubbed at his face. "Did I tell you to touch yourself, Sub?" Pokey's voice was clear in the night air. *Well, that cleared that up.* His hand dropped. "I've got something for your ass." She turned around. "Lick my ass, asshole, and you better not miss one fucking inch." David dropped to his knees, face welded to her ass. Pokey held onto the rail, rolled on his face.

Elena had been correct about them, since Pokey now had a smile on her face. She cupped her breasts, squeezed the wide areolas, released. Elena's breathing changed, became heavy as we watched. I knew what that meant. I cupped Elena's breasts, tugged at her nipples through the skimpy T-shirt fabric. Elena leaned back on me, kept her eyes on Pokey.

Pokey grabbed her slim ass cheeks, pulled them apart. "Ssshhhiiitttt . . ." My cock rose two inches in my pants just watching that. I hugged Elena closer; made the rock in my pants push into the small of her back.

She turned her head, said, "Pinch them, baby. *Hard.*"

Your wish is my command. I pressed the nipples hard. Elena lifted her ass and pushed into me. I pinched, released, pinched, released. Elena rolled and ground on my cock.

If somebody walked up right now, they'd get an eyeful, fa sho.

"Turn around, Sub." David complied. "Get on your knees." He dropped to his knees. Pokey picked up some contraption from the table and stepped into it. *What the hell is that?* When she turned, I saw the penis-like protrusion sticking from her pelvis.

"Oh!" Elena ground harder.

Chick was about to screw David. My mind was tripping. I wasn't into watching men getting boned. Wasn't natural, I don't care if you *are* doing this S and M stuff. Hell, I was halfway mad when I had to get a physical and the doc stuck his hand up my ass feeling for the prostate. So having Elena screw me? Not this man's cup of cola. No indeed.

My thoughts must have telepathed to Elena. "Keep your mind open, Chaz," she urged. Shoot, me still standing here watching already meant it was open—just a crack, mind you, but still open. I only said I would try to be open, not embrace everything.

Pokey squirted something onto her small fake cock and rubbed it around. David remained on all fours. A lamb about to be slaughtered. She squatted over him, pulled his butt wide, pushed. David grunted. With that sound, my cock deflated while Elena's undulations picked up tempo.

Pokey slid back, pushed again. David grunted again. I gritted my teeth in sympathy, really not feeling this scene. At all.

When she began pumping into him, slapping David's ass . . . I couldn't take it anymore.

I released Elena. "I'm out of here."

"W-what . . . what's wrong?"

"This stuff . . . baby, this ain't for me. I can't get with it."

"You said you'd keep an open mind."

"I have. It's just"—I gestured toward the humping couple, decided to give her the naked truth—"that kind of stuff turns my stomach." She could call me a homophobe, insecure, whatever, as long as she understood I couldn't fathom anal sex *on me* as a wanted and acceptable pleasure. Not me.

I walked toward our suite, not caring if they saw me or not. When I reached our door, I saw Elena hadn't followed. *Fine. Watch as long as you don't try that stuff.*

I'd finished a mini of Beefeater before she returned, face flushed. "You got off, didn't you."

"Yep." She grinned at me as she secured the door. She walked over, sat on the arm of the couch, and massaged my shoulders. "It got wild toward the end."

Spare me the details. Please. "I'll bet."

"You should have stayed."

"Nope. Told you it wasn't for me, but I ain't mad that you enjoyed yourself."

She spread her legs. The scent of her post-climactic pussy pushed into my nostrils; the want for some loving shone in her eyes. My cock woke up, then I had a flash of David getting screwed . . . and it went back to sleep. Not looking her in the eyes, I lifted and said, "I think I'll take a shower and head to bed."

"Want me to join you?" she asked, suggestion in her voice.

"Naw. I'm good. Maybe in the morning." I didn't even look back as I strode to the bathroom. I'd seen the sad face she was making a thousand times or more. One more time wouldn't break the camel's back.

11

Elena

I was frustrated, frustrated, frustrated as I lay beside Chaz. I'd watched as he took his shower and hopped in the bed. Then I took my shower just thinking that this was sex delayed only to exit the bathroom to snores. Play snores, in my mind. Shoot! I wanted his fingers, his mouth, his cock pulling and stroking, rubbing and kneading, sucking and . . . *pinching.* He knew I was horny . . . and he faked sleep.

My feet flexed, toes curled just thinking about how my nerve endings fired as he pinched the hell out of my nipples. I rubbed across them, enjoyed the soreness-pleasure that pain elicited.

Damn! Why'd he just shut down? We agreed to be open, and now at the first turn down Alternative Street . . . he just checks out. Gone. Poof. He knows how I feel about that. It's the reason this whole odyssey started in the first place.

Honey, we need to talk. Shut down.

Honey, can we try something different? Shut down.

Finally, *Honey, I want a boyfriend.* Sit the hell up.

Yeah, the whole Fem/Dom S&M was on a whole other

planet from the stuff we normally did, but honestly, watching it tonight made me want to try it. See how it felt to truly be bound . . . and gagged . . . and have my ass spanked and not be able to wiggle away when I wanted.

Maybe that's why you didn't fight those guys holding you at the restaurant when they stripped your bra off, my mind chided.

Maybe it was, but damn, this was a Sexolympics! Expansion of the sexual mind—*nothing* off-limits.

I fumed a bit, but then my finger ran across my clit and tugged my mind elsewhere. I licked my fingers, wetting them, and placed them back under the covers. I let my mind replay the Pokey/David scene; felt the labial tissues swelling in excitement.

Pokey got her ass slapped like she'd stolen something—my pussy wept, slicked my fingers.

David yanked Pokey's hair—I tugged my berries.

Pokey . . . fucked . . . *David*—I squeezed my legs around my hand, stroked my clit.

Flash. New Orleans intruded. *The woman sucked my tits, milked them*—my "man" stood up in the boat, pulsed.

I wiggled and squirmed around my fingers, letting the waves of pure enjoyment ebb and flow up and down my hot flesh. I bit my lip to stop my moans, not wanting to wake Chaz.

Flash. Beret's house. *Sucked Chaz's cock, saw his hands clenching, feeling me*—I mashed my magic button, felt my juice push out and over my fingers, swirled, tugged in abandon. My stomach spasmed; pushed out more juice. I captured it, applied it, aiding my nimble fingers in their quest. Heat played across my belly . . . over my pube . . . felt new flesh in the mix . . .

I opened my eyes and watched Chaz's tongue drift slowly down to my abdomen. My abs contracted, jumped as his whiskers brushed across them.

Thank you, baby.

My hips lifted, legs spread, guiding him to the motherlode. Chaz took his time, nibbling, sucking, lapping over my tummy. He pulled my hand off my clit, held it to his mouth. "Let me," he said before licking my pussy juice–slick fingers one by one.

He dipped his head, kissing my outer thighs, then the inner. My clit stood at attention—ready, willing, and able to shoot at the merest errant touch. He ignored my throbbing nub, kept circling around and around, left it wanting.

He parted my hairs, licked the sensitive skin beneath. Taunted me mercilessly.

"Please, baby," I begged. Just a slight touch was all I needed.

He refused, ignoring my request as if it had never been uttered. "Tell me who you were fucking in your head just now."

"Y-you, baby. You."

"Liar." He bit my thigh. "Tell me who you were fucking in your head." Firm; brooking no argument.

His nails scratched my inner thigh; lit a fire up my belly. "Pokey."

"Hmm." His finger slid closer, closer to my burning core. I spread wider, needing something in me. "Just as I suspected. Turn over."

I turned.

Whap!

The slap to the ass was expected, the sting not so much. I clenched my teeth and ass, readying for the next contact. I felt a tongue, surprising me. He bit my globes, scraped his teeth across them, sucked the skin. I lifted my ass higher toward him.

Whap. This spank was with less force, tolerable. I lifted my ass higher still.

"Oh, you like that, do you?"

"Uhmm-uhhh," I moaned, pumping my butt a little.

A finger coursed from my pussy to my upper anus. I shuddered in pleasure. His tongue licked at that sensitive spot between the vagina and anus, making the nerve endings pulse, throb. They sent out splinters of electric jolts to my nipples, clit, earlobes, toes. I wanted more. I rolled over.

"Turn this way."

A number of emotions ran across his face before he turned and slid his pelvis toward my head. He already knew what was coming.

His cock was stiff, ready for loving. He lapped closer to my clit; I licked around his head, nipping at the skin.

He stiffened. I pulled a ball into my mouth, sucked slowly. His cock tapped my cheek rhythmically, cum leaking as I swirled, then pushed him out.

Chaz returned to my clit. I squirmed; my legs trembled, blood pulsed in my temples when his whiskers scratched across it. He held my legs still, slid his tongue up and down, around and beside my folds.

I pulled his dick to me and blew on the head. I felt it engorge beneath my hand. I lightly licked his slit, let his precum slide down my face, smiling as I felt his body tense.

He pulled all of me in his mouth, sucked.

I screamed from the pinging and zinging flitting to every inch of my being; pumped on his mouth; wanted him to devour me. His cock lurched, telling me it needed attention. I stuffed it inside my mouth.

Chaz moaned loud and long, toes pointing and curling involuntarily. I rotated, sucked, gripped, lapped, nipped, slurped, and swirled on his fat red head. Clockwise, counterclockwise . . . I put my recent lesson to good use.

Fingers slid inside me, pumping. I squeezed the pseudo-penises as they moved in and out rapidly. He pumped fast then slow, deep then shallow.

I pulled his head deep then shallow, fast then slow, my body humping along in time to his rhythm. I cupped his ass tight, sucked him past my epiglottis, past my uvula to touch the back of my throat.

"Damn, baby, *dammmmnnnnn*!"

I let him feel *my* rhythm as I pulled him deep, bounced him, then backed him out. His mouth moved over my pussy, tongue pushing, stabbing inside me—hitting my *spot*. Damn. I clamped down on his head, kept him immobile, wanting the pleasure radiating from that spot to never end.

Black spots danced in my vision. Sweat poured between our bodies, our chests heaved from the exertion. We both kept up the loving, no one giving one damn inch. He sucked me, finger-fucked me, licked me, and flicked me. I vised his cock. His balls tightened, begged my mouth to allow release of a few million sperm down my throat.

I refused.

"Baby, please, please, baby, please." I heard but ignored him; I planned to let him cum when I said so.

I sucked that head like I was a newborn baby on a tit; impaled my mouth on it; wrapped my tongue around it, memorizing every ridge and dip he'd been born with. His head was about to burst!

Chaz bit my clit. Yowza! I couldn't help my body undulating on his mouth, juice shooting into the air as my body locked; mouth lip-clamped around his cock, an ocean of cum avalanched down my throat. A cannon boomed, firecrackers shot into the sky, music played along in my head . . . growing louder . . . *what*?

Chaz's ring tone. Getting louder. He moved, reached for it, answered. "Hello?"

"What the hell happened?" He sat up in the bed. I already knew it was some client doing something dumb that would require Chaz taking some of my allotted time. "Shit!" I waited for him to finish to get the bad news I felt was coming.

"Give me the number and tell him to keep quiet!" he roared into the phone before snapping it closed.

"Who did what this time?"

"My favorite dumbass."

I chuckled in spite of my being in a state of suspended masturbation. "Let me guess. Barney Phiffe."

"Yep. He just beat up a taxi driver because he didn't have change."

The dumbness of youth. "Par for the course. I guess he's in jail?"

"You know it, and the press have already gotten wind of this. Cathy said they've been blowing up the phone the past half hour."

Cathy, his assistant, was the epitome of well organized. If she couldn't handle it, it must be over the top.

"How bad did he beat the cabbie?"

"Put him in the hospital and they're doing emergency surgery now." Shit. That was pretty bad. Chaz scrolled through his phone, stopping at a number and pressing the Send button.

"Yeah, Mike? Chaz here." He listened.

"It's made the news already, huh? . . . How soon can you get to him? . . . I know what we said after the last time, but you're the best, and he needs the best . . . As usual, just send me the bill." He clicked off, pissed like hell. "Fuck!"

I rubbed his tense back. "It will work out, babe. It always does."

He looked back, face changing into a slight sorry smile, trying to soften the blow before saying, "We've got to go home."

My eyes widened. "You think it's that serious?"

"If he gets kicked out, we can kiss the twenty percent of his five million signing bonus plus the rest of his twenty mil contract good-bye."

I was mad . . . not crazy. If we needed to go home to save Barney's narrow ass, for four million dollars, we'd do what had to be done. "I'll start packing and you change the flight."

The rest of the Sexolympics would have to wait.

Chaz

I was glad for the four-hour flight home—relief from the constant cell phone ringing, answering questions, making statements about Barney Phiffe. I would cut his ass off if only I didn't stand to make a good chunk of retirement change.

Elena bunched her pillow, getting ready to sleep, as usual. Damn. I'd cut this holiday one week short—again. We didn't get to Juanita's or the Cayman Islands or Amsterdam. And I'd *really* wanted to see Elena on one of those swings, sitting in the window, playing exhibitionist. I'm sure I would have had to tell some joker to step off when he'd tried to purchase her for an hour of sex. I chuckled.

"What's funny?" Elena asked, just as her head hit the pillow.

"Just thinking about what we missed out on."

She lifted her head. "And that's funny to you?"

"No. The thought of having to whup some guy's ass when he tried to buy you for an hour after seeing you in the window in Amsterdam was, though."

"Oh." She relaxed. "And the show I had planned, you would have had to whup more than one."

"Really."

"Trust."

I chuckled again before turning a bit somber. I gave up a small prayer of thanks for my blessings—a wife who was understanding, sexy, strong . . . my backbone. And I couldn't manage to clear my calendar for two weeks to give her this little thing she'd asked. How long before she *did* turn to some other dude, get herself that boyfriend she'd joked about? I shook my head, damning Barney all over again.

I made a promise right then: Never again would I allow things within my control to affect our vacations. Unless somebody died, my clients would get "long distance" assistance.

I opened my laptop and made notes for the rest of the ride.

12

Elena

Three weeks later

I scraped the varnish off the chair I'd been refinishing and straightened up. My head suddenly swam, the room rotating at faster and faster speeds. I grabbed on to the chair, slumping to my knees as the vertigo increased. Closing my eyes made it worse; my stomach lurched and bile pushed at my esophagus. I held on as my body rebelled, tried to repel my lunch up and out. In a few minutes, it passed.

What was that? I struggled to my feet gingerly. The room was fine; I felt fine. Probably the varnish. The bottle did say to ventilate well. Even though the windows were open and I had a fan running, maybe that wasn't enough.

I pulled off the smock I'd worn over my jeans and T-shirt and scratched at my itching breasts. *A shower?* I wasn't in the mood right then, so instead, I flopped on the couch, deciding that I'd done enough for today. I'd move outside tomorrow. I snuggled into the couch and opened the book Beret had given me. I hadn't had time to thoroughly read it while we were gone. Too much to see and do. And when we returned, life intruded.

I smiled as I read her inscription: *Life is best lived . . . now.* And live it I planned to do.

Chaz had been a ghost since we'd returned. The whole mess with Barney had threatened everything—the Walruses, the team that had signed him, were hinting that Barney was about to be toast. Chaz had spent nights at the office trying to reach some type of settlement with the franchise to keep his errant client. So far, they weren't budging. The Walruses had withheld the second payment on Barney's signing bonus and demanded he have a number of rehabs—alcohol, drugs, sex—as well as anger management classes. The NHL commissioner had alluded to an impending suspension and potential fine. After all, Barney had smeared the league just by association.

I know Chaz was staying with Barney because of the big payday, but sometimes I thought maybe, just maybe, he should tell these overgrown babies he represented to kiss the crack in his ass. I know one or two . . . or maybe three would have been told to kiss mine.

I turned back to the book. I perked up as I read there were forty-two ways to perform fellatio. Forty-two, and how many had I done? Probably no more than ten, if that. Seemed like I had plenty of catching up to do.

The book was a quick read, and after I finished, I was hungry—again. I'd been eating like a pig for the past few days. My waistband would need letting out if I kept it up.

When was your last cycle?

Whoa! Where did that thought come from? I mean . . . I grabbed the personal calendar—the one where I wrote down things of this nature—from my purse. As I flipped back through this month and the previous one, I saw it had been five weeks since the last cycle.

No! I couldn't be pregnant.

Remember finding your IUD on the floor? The mood swings in Hawaii? Eating like a pig here? Your "itching" breasts?

Other than the IUD episode—which I'd completely forgotten—I'd attributed all the rest to symptoms of my impending period, not anything else. But . . . could I be preggers? Time to find out. I grabbed my purse, slid my feet into flip-flops and headed for Wally World.

My heart accelerated as I watched the second line cross the first.

Yes, I was pregnant.

Wow.

Chaz and I had talked around the idea, but were we ready to be somebody's parents? Guess so. I stared at the plus sign again.

Chaz arrived after ten. I heard his slow steps walking to the bedroom, knowing that he must be exhausted as hell. He stopped at the doorway and looked around the room. I'd placed candles all around the perimeter, lit incense, and had jazz playing from the stereo. Tonight was a special night, after all.

"Cathy called you?"

I sat up in the bed. "No. Should she have?"

He glanced around before saying, "Looks like we're celebrating, so I thought you'd heard the good news."

"We are celebrating. What's your news?"

He opened his tie, unbuttoned his shirt, and sat on the edge of the bed. "I got the Walruses to keep Barney."

I nodded. "That is good news." Actually it wasn't. It meant Barney would continue to be a pain in our ass—on demand.

"He has to complete only one rehab—alcohol—take the anger management class, and the commissioner backed down from the suspension. Oh yeah, they sent the remainder of his signing bonus."

"That is good news, baby!" I hugged him.

"So"—his fingers ran across my lips—"what are we celebrating?"

"Once upon a time there was a man and a woman who were in love . . ."

He held up a finger. "Uh-uh. No fairy tales tonight. I'm too spent, so just tell me."

"Okay." I took a deep breath. "We're pregnant."

His eyes widened. "Seriously?"

I nodded slowly. "Seriously."

He looked at the bed, then back at me before pulling me close. "This is wonderful, baby." He rubbed my belly. "A baby. Our baby . . . in there." He leaned his ear to my tummy.

"Yep, the stork retired so we have to do it this way." I laughed.

He lifted from my tummy and looked in my eyes, face now serious. "I do have one question, though. With all those folks running through your head while we have sex . . . is it mine?"

"I tell you what. If it doesn't look just . . . like . . . you . . ." I grabbed his chin and kissed his lips, "we'll feed it until it does."

He captured my face. "I love you, baby."

"Back atcha. Always and forever."

And thus the Sexolympics officially ended . . .

And new life began.

BECOMING ONE

1

The kiss was nectar from the goddess of love. Soft, quick brushes at first, followed by the pressure of lips as the tongue pushed inside my mouth.

Plundering.

Turning.

Stabbing.

Pulling.

Hands followed. On my breasts, up my spine, over my hips, across my belly, each one igniting a path of fire in my soul. Lips pulled at my earlobes, licked the back of my neck, nipped at my flesh.

Erik smiled as he turned me around, my back to his front. His fingers pulled at my tight nips before he sat on the bed. Hands kept rubbing, creating hot friction, as I positioned myself over his throbbing cock. The K-Y was cool, but only briefly. Fingers slid inside me, lubricating me, before strong hands pushed down on my thighs.

The first pain was always the hardest.

Intense . . . shooting . . . felt like I was being torn in half.

But the amazing pleasure that followed the pain was always worth it.

Erik worked his head inside slowly, waiting for me to relax. My clit was a pulsing button—too stiff to touch but wanting contact anyway.

It came . . .

I lurched as the tissue engorged even more from the wet tongue lapping around its edges, pushing Erik in deeper. It tantalized me, energized me. A few more laps and strokes and I'd found my rhythm.

Terrance lifted his head then, stood above me as I rode Erik's cock. I turned a bit so my breasts could be sucked into a hot mouth, increasing my pace when teeth pinched the sensitized berries. My hands roamed over the head, stroked the heavy cock in front of me in expectancy.

Erik pulled me backward. Terrance squatted a bit, aligned his cock with my pussy entrance, and with his own rhythm, entered me slowly, gently. My legs wrapped around his back as he drove deeper, to the hilt, balls to balls.

I was slowly inched upward. Erik began his stroking again, coordinating his pumps with Terrance, driving me out of my mind.

Domino claimed my attention. Not surprised. His young ass could never wait, always wanting to move up to top-dog position before paying *any* dues—sexy ass. He turned my face to him, lapped my open lips as the two cocks drilled me deep. I moaned from the twin stroke and the tongue play. The shit *was* just . . . that . . . good.

Erik offered my nipples up. Terrance latched on, milking them with his nimble lips as Erik caressed them. Domino, apparently tired of not getting his, stood and grasped his stiff cock in his hands. He moved closer, touched the purple head to my nose. I inhaled his musky scent, further energized by the smell of even more cock. My lips parted and Domino smiled as I licked around the head before pulling him inside.

"Take it all, Mama," Domino urged me on.

I appreciated the encouragement but didn't need it because my body was pinging and zinging from head to toes, and as a result, deep mouth strokes were already in the script. I rotated and slurped on his purple staff while I undulated, playing a double-fuck symphony with my body.

If I died right now, I'd be smiling so wide they'd have to break my cheeks to get rid of the smile. It *was* that damn good.

Domino rubbed in my hair before grabbing, wrapping my strands firmly in his hands. Gently, he tugged my head forward, pushing himself deeper and deeper, past my teeth, over my tongue. I gripped his stiff cock and rotated my head, eliciting a moan through gritted teeth. I was so feeling this session. I clenched my pussy, then my ass while head-pumping on Domino. Both Erik and Terrance showed their enjoyment in their clutching fingers and acceleration. I opened my mouth to allow Domino to push all his cock inside.

"Damn, that shit looks so good," Terrance groaned before he swirled his hips and drove deeper inside me.

My body hit a new crescendo in its fuck symphony—body writhed, slapped, and whipped as I stroked cocks buried into every available hole. The chorus of moans made me thrust harder, become rough—nails scratched across a chest, fist gripped the base of a cock. I was pushing the buttons, in control, taking them on my journey now. I gave them no release, took no prisoners as the spinning tornado of love whispered our names.

Erik was the first to break. His arms tightened around my waist and his cock swelled, stretched my chocolate hole. I felt the spray of hot jism even as he contorted beneath me. I screamed as the prickles washed over my body in waves.

Domino's climax swiftly followed, his cum spraying over my face and chest. Seeing this must have taken Terrence over his edge. His eyes rolled, face spasmed as I felt his cum splashing inside my sopping pussy.

Ahhh.

Another routine day in *my* life.

2

My name is Topaz November and I'm a polygamist.

Yes, a *female* polygamist. What's good for the goose truly can be good for the gander.

I live an unconventional life by any standards—yours, theirs, the world's, I know. Would I change it? Nope. I've got my cake, frosting, and a dollop of ice cream I'm eating all by myself—along with my three husbands: Erik, Terrance, and Domino.

Surprised? You shouldn't be. I'm doing what millions of women want to do—fuck a variety of men who are all in love with me—and nobody is complaining. Or if they are, they keep it to themselves.

Now, this lifestyle isn't for the faint of heart. In this game you either be the pimp or the whore. Oh yes, ladies, you got to wear your big-girl panties at all times. It takes a lot of energy to be married to multiple men. You've got to know you; dig down deep and see who you really are, your limitations, your sexual capacity. You got to want the sex 'cause men love a woman who loves sex. So sex could pop off at any given moment, unplanned.

It's a delicate dance when choosing partners. Get two who have high sex drives, you might find yourself outpaced and then they are in the streets, looking for new cooch to marinate in 'cause you can't keep up. Now, that means slowly but surely, they're sliding you into the whore role . . . and nobody, and I do mean no woman, wants to be the married whore.

It's all good. Oh, don't think the "conformist" mouthpieces in my life didn't tell me about myself. My mother called me Jezebel and my father—recognizing how much I was like his philandering ass—gave me a trust fund to get me out of his hair. As he told me, 'Do what you gonna do, just keep it on the low low.' "

And I have. If one husband has a company function, I attend with only him. For family functions, I usually attend alone. Keeps the nosy folks out of my business, and they'd get real nosy if I attended this function with this husband and pulled another one out at a different one. At work, since I'm the boss, my personal life is off-limits. Try me if you're bad. You'll find out how long the wait is at the unemployment office.

How did I get this way?

Let's just say, I've always been a bit wild. Couldn't have one boyfriend and be monogamous. I was that creeper, needed a little something on the side at all times. Am I a nympho? No indeed. I was selective as hell in the cocks I rode. It was that I realized "Two is better . . . three just right" was *my* unspoken motto, and I had no plans to change it any time soon.

Now let me say this. Long, long ago, right after the dinosaurs roamed the earth, I *did* try to be that one-man woman. I tamped down on my nature, fooled myself into believing I *could* ride the same one dick off into the sunset. Even married my first love *and* first husband, Terrance, with the full belief I could and would be his only wife and he my only husband, till death do us part.

And was he every girl's dream? Sure was. He had a construction company raking in the high six figures yearly, provided well for us, made me feel like I was the Queen of the World, and most importantly, had a nine-inch fat dick.

Regrettably, he suffered from that ailment too many husbands suffer from: He didn't invest the time. He believed—foolishly, I might add—that if he made enough money, he didn't have to be present. I'd find enough lunches, brunches, and committees to keep me busy. Or I'd buy enough purses, shoes, and jewelry to wash away any disappointments I had about the absence of his cock rocking my pussy on the regular. Let me tell you right now . . . the devil *is* a bald-faced liar.

Three years of that . . . sameness . . . and I got "the itch." Every woman knows what itch I'm talking about. That we're-in-a-rut-need-to-spice-it-up-*shit*!-I-gotta-have-some-new-dick-in-my-pussy itch. And when that itch rears its bulbous head, a woman's gonna do one of two things: overhaul her man or find her some new dick.

I did a combination of the two. I talked to Terrance. Let him shout, scream, cuss, fuss, and make promises to improve. The word wrangling went on days, weeks, a month or more. But in the end, we reached an agreement.

Terrance wasn't ready to let go—love is a mind fuck, ain't it?—so he agreed to this: I could sex another man . . . as long as we screwed in front of him. Right down my alley. I thought the shit was kinky and since Kink *was* my middle name, I latched on to the idea like a duck-billed platypus in water.

Now, as any woman knows, a man will say one thing when his back is up against the wall and do something else when what he said shows up at the door. Terrance was no different.

I brought the first "new sex" man home three months after

our conversation. Terrance had looked gut-punched when I'd told him that morning, but he'd agreed and I expected him to go through with the agreement. A man's word is his bond, right?

Wrong.

Terrance took one look at that tall, hunky stick of licorice I'd planned to dick down and slammed the door in his face. Pissed me off! Hell, who did he think I'd bring home? Some Elmer Fudd–looking dude?

It was back to the negotiation table—more promises to change, more putting off the inevitable. I backed down, gave him the reprieve he asked for. Allowed him to see if he truly *could* commit the time and energy it took to keep me satisfied.

He tried. Oh boy, did Terrance try—coming home early, flower deliveries all the time, us going out and sexing all over the place . . . It was like we just got married all over again.

But like they always say: No use in trying to be somebody else 'cause the real you is gonna show up, sooner or later. And it did.

Less than a year into our marriage rehabilitation, Terrance was back into his old routine. I saw the signs—working later and later; then taking on more and more projects we didn't need but he wanted, for whatever reason, that kept him out of town; next, the tsunami of flower deliveries decreased to trickle level; and our weekly dates became an occasional night out here and there.

The biggest hit was, as it always is, the sex. He knew, just like I knew, it wasn't frequent enough, and when he finally broke down and did give me some, he didn't bring his A game. More like the C game—surprise attacks in the morning instead of the long lovemaking sessions at night he knew I craved.

Time out, back the hell up, 'cause this ain't working!

A woman has needs just like a man, and this woman's needs were not being met. I told him it was time to go back to Plan A.

His blood pressure spiked! Even got put on meds for it. When the day came I'd found another dude I wanted, I told him to double up on the meds . . . just in case.

I'd chosen someone different from the first—looks, coloring. Hoped it would make the situation more . . . palatable. Terrance resembled a crazed he-devil when Isaiah walked in, eyes boring into dude like he was a denizen from the dark recesses of hell. Isaiah almost changed his mind . . . but I pushed him against the door and tongued him into submission.

Terrance was a marble statue as Isaiah and I rolled, rollicked, sucked, and fucked—but his cock rose.

Somebody was an eensy, weensy bit turned on.

The third time Isaiah visited, Terrance surprised us both. It was while Isaiah was apparently trying to earn the title of King Cunnilingus of the Decade that Terrance disrobed, strode to the bed, and stopped. My mind wigged out, made me wonder if I was about to be the latest victim of a crime of passion . . . when he leveled his polished tan head with my mouth and pressed against my lips. No thought required. I opened wide, slurped him inside.

He watched Isaiah as I dragged my lips up and down his shaft. Cum dripped on my chest at my moan when Isaiah drove his cock deep inside me. Terrance pummeled my mouth, shot his wad over my face as Isaiah came over my belly. Surprised me further when he'd joined us in the Roman tub, even made small talk with Isaiah—a bonding of sorts.

We'd turned the corner.

The trysts with Isaiah became a weekly ritual, lasting for two years until Isaiah got transferred. Terrance and I resumed our former one-on-one sex pattern. Unfortunately, there was mutual dissatisfaction with the results. Oh, we worked, but it seemed like we worked *better* with another person—another cock in the mix, an overdose of testosterone in the air.

Discussion time again. And before you ask, no, I did not

suggest another woman. *I'm* the *only* pussy gonna be up in here, got that?

Now, I didn't want a string of casual partners running up in me and then out of my life. Hell, I'd gotten emotionally attached to Isaiah, and my heart still ached. I wanted something more . . . permanent. My solution? Another husband.

Terrance—used to the other man in our lives and still wanting me . . . bad—acquiesced. He reverted to his previous absent-most-of-the-time pattern, left me to my own devices in finding this husband. I got right on the assignment. No need to let grass—

A car horn blew, snapping my thoughts back to the present. The taillights from the car in front of me were close! I slammed on the brakes, tearing off an inch of tire tread, trying to avoid a collision. The car skidded sideways, stopping inches from impact.

I sat there a moment, looking around. Curious eyes peered from windows, but nothing else. In minutes, traffic moved forward.

My mind shifted to the Women Are Polygamists Too—WAPT for short—meeting. I'd organized this group when I realized there were women out there just like me, living this *scrumptious* secret life below the radar. Who hasn't seen the male polygamists vilified and practically crucified for their lifestyle? Uh-uh. We'd learned from their sordid past; we knew discretion let you live like you wanted for longer than anyone could imagine.

I put the car in gear, the agenda for the night now churning through my mind.

3

"Ladies!" I banged the gavel down again, gaining their attention. "This meeting is called to order."

The women took their seats. Tonight was a medium-sized crowd, around thirty or so. All nationalities, religions, and age groups were represented. I was happy to see our octogenarian member, Mamie Willis, present. She had been a polygamist for more than fifty years, had seven husbands so far, burying four of them. I was considered one of the "newbies"—active polygamist for less than a decade. I made a mental note to invite her to high tea. I'm sure she had plenty of wisdom to impart to keep me walking in the same shoes she'd worn.

I glanced down at the agenda I'd scratched out in the car. "First up, discussion on the ratification of our constitution, specifically the modification of amendment sixteen, which deals with divorce, which states, 'A husband can be willfully expelled from a marriage due to creation of children with women outside of their lawful wives.' Do we have any conversation?"

Sue Parker, owner of the trendy She/He boutique, stood first. "Yes. I feel that should not only include children but infidelity as a whole." She was dressed to the nines in one of her trademark pieces, shoes and purse matching. "So why not back this up to the inciting cause in the first place—adultery."

"I agree." May Harris, our youngest member at twenty-nine, stood with her. May currently had two husbands, both damn near senior citizens, if not already there. After meeting the gentlemen, I imagined Viagra was a staple in their household. But everybody seemed cheery whenever I saw them, so who was I to complain? May added, "A man would put aside a woman in a heartbeat over infidelity, so the reverse should be true."

The pros and cons flew about the room with those wanting to amend the amendment having the larger say. We finally agreed to table it until the next meeting, with the Amendment Committee revamping the modification to include all points voiced.

"Next, new business. Anyone?" I glanced around, wondering who had a complaint about what. A hand was raised near the back. "Yes?"

A tall, middle-aged woman stood. "Karen Smith here." She owned a booming real estate business. You couldn't tell it by looking at her. The clothes were off the clearance rack, the shoes well worn, and the hair saw a stylist whenever the desert got rain. Just dumpy frumpy. The room greeted her politely and waited. "I'd like to present my choice for husband number three."

Murmurs ran around the room. "Bring him in."

Karen walked to the back doors, pulled them open, and drew a man into the room.

"Take him up front where we can see him good. You don't want none of us to put the moves on him by mistake, do you?" someone heckled.

"Yeah, take him in the light," another one urged.

The male specimen strode into the light. Every woman in room gasped, and . . . pussies wept.

Dude was a *damn* good-looking male—skin that red-brown color of mixed-race babies; hair shorn close to the head; face, neck, chest, waist, thighs . . . chiseled chunks of malehood. I looked at his feet. At *least* a thirteen.

If I were in the market, he would have been mine.

I smacked my lips; my nips tingled . . . and I hadn't even heard his voice. "Introduce him, Karen."

"Ladies, this is Waldo."

"Glad to meet you, Waldo. Know what you are getting yourself into?" Some men thought this was a game. It wasn't. Watching your woman, *knowing* your woman was sleeping with another man could be hard to handle. It's not for the weak of heart or the mentally unstable.

He nodded. "Yes, I do. I've been married before, got divorced when she cheated on me—"

"I told you!" May Harris pushed her point home.

"—but then I met Karen . . ." The look in his eyes said it all as he pulled Karen close and hugged her. "And I'll take her any way I can get her." He kissed her forehead.

"Ahhhhhhh . . ." The room sighed.

"Okay then. Anyone here have any objections? All in favor say aye. Opposed? The ayes have it." I slammed the gavel down. "Best wishes to you both. When do you expect the nuptials to take place?"

"Two weeks from this Saturday in Aruba," Karen responded. She seemed ten years younger standing beside him.

"Good destination." Getting married anywhere outside of the United States was a great destination. Bigamy in the States; outside, like Vegas—what was recorded in that country, stayed in that country. "Okay then, any more new business?"

No hands were raised. "Going once, going twice—"

"Wait." Topper Henley, new-world-order Indian, stood, jewel in her forehead, scarves billowing around her. "I have something I need to say."

"Go ahead."

She twisted her hands, an uncommon action for this normally calm woman. She was a pediatric surgeon, and steady hands were her trademark. "As of today, I renounce all my husbands."

"What!"

Topper stood taller; her voice grew stronger. "Yes. I am renouncing any and all marriages I have after my first husband. This thing we are doing—it is not right. Not by our land's laws, not by God."

"Now you wait one minute, girl. Folks had plenty of husbands and wives in biblical times. This is the same thing!" Mamie Willis admonished.

Topper shook her head. "No. *Men* had plenty of wives and concubines. Women were stoned to death because they were considered . . . whores. Now *we* are the whores."

Polygamist woman rule number one: Never ever *ever* call us a whore.

We all got hot. Comments and recriminations were slung about.

"You traitor—"

"I can't believe you are saying this, you—"

"Oh, so we're whores now?"

"Heffa, you take that shit back right—"

Somebody ran from the back, slung her purse into Topper's head, flipping her over the chairs. It was bedlam from that point. Chairs slid, arms windmilled about, weaves flew in the air. I banged and banged and banged on the gavel with no one paying me any mind.

I stood back, let them have at it. It wasn't that I didn't fight.

You should never feel too old to fight if there is a need, but I wasn't one to get scratched up about a comment that didn't truly affect my life. I finally just grabbed my purse, skirted about the still-battling women, and headed to the car. If they killed one another, they were dead. *I* was done.

4

November Manor.

Home sweet hacienda.

Lights were on throughout the house. A Jeep Wrangler and Mercedes coupe sat in the circle drive.

At least two of the hubbies were home.

Good food smells assaulted my nose when I entered. Pots banged in the kitchen along with humming off-key.

Erik. My Cordon Bleu chef—and husband number two. He stood at the six-burner stove, thigh shorts covering his toned ass; an apron protected his naked gold chest.

He spotted me as I dropped my satchel by the couch. "Hey, baby! How were the WASPs tonight?" A flame rose from a pan he was vigorously shaking.

Glad the insurance was up to date.

"That's WAPT, and crazy as usual." I walked over and got a chaste peck to the lips. "Smells good. What is it?" I had no idea what the black lump was he was swirling.

"Seared duck flambé."

Okay then. Restaurant's guinea pig night. "Looks . . . interesting."

"It is." He set the pan down, doused it with some cooking wine, and put a lid on the whole concoction. "Got to let it simmer now."

I shook my head. "You got a lot going on with that dish."

He walked behind me, fused his pelvis to my ass. "Not as much as we're gonna have going on later tonight."

"What was that about tonight?" Domino, hubby number three, asked behind us. He wrenched me from Erik's grasp, pulled me to him, stabbed his tongue to the left, the right, and around and around in my mouth. The kamikaze-style kiss forced my toes to curl. I grabbed his shirt in rising lust before he released me. "What was that again?" Domino frowned at Erik.

Erik held up his hands. "Hey, man, just trying to help a brother out. I know you been busy with all your Twittering and Facebooking, poking folks and stuff." His fingers danced in the air.

"That's SkySpook asswipe. Twitter and Facebook is for beginners . . . like you. My crowd mastered that a week after it came out and moved on."

"Whatever. But since you're usually tied up with *SkySpoofing*, I didn't want Little Mama to go lacking 'cause you got a busy schedule."

"Chile, please." Domino's favorite new phrase since he'd heard Chad Johnson, aka Ochocinco, use it. It meant, literally, "fuck you."

Erik wrinkled his face; he knew what it meant. "I'm just saying, you'd best be on your j-o-b when it's time for you to be, or I got the slack. Believe that." He turned back to the stove, shaking the pan again.

"I got me, Uncle Ben. You just keep stirring that rice."

I flipped a finger over Domino's lips, sealing them. "That's enough." Wife, mother, two for the price of one on any given day. He rolled his eyes heavenward.

Frick and Frack, Night and Day—sometimes I had to wonder what it was I'd seen in these two that had entranced me enough to husband them. Dithering, sparring . . . day in, day out, always a competition between them about any little thing: careers, cars, trips—me. Hell, they needed a time out . . . or maybe I did.

They didn't heckle Terrance, though. I haven't quite figured out if they knew better or had just written him off as a lame bull one step from slaughter. He was like me, watching, shaking his head, breaking up arguments only when it looked like someone was about to damage the house. And one thing he wouldn't stand for was damaging this house.

Ten thousand square feet of the finest materials he'd been able to afford—porcelain ceramic tiles, granite countertops, and marble sinktops, onyx waterfall showers, a Jacuzzi, and a pool, for starters. This was his baby, his love he'd brought alive.

Seeing it for the first time took my breath away. It was the fairy-tale palace all girls dreamed of . . . and I was living in it.

Domino looked back at Erik, saw him chopping up onions and garlic, and said, "If you don't quit putting onions on everything—"

"Man, you want to cook?" He eyed Domino with flinty eyes.

"Not like I can't match that crap in a pan like you."

"That's right." He nodded in assent. "Who could forget those wonderful Sloppy Joes that gave us all the runs." Erik snorted, shook his head. "Shit, flush, shower. Water bill was sky high that month from all the flushing and showers we needed to clean ourselves up afterward."

"Oh, you got jokes. You just go easy on the onions," he lowered his voice, "you fake-ass Chef Boyardee."

I left them to their squabbling. It was obvious jocking with each other brought them pure pleasure since they didn't even notice me leave.

The door closed behind me; I sighed.

My room, my sanctuary, my slice of calm in the storm.

Red suede walls, gold curtains, onyx floors—I was a woman who liked to mix hardness with boldness . . . just like my personality. The bed sat center stage, majestic, regal in its bearing: canopy sheers floating around every side, the silk duster, the bloodred coverlet over plump feather mattresses that required steps to get into . . . me everywhere I turned.

In its first life, it had been the master bedroom Terrance and I had shared. But once life changed, it changed. I'd redecorated it to my liking; Terrance moved down the hallway to a smaller room with a view of the endless pool in the backyard and the glimmering lake beyond. It was a necessity born of our need—no, scratch that, born of our wants. Enough of that.

I shucked off my clothes and strode to the bathroom, stopping once to survey my butt. It drooped on the right side as compared with the left. I already knew the cure for that. I squeezed and released my thick hind muscles a hundred times. I might not be able to overcome gravity completely, but I'll be damned if I give in without so much as a fight. When I was finished, I added an hour on the treadmill and a half hour with the punching bag to my exercise list for my morning workout session.

I was in "massage shower" mode. Yes, I know. With three husbands, one of them should be doing this. But apparently, whatever Domino and Erik were doing was more important, since neither had followed me.

The shower spray pulsed onto the floor; needled my skin. I wet my hair, lathered it up, felt the tea tree oil make my scalp tingle as it worked into my open pores. I loofahed my skin until it felt polished. I lavished oil over my skin, rubbed it in thoroughly. I hated being the "ashy sister" folks always joked about.

I leaned over, flipped my hair forward, blotted the water from it with my towel . . . that's when cock tapped me on the hips. A chin needing a shave rubbed into my back and up my spine, shooting off frissons of sparks into the air. His scent rose in the air—Grey Flannel. An old scent for sure, but one that suited his body chemistry perfectly.

"Knock, knock," the gruff voice said.

I knew this game well. "Who's there?" I tilted slightly, lined up my split with his head.

"Cock." He pushed into my left buttock—dickhead moist already—before sliding into the valley of cooch.

"Cock who?" I slid the moistness around; added my own.

"Cock for . . . you!" Deep, deep, deep he drove, stopping when balls touched bush. Reversed, cock dove again, marinated in my nectar, imprinted my scent onto spongy folds.

He lifted me then. Bulging biceps gathered my legs by each thigh, held me high while cock spiked into me. My arms imprisoned his head, pulled his thick lips to mine. My tongue stabbed inside braces-refined teeth; flipped, fluttered, was fire to his tongue.

He fuck-walked me to the bed, strode up the steps, let my feet touch the cover, cock never missing a deep stroke. I writhed, gasped, grasped any bit of skin my nails could catch hold of, and raked.

He pushed me off and rubbed at the thin red lines I'd created. He waggled a finger before my face. "Tsk, tsk, tsk. Keep us straight, okay?" No censure, but still, I felt censured; I knew I'd known better; got caught up.

My legs were snatched from under me and I flopped backwards onto the bed. My legs were snapped open. Cock pushed home.

"Oh, baby," I wheezed through clenched teeth.

Sweat coated my body, rolled into my navel, down the creases of my thighs, and pooled beneath my hips. My hips were lifted as my husband of thirteen years, Terrence, slowly plundered my pussy. My hands drifted up, plucked his stiff nipples, elicited a deep groan. I smiled, knowing that after all these years I still made him feel as good as he felt to me right at that moment.

He shifted, threw my legs over his shoulder. My pussy clenched and tightened furiously around his thick muscle—he was going in for the double clutch.

Fingers were wetted before sliding over my clit. My back arched as the sensations pinged through my body. Gawd! He was sexing me righteously!

He smiled, then bucked me.

My stomach knotted as I felt him caress the back of my walls, play slide tag with my cervix. My womb convulsed as he stroked precisely in and out. In and out. I squeezed my eyes shut; my fingers gripped the sheets as the glorious waves of desire washed over me.

Our eyes locked. Terrence licked his succulent lips, never missing a stroke or swirl with his long dick. I knew he was searching for my "back room," that part at the rear of my pussy that once he entered, it would suck him dry.

My lips curled unwillingly; his nostrils flared as my juices squished, the scent wafting between us. Musky. I was definitely . . . there.

He knew the signs.

His head flung back as his pelvis pushed forward. I bit my lip, grinding my hips to his thumping rhythm. My uterus swelled, my stomach hardened as his meat sopped in my juice.

My eyes began their joyous roll backwards. I grabbed my own tits and pulled the tight nipples between my snapping teeth, needing to heighten this release. His head dipped, lips closed around my stiff clit—

Pounding on the door.

"What the hell is this!" Domino . . . and he was pissed.

Terrance's grind hit a misstep; our rhythm was thrown off as the pounding and yelling increased.

"Open this damn door, man! It's my night!"

He closed his eyes, held his hands over my ears; tuned him out. I ignored the voice and focused on the hard meat sliding inside me.

The knob jiggled, hands pounded some more, then a kick before . . . silence.

Terrance pushed down on my thighs, spread me wider; defied the laws of body as he slid past my womb to my "back door." My lips curled; I made a Bride of Frankenstein fuckface as my pelvis pulled and sucked, rocked and rolled around his fat-assed, swollen, mmm, mmm good motherfucker of a cock.

His tongue hung from his mouth. Sweat dripped onto my forehead. Our hands intertwined, held fast, gave purchase to his magnanimous thrust which quickly, amazingly, lovingly spewed out cum, blowing the roof . . . off . . . my . . . cock . . . sucking . . . house.

"Uhh!"

Stomach was tight.

"Uhhh!"

Cock was deep and wedged tighter.

"Uhhhhhhh!"

Convulsion upon convulsion before . . . relaxation.

The scent of us was heavy in the air. I turned to him, "Domino is mad as hell."

Terrance wrinkled his face. "He'll get straight." He pulled me into his armpit, let his finger trail across my breast. "You'll always be my first love." He kissed my cheek.

My heart expanded; my mind drove down Memory Lane,

seeing us before there was a "them"; made me wonder if I'd jumped the gun. I didn't get the chance to sort it out before the pounding resumed.

"What the hell are you doing in there?" Pound! Pound! Pound! "Open this damn door!"

Terrance squeezed his eyes shut and shook his head. I lifted and said, "I'll handle this."

His hand stopped me. "No." He rubbed across his face. "I'll just get out of the way." Eyes weary . . . disappointed.

He strode to the door and flung it open. "Dude, that shit was so foul! You knew this was my night!" Domino yelled, spittle flying.

"Back down, boy." Terrance clenched his fist.

"Got your damn boy!" Domino stepped closer, eyes shining. "You broke the rule, dude."

"And?"

"Don't get checked, old school."

"Who's gonna check me? You, young buck?" Terrance rolled his head around his neck, popped his back, widened his legs—classic fighting stance.

Domino might be young, but he wasn't dumb. The best fighters in the world knew when to walk away. So did he. He took a step back, chest heaving. "I'm just saying . . . It was my night and you knew it but didn't respect it. That's foul."

"Here's a piece of information you need to ruminate on: This is my house, and that was *my* wife first." He pointed at me. "Your narrow ass is here *only* because I *allowed* it, no other reason. I am the top dog in this pack and I'll break the goddamn rules whenever I goddamn feel like it, and you know why?" Domino said nothing. "Because I made the rules up in the first place. Understand?"

Domino wanted to try him; I saw it in his eyes.

"Now, you need to grow some bigger balls and stop acting like a two-year-old chap having a tantrum when shit gets switched up. Bottom line: If you got other shit to do and can't do this job . . . I know somebody who damn sure will."

Domino whipped around, stomped down the stairs. Erik lifted from the shadows and followed silently. Terrance pulled the door to close it.

"Don't leave."

Two bulls had locked horns; the young bull was sent packing. The tang of their heightened testosterone aroused me.

Surprise was evident on his face. He hesitated, searched my face.

"Please. Stay with me." I crooked my finger, beckoned him.

He pushed the door close, walked slowly over to the bed, climbed in. We said nothing, just snuggled closer, falling asleep in each other's arms.

5

The wind whipped the flakes into the air. I stared at the threatening wonderland. I hugged my body and shivered.

I hated cold weather. It made me sad, depressed as the naked trees looked.

Terrance had left early, needing to check on a job. The usual. The rest of the house was quiet; Erik and Domino were probably still snoozing. I yawned and thought about returning to the warm covers myself. Hunger changed my mind.

No food smells tantalized my nose this morning. It was all good. Cereal was fine. I padded downstairs to the kitchen. Empty. I'd grabbed a bowl when a moan snapped my head up.

I did say I was the only pussy up in here, right? So who was moaning and why?

Curiosity led me to the computer room, Domino's domain. The door was cracked a few inches. The light was off but the screen glowed.

Pornography.

An addiction I'd never admit to.

Domino clicked a thumbnail, enlarging it. The photo was of

an orgy. A busty black lady was impaled on a pale cock. Her eyes were closed; another woman sucked her nips. He leaned closer to the screen. He nodded, then closed out the photo, enlarging another thumbnail. The same woman lay on her back, legs hoisted in the air, the woman who'd been sucking her now sitting on her face.

The changes in my body were noticeable—pussy got slippery, breasts lifted, swelled.

He moaned, pulled his rod out, spat in his hand. He lubed the purple head while staring at the photo. He jerked, grunted, choked the head. His hand twisted the pole, stroked it fast, then slow.

The robe slid to the floor. On silent feet, I walked over and touched his shoulder.

He jumped out of the chair and tried to shield the screen, eyes darting about my face.

"It's cool."

His body language said he didn't believe me. I gave him assurance. I smiled, then dropped to my knees and slid my lips around his cock. He backed up, met the chair, fell into it.

The photos sparked me; they put me in "rough rider" mode, kicked nice wife to the curb. I suctioned hard and deep, trying to reach his root on each and every bob.

"Awwaaawwwaaaawww!"

The knees moved to the side, giving me more room to work. I sucked his snake like it was shedding skin—methodically, purposefully, no inch left unsucked. I scraped his foreskin, pulled it back tight; scraped his head.

His hand balled, unballed. He wanted to grab my head, control my mouth.

I spat on him; his respondent grunt empowered me. It fueled my tongue, made me whip the head in frenzy.

Legs stopped on either side of me, knees pressed into my waist . . .

Erik had joined the mix.

Erik rubbed my back, then stepped back to let his hand rub my ass. My panties were pulled down, revealing the soaking mess that was my snatch. My knees were dragged apart; strawberries to treat later.

Saliva dribbled over my bum hole. I knew what came next.

The finger skittered, teased, circled, scraped; grew bolder still. It pushed past my tight rim, twisted and stretched me.

Domino's hand found my hair.

Erik's cock unlocked ass heaven.

Erik wasn't slow or careful. He'd already perceived rough trade was the order of the moment and lacked any semblance of self-restraint. He hump-walked himself into my chocolate grotto.

I slurped the cock and panted when cock sank deep. Sucked the head and puffed as cock retreated. My body danced the frenetic dance of lust—head bobbed, ass pumped backward.

Domino sneered; he couldn't take much more of my oral vacuum. His leg lifted, toes pointed. My lips tightened. The friction taunted him.

Erik reamed my ass like nobody's business; his movements were considered . . . perverse, even. Squatting now; hand in the small of my back. Riding his cowgirl—to the depths of his depraved need.

Hand twisted my strands, beat my head on his belly. "Unnnkkkk!" Spunk spurted in my mouth, filled it. I swallowed.

I focused, lifted my ass to meet the drilling cock. Erik needed no further enticement. His knees clasped my body as he sat on my back, stroked deep. Fingers dug into my back; cords stood out in his neck. I felt the heat, felt the head notch and hold.

It was time.

I twisted when jism back flowed; panted and blissfully

arched when it scalded my pussy's lips . . . shook him to the floor as cock lava scorched my clit.

"Hurry up with the fire, Dome!"

The room was freezing! I cupped my hands and blew in them, trying to get warm. He gave me an eye, returned to stacking the wood in the fireplace. "You know, the thermostat *is* on seventy."

Only a man would think seventy in the winter was warm. "It might be, but I'm still cold," I whined. My mama called me "cold-natured" since I could never get warm; said it was all in my head as I shivered while hugging the fireplace. I couldn't help it. I felt chilled to my marrow in the winter: my nose, toes, fingers—icicles.

"Would you hurry the hell up?"

"Woman! Don't make me take you in the back room, hear?"

The back room aka sex you down—a man's cure to whatever ails a woman. "And do what we haven't done before?" I baited.

He smirked before answering, "Keep on and you'll find out in a hot second."

"Humph." I gave an eye roll for good measure.

Domino took his time grabbing the box and striking a match. The flames danced along the fire log before—thankfully—igniting the twigs above it. I leaned in, hands splayed, trying to let the warmth seep in.

"Happy now?"

"Yep." I watched his ass bunch as he walked away.

"Will you hurry up, Emeril? I'm hungry," he yelled at Erik as he crossed the kitchen. Erik ignored him.

Domino.

Enigma.

Educated thug.

I thought it was a joke—the posturing, the tattoos covering

his body. I imagined he was brought up middle class and just *wanted* to be a thug. Fronting. However, a too-long trip to visit his family squelched that thought. Can you say hood? Yep, he was the real thing, with one little difference: he'd gotten out. Learned that hustling and slinging dope was a short-lived profession with a typical ugly ending—prison or death.

Despite his poor high school education, he'd enrolled in college, found his niche in computer programming, and made a success of it all. His social media site—SkySpook—had taken off like a shot . . . and made him a millionaire by twenty-five.

That's when I met him.

My mind remembered and I smiled . . .

It was Labor Day weekend. Terrance was out of town overseeing another project and Erik was tied up at the restaurant. I was alone—and horny. Not a position I cared for in the slightest. Holidays were meant for loving. But alone they'd left me. They knew better.

"Hey, beautiful," were his first words, "Why is a fine chick like you looking so down?"

There he stood, Nino Brown from *New Jack City*, down to the shades. I looked up from my cappuccino, then glanced away; I figured he was talking to someone behind me. He set his shades on the table and pulled out a chair, settling the misdirected thought. "You always this antisocial?"

I sipped my drink before answering. His eyes glittered. This one was trouble for sure. "Wasn't sure you were talking to me."

"Well, I was."

"So you were." I extended my hand. "Topaz November."

"Domino Johnson." He pulled up his sleeve, let me read his tattooed name; made sure I had it correct. "Yeah, just like the game—a chance."

I nodded, thinking the name seemed perfect for the person in front of me.

His eyes roamed all over my face, searching, piercing, dissecting. He threw a twenty on the table. "Let's you and me blow this joint, have some fun."

"W-what?" I almost choked on my drink. I didn't even know this dude.

"You look bored, so let's find some fun to spice up your life."

Pegged down to the last hair. "You read all that just from looking at me."

"Did I tell you my middle name was Nostradamus?"

I gave him my you-*must*-be-crazy look.

"It ain't crazy. It's called adventure." He placed his hands on the table and leaned close to my face. "You like to fuck. I can tell from your body. My cock smelled your scent, made me pause." He narrowed his eyes and looked at my hand. "You married?"

"Yes." Left out the part about the two husbands, though.

He shook his head. "And that dumb sucker left you alone? *This* weekend?" Labor Day weekend was always a wild one in this town. There was no reason to not be full, drunk, or well sexed with all the parties, barbecues, and smorgasbord of people milling about.

"Hey, life is short, and it would be well worth your time—and mine." He closed the distance, was inches from my face, from my twitching lips; letting me smell the Doublemint gum on his breath. "Why don't you"—a calloused digit trailed along my lips—"let my magic stick work its magic on you?"

I hesitated. Deep down I wanted to, but I hesitated. Why? It wasn't the fact that I was contemplating being unfaithful to my husbands—again—on my mind. It was the very real intuition screaming from the depths of my cells that if I tottered into this lion's den, *I* might end up a captive . . . willing . . . love slave.

He drew in a deep breath. "Looks like you need a minute to consider everything." He pulled out a business card and scribbled a number on the back. "I tell you what. This is my address." He passed me the card. "I'll give you an hour to meet me there. After that, I'll just assume you really weren't interested. And, Topaz, I'm don't believe in assumptions." He placed the shades back on his face and strode from the store.

I watched, interested, energized . . . then avoided the temptation as I let the time slip away. Spent the rest of the weekend bored out of my mind. Wondered if I'd missed out on something . . . special.

Fate is a trickster, though.

It looked like I was headed for a repeat of Labor Day weekend on Thanksgiving—both husbands were tied up and I had plenty of time on my hands. I was cleaning out my Rolodex when Domino's card dropped to the floor.

An omen?

I called before I could change my mind.

He didn't seem surprised to hear from me. "Twenty-five minutes," was all he'd uttered.

I made it in twenty-two. He said nothing as he opened the door—naked.

I thought about what he'd said to me before. This one was young . . . way too young for a mature woman like me, is what I'd said to myself as he pulled me inside. But that's neither here nor there because there he was, ebony skin shining in the full moonlight, muscles rippling from neck to ankles, sweat just beginning to break through as he ran his hands over his stiff black rod . . . before pulling mine down to cover the same path.

It was the beginning of . . . *us.*

I thought he'd be a booty call, a little something on the side. A diversion when hubbies couldn't get the job done—and I won't lie and say it hasn't happened before. Not much, but enough.

He and I were on different planets . . . so I found out. I'd held out, ignoring him when he'd continued sniffing up behind me after that first encounter.

Yes, he knew how to use his magic stick, but he's just a baby, I reminded myself.

"Get on, you still got milk rings around your neck," I'd reiterated to him.

Over time, though, his protests that the rings I thought I was seeing were really "love johns" neck chains became a joke that slowly and insidiously morphed into a challenge. And those career-building husbands of mine didn't seem to know how to keep this cat away from the tuna; they were focused on the money and not the prize—me.

Three months in and I knew what I wanted, he was about to be husbanded.

Valentine's Day found us together again. The bouquet of roses he'd gallantly brought lent a heavenly scent to the room. The champagne we'd toasted each other with lay chilling in the tureen. The sheets upon which I reclined were scattered with petals. I couldn't help but smile at him, at this situation, since I never expected any of *this.*

"Topaz," Domino whispered as he tore open the condom wrapper, "slip this on for me, baby."

I lazily sat up and exchanged places with him. His hands grazed my breasts and lingered. His fingers pulled at the erect nipples, stoked the fire in my belly. He leaned up from the pillow and caught a dark circle in his mouth. I hadn't ever produced milk, but his suckling caused a pseudo-milk letdown; my breasts swelled from the attention of his magnificent mouth. I sighed in contentment as I watched the cheeks suck in and out. In and out.

After long minutes of exquisiteness, he released my nipples. Hands massaged my stomach; I shifted between his legs. He slid one hand under his head, the other stroked my long, color-rinsed mane as I unrolled the condom down his blessedly long, backward-tilting shaft.

"I love watching you do that." Domino smiled, showing his

chipped eyetooth. From some fight, he'd vaguely explained. "Come here." The hand in my hair joined its twin on my waist and lifted me high. Succulent lips parted before his tongue tangled with mine. My eyes closed against the luxurious sensation. Time ceased as *this* moment loomed larger than all the previous moments of the day.

My mind committed every detail of his body, his being, to memory. From the short hair, his goatee, the bobbing Adam's apple to the taut muscles of his neck, tattooed chest, and I-want-you-to-hold-me-forever thighs, I remembered. His hands did the same with my body—a slow caress from hair to lips to nipples to belly to bush to thighs. I felt his fingertips pausing, clogging the neural pathway with information as they imprinted *me* onto his brain. One thing was for sure: if he turned me down and I never again rode this road, I would at least have the memory.

Domino's hands cupped a hip, squeezed, and released. Ahhhh. A man with a slow hand. That song was so true. A man with a slow hand might be ugly as homemade sin, but his ways will take him a long piece down the road. Domino wasn't ugly, but he was definitely a slow-hand man. The hand inched its way past my butt cheeks and around my thigh before slipping inside my K-Y Jelly–assisted nether lips. The lubed fingers stroked and swirled deeper and deeper in my juices.

I claimed his lower lip before nipping decisively on the upper. He reciprocated with sharp teeth on soft skin, and in milliseconds our kiss evolved into aggressive lip play.

Aggressor. Submitter. Leader. Follower. Dominant. Subservient. Our dueling lips propelled us closer and closer to dangerous territory—almost revealed that impatient aggressive side I'd become familiar with later—before a well-timed tongue quelled our fervor and the lip play returned to the state of a kiss.

The slickened fingers retreated slowly to the outside world, tiptoed through my bush, found my nub. My belly clenched at the first touch and I gasped, back arched. The fingers pinched, stroked, mashed, rubbed, and pulled at the overly sensitive flesh. My pelvis moved in an erotic octagon irrespective of my brain. I covered his hand, and as my juices trickled down to my fingers, I found myself first guiding then aiding his motions. My eyes rolled in my head. I was *definitely* drunk on the moment.

His other hand pushed me downward, and down I slid onto his love. Our bodies moved in concert to an ancient, innate rhythm, the squishing and popping sounds fueling our movements. He stretched me languidly, my legs spaghetti. I saw the impression of his rod beneath my navel, yet I never stopped a stroke, never held back from impaling my loins on his staff. Instead I leaned back, allowed myself to suction him deeper and deeper into my center of ecstasy.

As his fingers groped, frissons of electricity zinged down my spine and around to my still distended areolas.

I couldn't help myself . . . I clenched deep within.

Hard . . . then harder.

His face scrunched into a Freddie Krueger mask accompanied by werewolf growls.

My mouth opened in an "O" of ecstasy.

His hips trampolined me into the air.

Synapses cross-fired throughout my body.

And blissfully, that "O" became a long, drawn-out mewl when his cock erupted, burned my tissues . . . over . . . and over . . . and over . . .

Sweat still lay on our bodies when my proposition was presented and accepted. Domino became hubby number three.

Hands in my hair pulled me back to the present. "Whatcha thinking 'bout?" Domino plopped down beside me on the couch.

"You . . . us."

"Me too." He winked, tugged my arm, lifting me. "Come on. Got something I want to read to you. Wrote it just for . . . us."

"Hmmm. Sounds delicious."

He lifted an eyebrow. "I'll let you judge that."

I followed him to his room. The Cave. The walls, black; the carpet, black; the bedding, black; cavelike. Unlike my other husbands, Domino preferred I join him in "his" space versus mine.

I lay on the bed while he fished about his chrome desk and pulled out a sheet of paper. "Here it is." He glanced over at me, a peculiar expression I hadn't seen before on his face. "Now"—he stared at the ceiling, then back at me—"I wrote it a while back, afraid to just put it out there . . . let you know what was *really* in my head." He shrugged.

I was surprised and *moved.* "I'm your wife. If not me, then who?"

He nodded, cocked his head to the side, considering. "I hope you still mean that after I read this." He shook the mysterious page. "You *sure* you're ready for this?"

I sat up. "Try me."

"Okay. I call it 'Gold.' He took a deep breath and began. His voice started low, got stronger.

"Nether lips moisten as she enters the car.
Panties drip pulling into the driveway.
Anticipation. Longing. Need.
Fulfillment behind my door.
Eyes meet; lock.
Words unnecessary.
No air moves, just bodies.
Tongues digging trenches down throats.
Buttons popping into the air.
Clothes left where they fall.

Skin on skin.
Fused.
Flushed with desire.
Love-walking down the hallway.
No crevice missed by frantic lips and hands.
Turning the tables . . .
A shove into the bathroom.
Knowing what I need.
Giving it freely.
Hips forced against the vanity.
Wet lips encase my love muscle.
Hands entangle in her hair.
Drawing deep.
My glans expands in the back of her throat.
Her slurping . . . intense.
Pushing me to the brink.
On the edge.
Knowing she's taking me there.
Leg muscles tense.
I'm nearing Utopia.
NOW!
My anguished cry.
Lips release me from the wet prison.
Hot yellow liquid spews from my tip.
Spraying her face, her neck, her breasts.
Splashing onto me.
Dribbling down her back.
Scalding her love lips
Which clench in their own release.
Spilling their own juices
To mingle with mine.
Contented sighs in the afterglow.
No regrets.
A Golden Moment."

My eyes searched his face. It was open, wanting acceptance. I gave it to him. "Dag, that was deep. Want to give me a golden shower, huh?"

He shrugged again, a smile lifting the corner of his mouth. "Or you give me one. Doesn't matter to me."

A knock on the door. Erik dipped his head inside. "Hey, food's up, guys."

"Cool." Domino folded the paper into quarters; his face returned back to placid mode. I slid off the bed and stood. "You go ahead, baby. I'll be there in a moment." The moment of deep openness had passed.

"We'll talk some more later, okay?" I rubbed across his tatted mane.

"We will."

I joined Erik in the hall. He grabbed my shoulders and pulled me into his chest. "When am I gonna have some me and you *only* time?"

Erik was my most patient husband for sure, and I hadn't been neglecting him. No indeed. He was just too damn mannerable, never pushing the others out of line, no scooping me from under their noses just for his pleasure. He worked by the rules and felt bad if he broke them. I'd told him time and time again, the squeaking wheel always got oiled, but he apparently wasn't wired that way. So he shared me more than he got "alone" time with me.

"When you want it?"

"Oh, I want it all the time." My Latin love stuck out his tongue.

I tweaked his nose. "Better act like it, then."

"That's what you always say." He smoothed down my hair. "But on the real, I want to take you out, just you and me."

"When would you like to go on this date?" I kissed him lightly.

"Tonight."

"Damn all that giving a girl advance notice, huh?" I knew Domino and I still needed to have that talk about the whole golden shower issue, but I hated to put Erik on ice when he looked so earnest.

He squeezed me to him. "Maybe if you were still a girl, I'd feel bad." His hands roamed my arms. "But you, baby, you're all w-o-m-a-n, therefore, you're big enough and—might I add—*bad* enough to swing with any punches I might *want* to throw." His hands moved to my wrists. "I'm thinking something delicious . . . dirty . . . *nasty* . . . just like you wanna get with me."

I was definitely feeling warmer. "Think you know me, don't you?"

"Just like you know me."

And I did have a good handle on Hubby Freaky Deaky. Don't let that smooth façade fool you like it did me—at first.

I was on the hunt . . .

Ready to exchange the casual extra male encounter with a regular occasion sex. I needed a cock that knew my body well enough to push *that* button, wetting *that* hole, without fumbling about hitting and missing. I'd been keeping my eyes open but, so far, had found no one worthy enough to go pass the Casual Random Dick title. Yeah, there were plenty of buff men, but if it wasn't this flaw, it was that one—no job, living with their mama past thirty, talked about participating in Madden tournaments on that damn PlayStation . . . uh-uh. Y'all might need that man, I just didn't.

Then the WAPT ladies decided to meet and have lunch at a new restaurant/bar and grill—Lorenzo's. May Harris had sworn by their Cosmos, and Blu Campbell enthralled us with her story of the Amateur Strip Night Contest where a guy "too fine to touch"—her words, not mine—had put on a show that had caused a riot. Apparently the gays and the women wanted a piece of him and they'd stormed the stage, trying to strip him naked. I was all for visiting the eatery after that.

It was a beautiful contemporary-styled restaurant—lots of chrome, mirrors, and colored glass giving it a sleek look. The music was tasteful and the service better than most I'd had the pleasure of visiting. We'd grabbed drinks from the bar while waiting for our table. I'd laughed at how fast May slurped down her Cosmos; I opted for a delicious concoction called Fuck Till Sunrise from the bald, sexy bartender instead.

"Now, you've got to take your time with this drink, little lady," he'd warned me as I hungrily pulled the sweet liquid through the straw.

"Wooh! I see what you mean." Embers floated in my bloodstream, warmed up my torso. I fanned my face.

I was still fanning when one of the ladies started tapping me on the shoulder, making me slosh my drink about. "What?"

"Girl, I think The Rock is up in here." She pointed to a fine specimen strolling towards us in a white coat. At a distance, he resembled Dwayne Johnson, but up close, he was a bit better looking. No, scratch that. A *lot* better . . . if that's possible.

I gulped the next sip, causing me to choke and cough. It wasn't on purpose, but it got hunk-of-man's attention. The Rock's twin strode over and rubbed my back. "You okay?" His voice, with a hint of foreign inflection, made my blood pump; his hands made my coochie snap.

I caught my breath—and a whiff of some totally male cologne in the bargain—as I stood upright. "Thank you."

"The pleasure was all mine. You sure you're going to be fine?"

"Thanks to you, I will be." My eye was itching to wink at him but I held it at bay.

"Have a good lunch." He looked at the rest of the group. "Ladies." We watched that fine piece of gold walk away, giving a collective sigh of want.

After receiving our meal, we were again rewarded with the sexy man's presence. We all cheesed as he introduced himself as Erik, the owner and resident chef. The spark was in the air.

I nurtured that spark, explained my situation fully. He coasted along, lay back in the cut, moving at a slow but steady pace into my heart. When we finally got around to sex—after six months of feeling each other out—it was more than I ever dreamed or expected.

Your boy was a beast! He slapped it, flipped it, rubbed it down before riding it, bucking it, and tying me to the bed. He didn't listen to any of my pleas for mercy. He turned my pleas into begs for more . . . and more . . . and more . . .

He squeezed my hand. "Let's eat and then get dressed and head out."

"Deal." We twined our fingers and walked down to dinner.

6

I tossed the gold bra and panty set to the side. Too tame. I sifted through the drawer, discarding the leopard set and the chain mail, still not feeling I'd found the right one.

A tap on the door before Erik strode inside. "Ah, chica, I knew you wouldn't be dressed yet." He, on the other hand, looked snazzy in khaki pants, Izod shirt, and square toes.

"You know I'm still a female."

His hand skimmed over my naked hip. "Aye, no doubt about that one." Kissed my neck. "Trying to decide on what underwear to wear?"

"Yep. I can't find a set that matches my mood."

He rummaged in my lingerie drawer and pulled out a silver lamé-ish thong. "How about this one?"

I shook my head. "No matching bra."

"How about . . . no bra?" He cupped my breasts and rubbed his thumbs over my nips.

I thought for a moment. "Sure. I'll wear the halter dress and just the thong beneath."

He held the thong and I stepped into it. Erik slid the halter dress over my curves and tied the strings at the neck. I turned. He whistled. "I have the strongest urge to bite into you." He snapped his teeth together.

"I'm sure you will later."

He snapped his teeth again.

The air flowed through my hair as we rode in the Jeep. We could have taken my car, but I liked the wildness the bumpy ride brought out in me. "Are we doing something wild and crazy tonight?" I yelled over the whooshing of the air.

"Yep." He glanced at me and smiled. "I want to see you in a new setting."

"What kind of new setting?"

"One we haven't been in before."

That baffled me. I didn't hold back with the hubbies. I let loose, "got mine." As a result, they'd all been up in every hole on my body many times, as well as all over the house, lawn, neighborhood parks (yes, I am well aware of the law against this) helping me get there. "This is going to be good."

"All the time."

I jumped about the seat in excitement. I wanted this experience to be hot, sticky, and nasty as hell like he'd promised. When he pulled into Chocolate and Crème—a strip club known for its big-booty chicks—I grinned and nodded.

It was on.

The room was dim, the music sultry, and the women had the requisite big cabooses. I was envious of the tiny waists, at least ten inches smaller than the hips—but only a little. I knew what I was working with, and work it I did. I did mention those three husbands, right?

Women and men thronged about eating, drinking, watching. Two girls swung around on poles, their only attire very skimpy G-strings. We secured a couple of stools near the stage.

"What would you like to drink?"

"Something with a kick, babe."

One of the pole chicks walked over. She was the epitome of a stripper: toned legs, small breasts, big bubble butt, and plenty of long weave. She dipped low, spreading her legs in invitation. She licked her lips, her blue-rimmed eyes holding mine. She pulled at her nips, stuck her tongue out . . . offering.

Interesting.

I'd been strictly dickly all my life, never walking the lesbian experimentation road. Not even in college. I just never felt it. She pushed her G-sting to the side, Kegeled her pelvis. From the strength of her Kegel, it was obvious she exercised this muscle religiously.

Chick ain't gonna be nowhere in whatever Erik has planned for us. Ain't no way.

I watched the chick turn around, bounce her hips, work her moneymaker.

"Somebody sees something they like." Erik stood behind me, bumped me.

"You mean, somebody trying to act like they like something to get me to part with my money."

"I don't know . . . she got that girl-I-wanna-fuck-you look in her eyes." Chick had turned back around, stared at me.

I waved that thought off and broke eye contact. "Are you getting us drinks or what?"

Erik held up his hands. "I'm going. I'm just saying . . ."

I shooed him on toward the bar. Chick reclaimed her pole, wrapped her legs around it, climbed high. She flipped over, locked her legs, held her arms out to the side. Then she dropped! I yelled, knowing she was about to shatter every bone in her face, when chick clenched those big thighs and stopped an inch from her nose hitting the mirrored floor.

Sheeeeiiiiiitttttt!

My heart pounded; my mouth was still sitting open. Then I clapped like hell because that *was* some wild stuff! I pulled a twenty out, flipped it on the stage.

Erik returned with the drinks. I was excited and animated. "Did you see that, babe? Chick almost smashed her face in!" I grabbed my drink and sipped deep. Sweet, tangy, salty—good.

"Yeah, I caught that. They say she has another set where she's lifting and dropping with a girl on her back."

"Dag! I hope she does it tonight."

The dancers milled through the crowd, doing what it took to get more and more money in their G-strings. A cute brown-skinned chick with red-blond highlights stopped next to Erik. "You ready?" she asked me.

"She is," Erik answered for me.

I didn't know what was up but went with his flow. Who knew? Maybe my life was changing and I was about to "get lesbianed" for a night.

Her hips began that sway that only island girls, belly dancers, and project chicks seem to have perfected. The ultimate combination of timing with body symmetry that made something so obscene as making your butt "clap" in the first place become that one thing many women aspired to do for their men. She stepped closer, hips inviting. "You a titty or ass chick?"

"Neither."

She laughed. "Believe me when I tell you every woman is a titty or ass chick." I gave her a noncommittal nod. She scooped her small high breasts in her hands, offered them up. I watched, not moving; I knew I couldn't touch if I wanted to. Rules and all.

"I'm Savannah," she said as she rubbed her pointed nips across the fabric covering my own stiff nips.

"Topaz."

She nodded and pushed her nips up higher, to my chin;

played around my mouth. "You wanna lick, don't you?" Licking *would* be the obvious next step. I stayed silent, but my body was wide awake. Savannah turned around and backed her voluptuous booty into my pelvis. She stared over her shoulder as she rolled and shifted, her hips briefly touching, then backing off. "I'll bet you never had something so soft rolling on your clit."

I had to confess, I hadn't. Her hips were soft and firm at the same time; it felt like a soft pillow was being rubbed and bounced off my clit. She turned back, faced Erik, and rolled and ground, pulling at her nips. Erik smiled but I wasn't a bit jealous. *She* might not know it yet, but I was the *only* one riding that dick.

Erik flipped two C notes beneath her nose. "Let's take this to a back room."

Savannah immediately stopped her roll—confirming that this was completely money-driven lust—and plucked the two bills from Erik's fingers and into her string band with magician-like skills before strutting toward the back of the club. We followed behind, soaking up the atmosphere, the out-of-control vibe in the air. "You okay so far, babe?"

"Better than okay."

Savannah led us into a plush, mirrored peach-colored room. I really do mean peach—curtains, rug, chaise, couch, mirrored glass, they all were a monochromatic play on peach. Heck, even the lightbulb was a pink-peach. Savannah sat on the couch, legs crossed, arms resting along the low back—the queen welcoming her subjects.

She bit her lower lip, gave that smile you give prior to saying something you think is sexy. "What's next?" She parted her knees, granted Erik a bigger view of her commercially honed lust.

"I want my wife to give me a lap dance."

Her face screwed up. "That's it?" Guess she thought she would ride this cock. Sucker.

She slid to the edge of the sofa and patted it. Erik sat next to her and I stood in front of him. "Well, girl, lap dancing is pretty easy. You already know what he likes, so you just tease him with it. Don't just put it in his face like *Bam*! You got to finesse it." She stood, placed her hands on my waist. "Relax your hips and start rocking."

I swayed left and right, eyes pinpointed on Erik. As my body warmed, I closed my eyes, let my sway become erotic. Erik's pants rose, encouraging me. I added a roll, an air grind.

"That's it, girl, now spread your legs, bounce your hips."

My legs widened, I bent my knees, let my hips began a slow dip. "Good position, just go faster." I put my back into it, let my hips drop rapidly. "You're doing good. Now turn around, tease him with it."

I turned my hips to Erik, began bouncing again. Savannah lifted my dress, exposed my booty. Erik slid to the edge of the couch, his face now inches from my bouncing globes. "Go faster! Clap it!" she encouraged. Just what I wanted to learn. I churned to Speedy Gonzales range, and was shocked and surprised to hear the clapping sound coming from my ass.

"Ooh, Mamio! Clap it for your Papi!" Can you say Slobber Monster?

Savannah lifted my drink to my lips. "You feeling this shit, ain'tcha?" I threw my head back and nodded, resembling a cartoon character. "I can see. Open and close your legs slow, then fast. Show his ass why men are willing to die for a taste of our pussies," she hissed.

I followed her guidance and was rewarded by Erik gluing his tongue to my hot flesh. His tongue slid around and around, teeth scraping occasionally. This made me bolder. His head bobbed as I popped him up off my hips. "He's feeling you, girl, but don't let him take charge just yet. Back him up, sit on him, and grind his ass like this was your first time getting the dick."

I circled my pelvis while bouncing my ass into Erik's chest. I slid down into his lap, felt his granite cock. He untied my strings and pulled my dress top down, palmed my nips. My pussy juice pushed past my thong, aiding my slow grind. I figure-eighted in his lap, drew a rectangle and a triangle, then back to the old circle again. His cock stabbed me as it pulsed, begging to be released. I slid from his lap, turned on my knees, began pulling down his zipper.

"You can leave. Thank you," Erik told Savannah.

She shook her head. Her eyes had glazed as she'd stood there watching us. "Y-you sure?" She licked her lips, eyes glued to my hand.

"Yes. Thanks. We'll take it from here."

Disappointment was written all over her face but she sucked it up, took her time turning, opening the door. She gave us one final glance before exiting through the door and pulling it . . . "Wait a minute." She turned and waited. "I changed my mind."

I stopped, surprised. Erik knew there would be nobody else getting sexed besides me 'cause that was in the rules, and Erik always followed the rules . . . and today would be no different. Otherwise, there was gonna be some furniture moving going on real quick!

Erik's freaky dark side rose to the surface. He focused back on me, wrapped his hand in my hair, dragged my lips up to his. "You trying to get off easy? Make me blow my wad like I'm a damn forty-two-second thriller?" His eyes were slits, his face serious.

My scalp stung as he wound my hair tighter. "Of course not, baby. I know you like it long just like I do." Savannah watched in silence.

"Seems like you trying to short me, my time."

"Never that."

"I hear you, but I'm not convinced. Why? 'Cause from what I've been noticing lately, I'd bet a week's receipts that you wish you were somewhere with that motherfucker Domino—don't you?"

I vigorously shook my head. "No, baby. I want to be right where I am. With you."

He sucked his teeth. "Let's see about that." He reached into his pocket and pulled out a plastic tie. "Take another sip from your drink." I grabbed my drink, sipped lightly. "A deep sip." I drew deep on the potent mixture, felt the burn as it tumbled into my stomach. "Turn around."

Savannah watched as Erik pulled my arms behind my back and secured my wrists with the tie. Hands reclaimed my hair, turned me roughly. Erik pulled his cock free. The light brown staff quivered, the head like a mushroom. He slid his belt free. It had been a minute since he'd really spanked this ass; he would be rough. "I can read your thoughts. I know you thinking about one of the others right now." He shook his head. "Not good at all." His face hardened. "Bend over the couch." He glanced at Savannah. "You too."

She stayed where she was. "That's extra," was all she said.

"How much?"

She shrugged her shoulders. "Another two hundred."

Erik fished into his pocket, pulled out three Benjamins and threw them at her feet. "The extra is for"—he turned to look at me—"incidentals."

Savannah moved the money to the side and stepped out of her G-string. She positioned herself beside me, her chest burrowed into the couch. "Now, that's a beautiful picture—two plump asses in the air, just for me." His breath was ragged. "But . . . you've been bad asses. Ever since Eve made Adam bite into that apple, you women have been nothing but big-assed trouble. I got a cure for that—for a little while, anyway."

The air whistled as the belt flattened across my ass. I grunted as the leather snapped my flesh again and again. Savannah yelped at the first hit. "Too hard, huh? You must be new to this game." He popped her ass again. Savannah writhed. Erik laughed. "You must still be dating young boys, girl."

The belt flew in the air between my ass and Savannah's. My ass was numb, my body strumming and humming as I watched the belt flay across Savannah's now crimson-striped butt.

Insert mind fuck here.

I lifted my hips, opened my legs. "Pop my pussy, Papi," I begged. I loved having my pussy lips and clit lightly spanked, and his ass loved being the spanker.

He complied, letting the stiff leather snap against my wet flesh. My lips swelled, engorged with blood as he snapped them over and over. I purred and dipped my belly, trying to expose more of my clit to the belt.

He dropped the belt and plunged his cock into my pussy. He grunted, the efforts of his deep thrusts pushing my cheek farther into the pillow cushion. My feet pointed; the tendons in my neck rose, strained in ecstasy. Savannah lifted from the couch, stood behind Erik, and wrapped her arms around his waist. She rode his back and hips, added propulsion to his thrusts as he rode me.

"Oh, yeah, boo. Fuck her good," I heard Savannah whisper.

Erik's hair tickled my ass; made me twist and turn to avoid it. Drove me wild. He misread my motions—on purpose. He stopped. "What? You don't like the way I stroke you now?" My arms were grabbed, I was stood upright. Erik sat on the couch, pulled me on top of him. I dropped onto his wide cock, let his arms pull my hips down deep. "Now work that ass, baby."

I ground and bounced, watched as Savannah fingered her own pussy. Erik took my "punishment" to a higher level. Clamps were placed on my nipples, tightened . . . the long chain tossed over to Savannah.

Savannah crawled over to the chain, picked it up slowly, let it slink between her fingers, then . . . she smiled. She gave the chain a nice yank. My back arched from the pleasure pain shooting through me. She yanked again, eyes shiny as any zealot, made me lean forward, trying to lessen the zings shooting from my nips.

Erik spread my legs over his and wrenched the last of my control away. He vaulted me off him, sinking deep on the rebound. I gasped and moaned from the fucking I was receiving.

"Lick her," he told Savannah.

I shook my head. "I d-don't know, baby. I haven't ever done this—"

Savannah ignored me and seated herself between my spread thighs. I sucked my stomach in, tried to delay the touch of her smooth-looking lips on my clit. She spat on me, let her finger tease around my stiff nub. I moaned—couldn't help myself. She hauled down on the chain; pain made my eyes close. She welded her lips to my lips . . . sucked . . . made my eyes flip back open.

Like most women, I've had my kitty licked by numerous men, but this right here . . . this was different. Hard for me to explain. The touch was lighter, on point; the correct amount of pressure around the clit, the usage of multiple fingers along with the licking, the flicking, feather-like tongue diddling constantly. I understood how these sensations could sucker you in, overwhelm you, overtake you completely . . . make you fall in love with it.

I tried to stand, to give my body some relief from the exquisite feeling rushing through me. Erik pulled me back and placed his prickly beard on my shoulder, rubbing deeply. "Ah . . . baby? You should really be feeling this shit here. Since you aren't, we've got a little bit of a problem. You're here with me but you still got one of those *other* chumps in your head." He bit the back of my shoulder. "Bad, *bad*, move." He never missed a stroke or stab in my pussy while talking. "Don't worry, though. I've got a fix for that. Let's see who's still at home."

Savannah lightly lapped at my clit, eliciting a loud, long powerful moan. A cell phone was held up to my ear. "Tell him what you're doing."

I pulled my head back, tried to bump the phone away. My hair was grasped in tight fingers, my head held still. "Tell . . . him . . . what . . . you . . . are . . . doing," Erik repeated in his "about to be a menace to society" mode.

"H-hello?" I gasped out while being bumped in the air.

"Who is this?" Domino. Erik knew what he was doing . . . who he was disrespecting . . . who he was giving the ultimate diss—and now making me participate.

"To-Topaz."

Domino crunched down into whatever he was eating, breathed in the phone. "O . . . kay. Thought you were out with Erik. What's up?"

Savannah pushed a slim digit between my lips, pushed into my pussy, nestled beside Erik's cock. I flipped my hair back, cried my pleasure loud and long to the mirrored ceiling.

"Topaz! What's going on! Where's Erik! What's happening!"

"He—he's making me—" Her tongue swirled at my pussy door, flipped, and snaked over and around Erik. "*Damn*! *Uhhhhhhh! Damn!*"

"Shit, girl, don't stop!" Erik was obviously enjoying the lip play.

"Top, baby, who's making you do what? Where is that fucker Erik?" Domino was up in arms; ready to save his damsel in distress—happy distress.

"Erik." Erik surged deep upon hearing his name. "H-he's fu-fucking me. Making s-some ch-chick . . . *Shit*!—" Savannah pinched my clit, lapped my slit, took me to the brink.

"Making some chick what! Where are you? I'm coming!"

"Fu-fuck me, suck m-me." I finished with a deep moan, couldn't hold it in; I had to let it and its cousin, the scream, out . . . but just a little.

"What?" His voice changed then; let the jealousy creep in. He wouldn't ask again, hoped it wasn't true.

"S-she's fuck-ing me."

"Tell him you like this shit, too," Erik said, hands pulling my ass cheeks farther apart.

"And I-I li-like it. Oh baby! Oh baby!" I moaned, grunted, gasped as all the little sensations met, combined into one big, monumental explosion of pure unadulterated lust.

I tried to hold back, lessen my body's reactions, but failed as Erik's head mushroomed inside me. I screamed as my legs became useless appendages hanging over his thighs as he bucked my pussy. His fingers mashed my clit and the pinging and zinging began in my toes and slipped rapidly up my legs and *Pow!* I sprayed Savannah's face with juice; relaxed my pelvis, rode as low and deep as I could go on Erik's cock. I was rewarded when he groaned, lifted us off the couch in his release. With a big thrust, his body tensed and I felt the jism pumping into my love hole . . .

I never heard when Domino clicked off.

7

Today was supposed to be a "Topaz only" day. No husbands, no work, nothing but doing whatever I desired. But like they say, no good plan goes un-hijacked. And I'd been hijacked by the WAPT.

An emergency meeting had been called. It seemed a member had a "situation" we needed to vote on immediately. I'd rolled my eyes, wondering what new hell had rolled into somebody's life. From what I'd gathered—half listening since I was pissed like hell they'd even called—somebody needed to ditch a husband, like, yesterday. Not that common, but hey, divorce between regular couples was over fifty percent, so we were due. If I hadn't been the president, I'd beg off. But duty called, and I was going. Besides, it irked me when others shirked theirs.

Our maid, Sonja, bopped her head, hips swaying to the music of her iPod while she vacuumed the hallway. An open trash bag was leaned against a door. My nose wrinkled in further irritation. *I've told her a thousand times about leaving open trash bags in the hall.* It was a hazard just waiting for someone to turn over. I held my tongue; decided to help her out.

The bag was packed to the brim. I wrinkled my nose again and carefully gathered one edge. I shook it, hoping the contents would drop at least a few inches, giving me plenty of room to close and tie it off. That's when I saw it.

The condom wrapper.

I ignored the fact that I was digging in waste and fished it out. Trojans—not our brand since I was allergic to Trojans. The dark blue wrapper was torn, so it had been used. Sonja turned off the vacuum. "I'm sorry, Ms. Topaz. I'll get it."

I waved her off, needing no one other than me to realize what I'd discovered. "That's all right, Sonja. I'm going down, so I'll drop it in the trash can." Her brown eyes were wide, worried. "Really, it's fine." I stuffed the wrapper deeper in the bag, tied it off, and hoisted it down the stairs.

My mind was reeling. Please tell me no body that lived in this house was bold enough to screw someone in *this* home?

In the garage, I reopened the bag, my mind needing absolute positivity about what I'd seen and now suspected. Midway down, I found proof positive—the used condom . . . with cum in the tip. I found a Kleenex in my purse and did some stuff I never ever thought I would ever do—I squished it. Yep, it was wet, meaning *recently* used.

What the frigging hell?

Or better yet . . . who?

I was rocked to the core. A used condom in *my* house? I think I was a bit irritated since I had no way to reasonably explain this away, to come up with a somewhat plausible, yet thin, excuse my brain would accept. The greater universe was not allowing me this psych save; I had to face the facts: the condom wasn't our brand, there was still wet cum in the tip, and it was found in my house. That meant one of only a few things: either someone was bringing a female over when I wasn't there, or the guys were sexing each other. Bile seeped into my throat at that thought. I'd heard of the down-low men, but wasn't no way in hell I was an advocate of it or about to be a willing accomplice to the practice.

My brain spiked down new tangents. Did the others know? Were they *all* sneaking women in my house? Was it . . . *Sonja*?

I rocketed back up the stairs, hearing old conversations about hiring maids and the resulting problems with your man—or in my case, men—in my head.

She was still vacuuming. I gave her a once-over—a typical Hispanic female, dark hair, dark eyes, gold blush skin . . . not bad. Her firm hips swayed, dipped with the freedom that only comes with youth and lack of an audience. I tapped her on the shoulder. She spun around, startled. When she saw it was me, she cut off the vacuum and pulled the iPod plugs from her ears. "Yes?"

"Sonja, I need to ask you something." She nodded. "Ah . . . I'll just get to the point. Have you had any friends here while we were away?"

She wrung her hands; tears sprang to her eyes. *My God! Was she the one?* My heart pounded and I took a step closer. Sonja's eyes widened; she backed up.

"Sonja?" Menace in my voice. "Have you had sex in my house?" I purposely left off the "with my husbands" part. I couldn't bring myself to just put it out there like that because I wouldn't be responsible for my actions if she confirmed it.

The eyes narrowed, looked confused. "Sex? Here?" she laughed. "Oh no, Ms. Topaz."

"I'm sorry. I fail to see what's funny." She wouldn't be laughing either if she realized how close she was to a beat down. I do *not* play about my husbands sexing other people!

She stopped the laughter. "I sorry. I thought you'd found out that my mama had dropped off my two kids one afternoon when she had to rush to the hospital for my sister. They were sick and had to stay home, but then my sister went into early labor, so you can understand my dilemma."

Oh. She had kids. I was relieved and ashamed. Relieved that she wasn't the female party getting sexed in my house, and ashamed that I'd employed her for almost a year and had no idea she had children—hadn't inquired about her life at all.

My silence seemed to unnerve her. She clutched her chest, eyes very worried. "Ms. Topaz, this is a good job. I make decent money and get home in time to get my children from daycare without having to pay the after-hours fee. I'd never mess that up. I can't afford to."

"That's good to know." I turned to leave, refusing to show my shame. "Keep up the great work!"

I felt her eyes piercing my back but I didn't turn or acknowledge her. I had bigger things on my plate.

Damn this meeting!

The officers were already seated around a conference table when I arrived. I wasted no time with pleasantries, just plopped my purse on the table and said, "What's the deal?"

The fact that I was in a poor mood wasn't lost on anyone. No one immediately spoke. "Well?" They had better hurry the hell up because I had things to do, information to shift through to get a handle on my own situation.

May was the first to speak. "A member has come before us to dissolve one of her marriages. Rina Stouffer."

The day had finally arrived.

I sighed. "Present your case." I waved Rina forward.

Rina was forty, full-figured, and apparently insatiable, judging by her decision to have six husbands. Too many for me, but she'd been juggling her passel of husbands for nearly two decades, so she knew a thing or two.

Her voice—raspy from her pack-a-day habit—always grated

my next to last nerve. "It's simple. Husband number four has become a bum."

"A bum? Explain further, please."

She shrugged her shoulders. "He can't keep a regular job, has been sitting around the house for the past few months, eating me out of house and home, playing that damn Nintendo day in and day out, won't pick up after himself or help with the yard work. Just acting like a diva, and I'm the only diva in our house."

She got a round of head nods at her speech.

"So, you want to divorce him because he can't keep a job and won't help around the house."

Rina nodded. "Yes. He is failing to uphold his natural role as husband. Instead, he's acting like a teenager still up in his mama's house. And I don't screw my son."

"I hear you. It's not the bad economy." Rina shook her head. "He's just wanting to be a kid again. No responsibilities."

She mimicked a gun with her fingers. "Right."

I looked around the table. "Discussion?"

"You need to think long and hard before you put your man out to pasture," Mamie cautioned. "That kind of stuff gets the others riled up, makes them believe they have choices, which we all do, but if it's not put out there, they usually don't think about it."

"You think she should just . . . put up with his mess?" May asked, anger inflecting her voice. "That's not right. He wouldn't do it for her."

Mamie put her hand in May's face. "You need to calm the hell-o down." May's nostrils flared but she held her tongue. "I'm just saying that she's setting a shaky precedent for her household. Today, it's this one, tomorrow, it may be another. Then what? You're gonna look up one day and they're all gone."

The room was silent now. It was one thing to get rid of one husband, another whole string of yarn for the whole lot to turn on you and leave. We'd be laughingstocks; female polygamists would become the brunt of jokes from every male walking the planet instead of the powerful women we truly were. That was unacceptable.

"Rina, perhaps you are being too hasty," Susan Thompson, trust fund socialite and wife of two, stated before I could voice similar sentiments. "Have you thought about marriage counseling?" I was a bit surprised at the suggestion coming from this source. Susan—sweet woman, but let's just say, the elevator gets stuck about halfway up.

"Whenever me and one of the husbies gets off track, we'll get counseling in a heartbeat, talk out what's bugging us. It's worked for us. I love them and they love me. Besides . . . the make-up sex after we overcome whatever hurdle is . . . just . . . amazing."

"No, I haven't," Rina informed her. "I've got *six* husbands. Six. When would we have the time to go, and just which one of the other husbands do you think would be willing to pay for this counseling?"

I understood where she was coming from. "That's right. No job, no health insurance." In this role-reversal lifestyle we were living, not everything is completely reversed. You can't overcome nature completely; can't change what's innately within a man—and few men would help their rival get counseling to stay in a multiple-man marriage.

"Exactly." Rina glanced around the table. "And I'm gonna say what to the others? Y'all pitch in and pay for marriage counseling for me and the bum? Hell, they're just thinking one down"—she wiggled in her seat, slid a smile on her face—"more of me to go around." We all laughed because it was a true point. Husbands always wanted more time when there was competition around.

"What if we found a low-cost counselor, ladies, and paid for it from the treasury?" Helen Reed, our secretary, suggested.

I'd never been a fan of paying for things from the treasury that benefited only one person. Wasn't fair to the WAPT group as a whole, especially if you never had a problem we needed to bail you out from. She needed help, but that wasn't the right way to get it.

"Ummm . . . I don't really like that idea. It's a nightmare waiting to happen because someone will feel or actually *be* slighted in the process. I mean, how much money do we put into counseling before we say no more? What if you two are almost there but not quite when we pull the plug? Have we really helped or just dragged out the process of him leaving anyway?"

"Good point, Topaz. When is enough going to be enough?" May agreed.

More husbands. More decisions.

The tears sliding down Rina's face surprised all of us. "Y'all just gonna not help me? Just leave it at 'work it out' when I've told you I don't think we can?" Her teary eyes dug into my soul. "Hell, this is the same thing the preachers do when a woman comes to talk about her man problems. 'Y'all can work it out. You be patient. He'll come around.'" She slammed her hand into the table, leaned up to the edge. "Damn all that! Y'all need to listen to me. I *have* tried to work with him but I *cannot* and *will not* continue to house a husband who will not work for the good of our collective family. If WAPT has no solutions to offer, then accept my divorce petition and let me deal with the consequences." She slumped back into her chair, tears sliding freely down her face now.

"'No woman shall be forced to remain with a husband she wishes to put aside for adequate cause, not even for the good of the organization.' Article Three of Amendment Two," Adrian Hung, parliamentarian, read from our constitution. She closed the manual, looked around the table. "Ready to vote?"

It was all there in black and white, just where *we'd* placed it since the beginning. I had mixed feelings—my own situation was clouding my mind—but called for the vote because it was the right thing to do. "All in favor?" The hands rose slowly, but they all rose. "No nays." I turned to Rina. "The ayes have it. You are free to divorce your husband."

"Thank you all."

"We done?" I asked the table, receiving nods in response. "Good. I'll catch you later." I grabbed my purse, Rina's pain fresh on my mind, and hoofed it out of the room. I definitely had my own stuff to work through.

Alone.

It was not to be.

"Topaz!" Adrian, our helpful parliamentarian, jogged over to me before I reached the car. I stopped, tried to erase the frown from my head before I entertained her. "Got a minute?"

I opened my door and put a foot inside, wanting her to know I was in a hurry. "Yeah. What's up?"

Adrian huffed, a chunky hand on her waist as she sucked in air before she spoke. "It's about Rina." Her breathing regulated, she patted her chest. "I know you were hesitant to vote for the divorce but"—she glanced around, took a step closer, lowered her voice—"there's a whole lot more going on."

"Really. Like what?" I wasn't being nosy, but if Rina had been lying and it was something that could ultimately affect the organization, I needed to know. Damage control and all that stuff.

"I've been friends with Rina since husband number three, so we go way back. Now, Romeo, husband number four as well as a jerk living up to his name, is a real piece of work. A few months back, Rina found a used condom in the trash in the laundry room."

Prickles of déjà vu crawled up my spine; I stiffened but kept my expression neutral. "That had to be a surprise."

"It was, and chick don't play that at all." Adrian shook her head. "She said she hadn't had sex with any of the husbands in the laundry room, so why would one be there? And get this: It was a fresh condom. Rina didn't fall off the turnip truck this morning."

"Right, right, so what did she do then?"

"What a real woman does—hired an investigator to get the dirt."

"And what did he find?"

"Romeo didn't have a job—had been fired a few months earlier for something petty, as usual—was sleeping with some rich girl across town who was giving him plenty of money and, as it came out, was four months pregnant . . . with his child."

"Shit." Point. Game. Grand slam.

"Shit is right." Adrian grimaced and shook her head. "Chick showed up at Rina's house last week and showed out. Pulled Romeo out the house, demanded he come with her—and he went." She shook her head. "Rina is just trying to get out of this mess without the other girls getting all up in her business. The divorce was the best solution we could come up with. Quick and quiet."

I now understood the tears. Rina *was* at her wit's end, trying to save face instead of crumbling. Avoid being relegated to the "typical, common" wife status where men do whatever to them and they just find a way to swallow it down, accept it as expected.

"I didn't mean to pull out the rule book, but it looked like we might not get the vote to go our way, and she's not wanting to just spill all her business in the streets to get it."

Nothing to do but nod. "I understand completely."

"Knew you would and, girl, just keep this between us, okay?"

"Always."

"You have a good one, hear?"

"Bye." I watched Adrian walk away, wondering if I'd be the one sharing the same type of confidences with her soon. Ugh! I fished out my phone, called over to the Sunshine Spa, and rescheduled my appointment for later in the day. I had another stop to make first.

8

I hadn't been to the brick-and-mortar building in a few years. I hadn't needed to. It still looked the same—chipped bricks, peeling paint, looked like the building was falling apart. But that was far from the truth.

The Break Down. The place to smash, crash, and hurl away your problems. Great idea, one I wished I'd come up with first 'cause it worked. If more people indulged, therapists would be out of business in a heartbeat. I pushed open the door and let the cool air rush over me. Not that it cooled me a bit.

"Hey, girl!" Connie, the proprietor, strode over, gave me a quick hug. "Haven't seen you in forever. You're looking great! Life must be great!" She was looking good herself. This business was born from a vicious breakup that Connie said "sucked the life out of me," made her want to commit suicide. Instead, she started throwing things, and no surprise, others wanted to throw things, too.

I gave her a half-smile that didn't quite reach my eyes. "I haven't had anything to complain about . . . until recently."

Her eyes summed up the situation in milliseconds. "You

know you've come to the right place to get things back on track, then."

"I sure hope so."

She squeezed my forearm. "What will it be today? One rack or two?" She wiggled her nose at me.

"Um . . . three, for starters."

Connie made a muscle-man pose. "Oh, you're mad as hell, then." She turned and clapped her hands. "Tommy! Grab three carts and fill them to the brim!" Something crashed and shattered. "Tommy! That had better have been a customer and not you!"

A muffled reply I couldn't understand came from the rear.

"He's new." She rolled her eyes. "Wouldn't have hired him at all but he's my nephew and needed a job." She sighed, gave a what-could-I-do-shrug. "So girl, you want just glass items or what?"

I looked at the menu hanging over the huge, ancient metal cash register Connie said she'd found at a yard sale. They'd been inseparable since. The selections were wide and varied—glassware, pottery, plants, food, water balloons. I chose quickly, though. "Give me one rack of glass, the second one full of potted plants, and the third"—my eyes scanned the fruit and vegetable list—"hmm . . . ripe tomatoes."

"A shard, fruit, and plant party, eh?"

"Sounds about right."

A rumbling sound made us turn. A pimply-faced redheaded teenager pushed a rack and pulled one behind him, bumping into every wall in its path. "Tommy! Can you be any more clumsy?"

"Sorry, Aunt Connie." The look on his face told me he'd heard this before. "I'm still getting the hang of things."

"Better tighten up before I hang you." She poked him in his thin chest. Tommy smiled. "Load up these babies with plants, glassware, and your favorite . . ."

"Tomatoes!" they said together.

"Come on, girl, let's get you into your plastic jumper." She pulled a thin vinyl suit from the shelf behind the counter and handed it to me. "What size?" She looked at my feet.

"Seven." We also got steel-toed boots.

"Twenty minutes, you think?"

I shook my head. "I'll need at least an hour."

"Big spender!" She rang up the cash register, peeked around the oversized side, and said, "Sixty dollars." Cheap-ass therapy.

"You need a stool." I peeled off three twenties with a smile.

She slid the money in the drawer. "Just as soon as I can afford one." Liar. "Follow me."

She had twenty rooms—six by fifteen foot cinder-block cells made to handle any frustration thrown at them. Twelve of them were occupied. The *fucks*, *hells*, *damns*, and *pricks* flew in the air as we walked past. All expected since it *was* the place to vent.

I slipped into my crinkly suit, anxiously anticipating Tumble Tommy's arrival. He rumbled down the hallway in a few minutes. He'd stacked each rack to overflowing with the items I'd selected. He took his time bumping and stumbling into the room. But eventually, the racks were in place.

"Don't forget to wear your goggles."

I gave a tight smile. "I will." I was *so* ready for him to disappear.

When the door finally closed, I hefted the biggest vase on the rack and hurled it forward. It shattered into a million diamonds, shards bouncing into the walls.

That felt good.

I rolled my head around, cracked my knuckles. Time to get down to the nitty and the gritty. I alternated at random between the carts, throwing a plant high, smashing a ceramic urn low—I would be ready to play pitcher for the neighborhood softball league if they had one as I threw a tomato fastball, then curved a green vase into the corner of the ceiling. My tension was lessening.

The used condom flashed in my head. Five tomatoes splattered in quick succession.

Rina's face followed. Three tall glasses mimicked suicide bombers as they crashed into alternate walls.

That couldn't be who I'd one day be, could it? I flung the pipettes to the floor, smashed them under my boots.

I let my mind slip down that slippery road of the "What If?" game. Which husband could it be?

Terrance. Who would he choose? Someone like me or totally different? A green tomato split in half on impact with the back wall. Either way, she'd have a big behind since he was, like most black men, an ass man. I imagined a huge-hipped chick riding his cock and glancing over her shoulder, egging him on. Him smiling, licking *my* lips, trying to dig *my* cock as deep inside her as he could.

The image was too real, too plausible.

Blood boiled in my veins. I grabbed the palm plant by the neck and swung it around, building momentum, before catapulting it down the narrow room. It exploded high up on the back wall, raining dirt five feet from it.

I was a marksman, aiming for the center of the bull's-eye with the dozen narrow-stemmed candlesticks flying down the length of the room like sharp knives.

But he'd been there from the beginning. Was he capable of this level of disrespect . . . in his own home? I caught my breath, let the thought rumble about my cranium. My final conclusion: doubtful. I bounced the tomato in my hand before tossing it high and light, the juice splattering back onto my suit.

Domino. A wild card for sure. Who knew what he'd hook up with. Project chick to the high-end call girl—he was the person with the suave manner, the chutzpah, the charisma to navigate any woman he wanted. But would he?

He'd been a bit salty since the phone-sex episode. Said nothing, but body said plenty. We'd never had our golden shower talk, either. He always seemed busy with this new project or expanding SkySpook or server failures and hackers . . . anything to avoid the discussion. But it was his to have, so I backed down, let it lie.

I couldn't give a yes or no on Domino.

Erik. Who would it be for him? The first thought floating into my head? Sonja, the most likely choice. Both Hispanic, both beautiful—golden bodies intertwined, him pulling her long hair, spanking her firm ass into submission—oh, hell naw! I almost had the Chinese juggler's act down pat as the stack of saucers flew from my hands, crashing and throwing up pieces of low-quality porcelain to the ceiling and back down. A stack of plates followed.

I leaned on the cart and huffed. Yes, Erik had a dark side, but honestly, he didn't have the sex drive despite his complaints about me not spending time with him.

Girl, he doesn't need a high sex drive to get occasional sex from someone right there.

I grabbed the nearest plant, swung it over my head, dislodging the pot, and flung it with all my might. I *hated* when my own logic kicked my ass. Was his lack of competition really a . . . *cloak* . . . for getting it elsewhere? I rummaged through my mind bank, tried to remember how we were when we first married. Was the sex that much more plentiful?

I swallowed as the response slammed into me. Yes, it was—before Domino. But that was expected, and besides, he'd verbally accepted, along with Terrance, the third marriage. I won't say they were happy as hell about it, but they were busy men, and as busy men they were unable to meet my pleasure demands, so they definitely seemed to . . . understand, to allow me a new plaything they could monitor . . .

Bullshit.

All of it was bullshit. I felt it down to my toes. I was being played just as men had played women for a million years. No matter who the culprit was, someone in that house was tearing down the intimacy bonds I'd created by letting an outsider into our inner circle. Introducing germs that might ultimately infect us all. I shuddered.

Boiled.

The wine bottle was pummeled into the wall, wine coating my goggles and suit. I wiped the lens clean, picked up a mirror, and hefted it to the middle of the hallway, shattering it into puzzle pieces. My fury swelled, necessitating the sacrifice of glassware, pottery, fruit, and plants flying about in haphazard fashion, slipping from my slick fingers, being tossed, slid, stomped, slammed into a wall.

Think you'll screw me over? The lamp hurtled kitty-corner into one wall before ricocheting into the adjacent wall.

Not as long as I'm breathing, baby. I played—Kerplunk!—with the remaining tomatoes, letting their redness paint the wall in variations of red pulp before sending the remaining glassware to its death, resulting in a kaleidoscope of crystal prisms covering the floor.

Drained.

I grabbed my knees, watched the sweat drip from my nose to the floor and splatter. I felt better, but that didn't change the reality—someone was stepping outside this relationship. I pulled myself upright, stripped off the ruined jumper, and slowly walked back to the front.

"All done?" Connie asked.

"Yeah."

"Whoa. You don't look much better than when you came in. Need another rack? It's on me. I want my customers satisfied."

I shook my head. "No more racks. Besides, my arms are spaghetti right now." I stepped out of the boots and slid my shoes back on.

"You sure?" Worry lines crinkled around her eyes.

"Positive." I gave her a warm hug. "I'll be seeing you around."

"Don't be a stranger, even if you don't need to blow off steam."

"I'll try." And I would. Connie and I had hung out a couple of times and I found her to be pretty cool and laid back. "You just stay busy and get a smaller cash register before that monster falls on you."

She smiled, shook her head. "Not even if they offered me a million bucks."

I chuckled. "Girl, if I hear of somebody offering you a million bucks for that thing, I'm gonna break in here and sell it for you."

"Only if you can get past Deuce." Her Doberman pinscher watchdog.

"Yeah. I forgot about him."

"You come in after we close, and you'll remember him forever."

We both laughed. "See you, girl. Bye."

9

I looked and smelled like crap as I turned into the Sunshine Spa's parking lot. The return looks and obvious sniffs confirmed it. I was shown to the back quickly, where I stripped down and donned a robe. From then on, I let my mind drift to strategies, possibilities, conclusions for the future.

There wasn't much I could write down on the customer satisfaction comment card as I checked out, because the entire session had been a blur. Shame, since I'd received a seaweed wrap, mud bath, facial, manicure/pedicure, and a shampoo and blow-dry. But I looked good and smelled good, and that was all that mattered.

Everyone was home. Erik was doing his usual cooking, while Terrance watched football on the flat screen. Domino glanced over, saw me and said something into his phone before closing it. I waved and spoke before moving up the stairs to my suite.

I didn't allow myself time to change my mind, just pulled the suitcases from the closet and began folding and rolling clothes into them. No one interrupted me during the forty minutes it took me to pack and make flight and hotel arrangements. However, once I rolled the suitcase down the stairs, I knew it would be Scotland Yard, third-degree investigation time.

Here we go.

Domino was coming up the stairs just as I was coming down. He stopped, foot midair. "You going somewhere?" His eyes bounced between my suitcase and me.

"Yes." I moved past him. He turned and followed, got in front of me; stopped me.

"Baby, is something wrong?"

"Yes."

"What is it?"

"Toppie, what's going on?" That was Terrance, who'd lifted himself from the television and saw the suitcase and Domino. He stood, arms across his chest, watching me and Domino.

Before I had a chance to speak, Erik spoke. "You leaving us?"

There it was.

I was leaving them—the person or persons who'd killed off my Xanadu simply by not flushing a used condom.

"Something like that."

"What?"

"Hold on, baby . . ."

"Wait. We need to talk . . ."

"Where is this coming from . . ."

"I don't get it . . ."

I held up my hand, halting the questions. "I simply need a few days away from home."

Terrance's eyes narrowed. "Top, this isn't about some"—he looked at Erik and Domino—"getting another husband, is it?"

Everyone held their breath as they waited for my answer. "No. I'm going alone and not hooking up with any other men." They all sighed after I'd given it.

"So you just need a few days away from your men to what?" Terrance held my eyes, tried to read my thoughts like he once could.

"Think."

"About what? Did we do something?" Domino fidgeted beside me.

I gave him my best, pointed stare. "You tell me."

He frowned. "What are we talking about?"

I looked at each husband slowly. "It seems that someone wants out. Feels the need to insert an outside party into our little circle—without telling the others."

The men glanced at each other, faces stoic and unreadable. "That's bad business all around."

Erik raised his hand. "Topaz, how did you come to this conclusion, one of us wanting out of this?"

"Yeah, baby, what made you think that?" Terrance asked.

"It's simple—"

The wailing smoke alarm cut me off. Erik ran toward the kitchen, Terrance and Domino on his heels.

"Man, you got the house on fire!" Domino yelled. From the smoke billowing out, I believed him.

"Grab the flour!" Erik yelled.

I stood at the fringe, watched Terrance slap at the fire with a wet dish towel, Erik and Domino squabble and pull at the canister of flour like two bad-assed chaps. Since there was no real danger of this becoming an inferno, I turned, left a destination brochure on the foyer table, grabbed my suitcase, and headed for my car. The fire could be put out without my help.

10

The plane landed in two hours and twenty-five minutes. Four hours and fifty minutes since I'd left home. I switched my phone back on, not surprised in the least at the fifty voice messages and texts in my in box. They'd finally stopped playing and realized I was serious. I switched the phone back off. I'd deal with that later.

I'd chosen South Beach, Florida, for my getaway. I needed someplace hot and anonymous. It didn't hurt they had offered a special on this trip, either. The taxi dropped me at the hotel, the bellboy took my luggage to my suite, and I flopped on my bed in relief after he'd gone.

Is this what every woman feels when her marriage is in trouble over infidelity? The aching, the betrayal, the wanting to know the who, the where, the . . . why?

My clothes felt like bonds. I pulled them off, threw them across the room to land wherever. I sat in the middle of the king-sized bed, tucked my arm under my head, and stared at the ceiling.

Three husbands. More than my share, if you asked any woman. Terrance and I were married the longest; thirteen years, Erik and I for eight; and Domino and I for four.

Did I enjoy my life? Truly enjoy it? Honestly, I had—until the condom incident. We all . . . meshed. The men were each different; brought different things to the table, touching different sides of me.

Terrance was steadfast, unmovable, the mighty oak. I could count on him to be there through ups and downs, through my new-husband phases, through almost anything. I'd never ever heard or felt in my heart he'd been cheating on me. Never. It's true. I know they say the wife is the last to know, but that's just a bunch of crap women spew to look good for the world. You can't spend time with a person day in and day out and not have a clue they are cheating. Something's gonna get missed in the cleanup details—a number in the pocket, a sexy text message, a phone call, a condom wrapper. But I hadn't ever felt or seen any of this with Terrance.

I did remember his face when I'd told him I wanted to husband Erik, though. I was bold, aggressive, not once considering he just might go ballistic, try to snap my neck . . . because I *knew* he wouldn't. I *knew* him. I *played* him. Pushed him.

The hurt, though he'd masked it quickly, was there, palpable. For a brief second, I'd almost recanted, told him it was a joke—but I didn't. I was full of myself, my swagger challenging, backing him down into acceptance. I was a damn bully for some new cock. Terrance took it all and had said barely a negative word about it in all these years.

Erik. Erik. Erik. He was the opposite of Terrance—the undercover bad boy who knew how to dress up and have a good time. Terrance was a homebody, liked watching television when he wasn't working; a night out only when I'd begged him for a minute. Not Erik. If the party was jumping, he was jumping to be there. His energy was a damn aphrodisiac.

His world was so different from mine, and I wanted mine to expand. Erik knew everybody from any and every walk of life, and I loved meeting and hanging out with them. It was nothing for him to call me at the last moment, ask me to meet him downtown at the restaurant for an impromptu party with some friends in from out of town. I was proud to be there.

Erik's sex took me to a new level also. Terrance wasn't into all the pleasure-pain activities. He stuck with the tried and true vanilla sex. Got him off every time. After Erik had opened my eyes and expanded a new hole or two, I'd put it out there for Terrance to enjoy. He'd only stuck with the anal. The rest of the S&M stuff he'd passed on; said it made him sick to his stomach to see me in pain.

And Erik was aggressive, like me. If he saw something he wanted to accomplish, he put his mind to it, got her done. Lorenzo's had grown from two thousand square feet into ten with four bars and three dining rooms over the past five years. He'd received the food critic's highest award last year. Was I a proud wife? Sure was. His drive fueled me, made me want to have him there, in my inner circle. Mine. All. Mine.

Did I feel or see signs of unfaithfulness? No. I'd been at the parties, popped up at the restaurant . . . nothing. He had no unaccounted-for time, his money flowed into our joint checking account, and he denied me nothing. I saw, felt, read, and heard nothing, not even a whisper, about Erik and some other woman. You know why? I was *his* second wife, the first being Lorenzo's. If I'd let him, he'd eat and sleep there, that's how much he loved his business.

Did Erik have opportunity? Sure. What person alive didn't?

I moved on to Domino. Domino was a chance meeting of opportunity plus curiosity. His approach had been unusual; his background seedy, scary even; his accomplishments huge. A walking antithesis.

Terrance and Erik never saw this one coming. When I'd made the announcement, Terrance had just walked away, not asking many questions at all. Erik, on the other hand, talked me to death. Grilled me. Met Domino and grilled us further. He'd gone away for a few days and surprised us by giving us his blessings upon his return.

We were still in the honeymoon phase—Domino was my most frequent bed partner. And his lovemaking was that of a young man: fast paced, vigorous, and abundant. Despite playing the offended party the other night, he'd scooped the other hubbies plenty of time. He just didn't want to deal with payback.

You don't, either.

Was that what this episode in my life was about? Payback?

I felt that gnawing deep down in my belly, confirmation that this was exactly what it was about.

These three husbands were about me. Their focus was to be on me. Their resources were to be used by me for whatever I wanted. Was I being selfish? Or just taking charge of my life and getting those things I needed and putting it all out front where nobody could mistake my intentions?

You just dressing up the truth.

No, I wasn't. I did need what I needed from the exact avenues I was getting it from. Up until I spotted that used condom, I'd believed the same thing—Enough! I was sick of the mind ambush. I decided to go down to the bar for a nightcap, let my neurons rest a bit.

The lounge was dark and smoky, half filled with patrons watching the game, nibbling on food, and talking. I slid onto a bar stool near the far end. I wanted to survey the room and chill.

"What will you have?" a Goth-looking female asked.

"Campari and soda."

"Coming right up." She slid the glass over to me in seconds.

The team on TV made a touchdown and a few of the men erupted in yells and slaps on the back. I really wasn't paying that much attention. Football wasn't my strong suit at all.

I sipped my soda and glanced out the door to the lobby area. I suddenly sat up straight. The man at the desk strongly resembled Terrance.

Can't be. Terrance doesn't know where you are, right?

Right. I leaned back into the stool and sipped more of my drink. When I glanced that way again, the man was gone.

"Why do you keep asking me that?" This came from a woman seated at a table behind me. I gave a sneaking glance their way. The woman was a twentysomething brunette, and her companion a twentysomething male. "I'm not interested."

"Come on, babe. What could it hurt?" I heard the chair scoot closer. "It would add spice to our relationship."

I didn't mean to eavesdrop, but it was interesting. "What do you mean, add spice to our relationship? I would never ask you to do something like this."

"See, that's why we are where we are, 'cause you don't like to explore shit."

"I like exploring shit just fine. What I don't want to do is to eat pussy."

"Tsk. It's no big deal, babe."

"Really? How about if I asked you to suck a cock, is that a big deal?" I got ready to leap out of my seat, because normally this question usually made things pop right off.

"Have you lost your damn mind? I'm not down with that homo stuff, you know that."

"Exactly. Neither. Am. I."

The chair was shoved back. "So let me get this right. You

would be willing for us to have another woman . . . as long as you don't have to eat her pussy?"

"You're just determined to be a moron, aren't you? I don't want another woman *fucking* your dick, *sucking* your dick, or even *looking* at your naked dick. *Understand*?" She slapped the table.

The man chuckled low and long. "That's kind of narrow thinking. It's the new millennium. All kinds of things to be experienced, all types of people willing to experience them . . ." He turned his palms upright to the ceiling.

"Is that a threat?" *I sure think so, chick.*

"No. I'm just saying." I knew he'd shrugged, given her that noncommittal look that behind it said, "If you won't, someone else will."

I heard the sound of someone reaching the bottom of their drink. "Baby, trust me. This will be good for us. The first thrill ride of many more thrill rides to come. Hey, one day it will be you. And if you tell me of something you want to do, I'll do my best to do it for you. Because I love you. Just . . . give this a try. Please?" He was good.

"I don't know . . ."

"She won't touch you at all, just me." Pushing his point home.

"No eating her pussy."

"Done."

She was falling. "Stop means stop."

"Done." Almost got her.

Another slurp. "And you promise that when it's my turn . . . you'll do it for me, right?"

"Already done." Wait for it . . . wait for it . . .

"When do you want to do it?" Gotcha!

"Tomorrow. I think I can find a chick, and we'll have a great time before we leave. Cool?"

There was a minute of silence, then, "Okay."

I smiled around my straw. He could have been me negotiating my marriages . . . that were now up in the air.

I finished up my drink, slid from the stool, and headed out onto the boardwalk. The wind was mild. I leaned on the wood railing, watching the surf crash, the joggers run past. My mind refused to allow me peace, though.

Who do you love the most?

In my mind, love had no outline. I felt what I felt. Had our feelings for each other changed? Certainly. I'd matured, they'd matured, we'd all had to see the naked truth about each other. Couldn't be avoided. But who did I love the most? I truly could not answer that question since I loved each one, just in different ways.

Which one touches your soul, makes you feel safe?

I'd have to say Terrance and Domino definitely tugged at my heart the most. Terrance because he was my first love, Domino . . . something about him made me want to be there for him. Like that orphan kid struggling in the world who's never had anyone have his back. He needed me.

Which one brings you the passion you need the most?

Domino was my most frequent bed partner, and when I thought of sex, I thought of him first. But was his frequency just overshadowing the others versus being what I truly needed? Terrance's lovemaking was deep. Vanilla, but deep. I could feel his passion for me in my toes.

If you were told tomorrow you could only have one husband, who would you go all-out to keep?

Not fair. Not fair at all. That's not the situation I'm in.

A ball hit the wall beside me, making me jump.

"Sorry, ma'am!" A teenager ran up, grabbed the errant ball, and ran back to his group.

My head ached from all the thinking. *Time to shut it down.* I headed back to my room. Switching on my phone, I saw my message count was now up to sixty-seven. I powered up the computer and sent each husband an e-mail with the hotel's name and phone number. I let them know I was fine and asked that they hold off on contacting me for a few days. I still needed to think. I powered down before any responses could come through. After a quick shower, I let television then sleep hold my attention the rest of the night.

11

My scalp throbbed.

I was beginning to rethink this whole "A Me Vacation to Think" because I felt drained, drained, drained. The day was beautiful, so I dressed and decided to walk along the early morning surf. Meditate.

Apparently the folks in Florida didn't sleep because the beach was full of the joggers, beachcombers with metal detectors, sunbathers, and a dog or two even at this early hour. I smiled as a Lab chased after the stick his master threw in the ocean and brought it back. The seagulls dipped and rose. I shielded my eyes as they passed the sun.

"Hello, Topaz."

I stopped, turned slowly. It just could not be . . . "Terrance!" He grabbed me into a bear hug, arms squeezing me tight. "Terrance, baby, what are you doing here?"

He looked down at the ground. "When I saw you'd left, I almost had a coronary. You've never run off before, baby." He stared into my eyes. "What's wrong?"

I pressed my fingertips into my eyes, rubbed my face. "I just needed time to think."

"About what, baby? Are you leaving me?" I was silent, watching. "Are you?" His pupils were dilated, his face grim.

"I don't think so. It just—"

"What?"

I shook my head, not wanting to reveal all I knew in case he was the condom wearer. "Nothing."

I could see from his eyes he wanted to ask more questions; drill me. "You had breakfast yet?"

"No. You?"

"No. They've got a buffet inside, though."

We walked in silence to the dining room. Terrance paid as he always did and seated me before grabbing us two plates. "The usual?"

"Yes." I watched my manly man fill the two plates with breakfast food. He'd done this for me since the first time we'd gone to a buffet. He took his time navigating past the patrons and tables on his way back.

"For my wonderful wife." He sat my plate in front me. I pulled it toward me, unrolling my napkin at the same time. "You forgot something." I looked up and he pointed to his lips.

"You're right." I kissed him lightly.

"That's better." He settled into the chair, said grace, and we began eating. "So, you through thinking?"

I had to laugh. He hadn't even given me a whole day to sort out my thoughts. "You act like I am. Shoot, I haven't been gone twenty-four hours yet." I remembered the man from last night. "When did you get here, anyway? I just sent out the e-mails telling you guys where I was around eleven last night."

"At eleven, I was up in my room, trying to persuade the front desk to give me your room number since you didn't answer your room phone. No luck."

I giggled. "Funny. I thought I saw you last night checking in but dismissed it since nobody knew where I was."

"Baby, you don't know who you are married to. Dome might be a computer whiz, but sometimes, it just takes good old common sense. I called up American Express and asked what the last couple of charges were on the card." He smiled because he definitely had me there. I'd charged the room and plane fare to the Amex card. Hadn't given it a second thought. "I hotfooted it on the next plane out and got a room here, hoping to run into you."

"Keep sneaking around, you gonna find out something you don't want to know."

He pursed his lips, nodded. "A chance I was willing to take." His face saddened. "The worst thing a man can see is his wife with another man—and I see two of them . . . every . . . day."

Ouch.

He sat down his fork. "Baby, what really happened to us? Where did we go?"

"South."

"Yeah. I married the woman of my dreams, you know that?" I smiled but didn't nod. "You were a spitfire! I loved how you talked shit with my boys and beat us at most of the games, and even when you didn't win, you talked so much yak that nobody could concentrate anyhow." He smiled, tucked my hand into his.

"I loved how you would cheer me on in whatever. I always knew that no matter how crummy things were going, you would give me the encouragement I needed to keep going. Never give up. I loved that you stood up for what you wanted. I knew that anybody messing with you and yours would catch hell! Then one day, it seems like out of the blue . . . you changed. Or maybe I did and just didn't see it."

Tears collected in the corners of my eyes and threatened to flow down my face as I knew he spoke the truth. He had wanted to land this big contract, so he worked the longer hours, took on the impossible tasks, stressed himself out to get it, thinking that he would slow down after he got it. But he never did. Bigger jobs came along; I was left alone more and more. Yes, I changed.

His lips rubbed softly together. "Remember that time we took my truck to the woods?"

The memory of that delicious day almost made me cry out. The tears ran in rivers. Terrance handed me a napkin.

"I'd just gotten the Toyota Tacoma and we decided to see if it was as rugged as they said. That summer day was golden and hot, just like you like them." He remembered well. "We splashed across that small river, ran a tire across a downed tree just to see if we could get through it like the commercials said, then stopped in that clearing by the cliff."

He looked at me expectantly. I remembered it all. Terrance slid his chair closer to mine. I smelled his aftershave and wanted to run my hands across his massive chest but restrained myself at the last minute. We *were* in a public dining room.

"Do you remember what you did then?"

I had to smile now. "I gave you the striptease of your life before I sexed you up like I'd never done before."

"You got that right! That has to have been *the* most memorable sex of my life! You in the back of that truck . . ." He grabbed my arms and crushed me to his chest. "Where did *she* go?"

"She's still here."

He sighed, in doubt, I thought. "Yeah, right. Let me ask you this. How do you know she's still in there when you're running back and forth between me and Domino and Erik?"

I knew I had no answer he truly wanted to hear. He tickled my back. I giggled into his chest, then caught my breath as his hand began rubbing circles into my back. Oh, I'd missed this intimacy.

Terrance rested his chin on my head and his hands roamed lower to my buttocks. "I'd love to see her again."

The subtle request was there . . . and I was up to the challenge.

"Oh you would, would you?"

His leg rubbed against mine; toes tickled under the balls of my feet. "Yes." A grin was now on his face.

"Let's go upstairs."

The elevator took its own damn time reaching us. When it finally dinged open, we were hot enough to make a firecracker explode! I smiled at the maids and put the Do Not Disturb sign on the door before closing it. He grabbed me up, slapped his lips over mine. I pushed him back.

"Get ready to be strung out!" I strode to the stereo and scanned the stations, selecting an R&B oldie one. I was hoping it would play something that would take us back to that period in time.

I was in luck when the Emotions' "I Don't Wanna Lose Your Love" began playing. As the trumpet intro began, I turned slowly, my hips rocking slowly at first, then faster to the beat.

I slowly unbuttoned my sundress and dropped it the floor. Pulled the pin out of my chignon and I shook the hair free.

Terrance walked close enough for me to see the bulge in his pants.

I don't want to lose your love . . .

I unbuckled my sandals and stepped out of them. Clad only in my underwear, I opened my legs wide and dipped low.

"Shit!" Terrance yelled.

I walked closer to him and grabbed a hand. I pushed him onto the couch, and with my tongue, I swiped him from crotch to face. He grabbed for me and I stepped back. I pulled my bra down, pushing my breasts free and up. I palmed one and offered it to his waiting mouth . . .

. . . then pulled back before his lips touched. I turned backwards and slid fingers into the sides of my panties. Slowly, I dragged them from my ass, then bent over.

Terrance sucked air loudly.

I pumped a finger at a time into my dripping cunt, punctuating the sentences. When the beat resumed, I booty-danced my hips like I *was* getting paid for this performance.

Terrance grabbed me from behind, his hands sliding, roaming, squeezing up and down my body. He bit into my shoulder and tweaked my nipples frantically. I arched my back and rubbed against him.

His fingers traveled over my butt and lower. He slipped a finger inside me and began pumping to the music. I opened my legs wider and twirled on his hand. His thumb tickled my anus before nesting inside its door. He twitched them together. The tissues stretched and the nerve endings jumped. My juices multiplied by five. It was my turn to yell, "Shit!"

I no longer heard the music, only our music. Terrance kissed down my back, then pushed me slightly forward into the mantel. His breath then followed the trail of kisses to his fingers. Ever so slowly, he withdrew his fingers and parted my lips. His tongue delved right in—swirling, lapping, stabbing—between my anus and my cunt.

My toes curled in ecstasy; my fingers found my clit. I rolled and rubbed as ripples of heat suffused me, swamped me, overwhelmed me.

His zipper slid down and I felt the head of his dick pushing at my opening. I leaned forward more. He sucked on my back before surging into me. *Damn, this feel good!* He pushed forward again, trying to fit every inch that God gave him into me. He began pistoning like well-oiled machinery. My head was bumping the wall so I put my hands up to cushion the impact.

There was no way I wanted him to change positions! I figure-eighted, Kegeled, swirled, and pumped back at him.

"That's it, baby! That's it!" Terrance yelled in pleasure.

I suckled my own jiggling breasts, drawing secretions from the tips.

"Baby, touch the floor." I did so without another thought. Terrance placed his knees between my legs, put his hands on my waist, and squatted slightly. He pushed down on the small of my back and began pumping again. His balls slapped my clit and the angle seated him even farther in me.

"Oh hell yeah!"

He fed me dick, my pussy eagerly swallowing him whole. "Baby, oh baby oh shit oh shitohshitohshitohshiiiiiiiiiiiiiiii-ttttttttttttttttttttttttttttttt!" His spunk burned, stung as he filled me to the brim. My clit flowered, pussy pumped juice over and over and over his cock.

Terrance and I lay spooned together, sweat cooling on our bodies. He shifted, then spoke. "Baby, I was wrong. *That* was the best sex I've ever gotten." I giggled, feeling surprisingly good. He kissed my hair. "You still need space?"

I shook my head. I knew what needed to be done. I kissed my husband on his lips. "Let's just take a few days and then we'll go back, okay?"

"Okay." He dragged me on top of him, lips claiming mine, cock wide *wide* awake.

What the hell have I been missing out on?

12

We were all seated around the dining room table. "Guys, I called this meeting because I need to put a proposition before you."

Erik sighed, leaned back in his chair, and crossed his arms. Probably thought I wanted another husband. Domino steepled his fingers, sat his chin on top of them. Terrace just . . . sat.

"I took the past few days to reflect on us, this unique situation we're in." I gave them a small smile. "I also know that every one here isn't completely satisfied."

"How do you know that?" Domino asked.

"Just . . . I know." And I left it at that. I'd decided to keep the condom info to myself—for now. "With that being said, I have to make this statement and pose this question: If anyone wishes to leave, they are now free to go. It does not matter the reason. If you are unhappy, dissatisfied, wish to be satisfied elsewhere, I will grant you a divorce."

Erik's arms uncrossed and he sat up. "What the hell?"

"Baby, you never said anything—" Terrance.

"You saying you don't want us no more?" Domino.

I waved them silent. "Husbands, I've said what I wanted to say. You have twenty-four hours to decide if you would like to continue to be in this polygamous marriage or I can grant you your divorce. It *is* that simple." I rose from the table and went to my room.

Twenty-four hours is a long time when you are waiting on an answer.

Twenty-four hours goes by slowly when your future is up in the air.

Twenty-four hours can seem like forever if you've never had to wait twenty-four hours for anything.

Shit, twenty-four hours can be a bitch!

I paced, gritted my teeth, worked out, paced some more. I saw no husband. Responded to no text, e-mail, or call from them. I didn't want to know their answer early. I wanted us all to be there when it was said.

The house was silent. No television on the great room; no pots and pans banging. It was as quiet as a dormitory over Christmas break. I surfed the 'net—purposely avoided Sky-Spook, updated my Facebook page, poked folks I hadn't ever met, and sent friend requests to a few hundred more. I chatted, bought e-books, and worked out some more. My sleep periods were brief, erratic, and filled with nightmares.

When the sunlight woke my tired body the next morning, I jumped up and rushed out of my room. Ready to get it over with.

They were already waiting for me.

I plopped into my chair and blurted out, "Who's staying?"

"That's how you gonna ask us, woman? After the hell you put us through over the past day, and you just run in here and ask, 'Who's staying?'" Domino was not a happy camper.

My mind was tired, confused. I just needed an answer; knew it was the key to me sleeping restfully. "Y-yes."

He pursed his lips, gave me a mean mug.

"Hell-ooo. Could you guys give me an answer?" They looked at each other; a silent message I couldn't decipher passed between them. My heart sped up. Were they *all* leaving?

I waited.

They made me wait.

And wait.

"Please! Would you give me your answer? Who is wanting to stay in this marriage?"

Terrance flipped his hand up. I nodded and winked. Domino was next. "You need to learn how to talk to folks better. That wasn't right what you did."

"I acknowledge that area of improvement. Thank you, Dome." My eyes swung to Erik. "Erik, you in . . . or out?"

He stared at me, gave me a slight "I'm sorry" smile. I knew then what I'd felt all along; was about to get confirmation—

"I'm in."

I was so far down my off-road brain path, it took a moment to understand what he'd said. "*What*?"

He cocked his head to the side and gave me a curious look. "I said, I'm in."

All three husbands were . . . staying!

When it finally sank in, I jumped up and whooped. "Group hug! Group hug!"

With all my faults, their faults, we each felt there was enough love to stay in this marriage and work through whatever. But don't think I'm a fool. While they were out day before yesterday, I'd had the entire house wired with minicams and mics. No space was private. So whether they were jacking off or having help, I'd know soon enough—and deal with it then.

"Time to celebrate. Hit the music, Pops." Domino being . . . Domino.

"Got your damn Pops, damn baby thug." He powered up the CD player, was scrolling through the extensive play list.

"And don't play none of that blues stuff. You got some Plies? Now that joker there, he knows some stuff."

"Man, don't nobody want to hear no Plies. Put on Santana," Erik suggested.

"Chile, please!" Domino again.

"Got some Richie Sambora, how about that?" Terrance asked.

"No!" Dom and Erik yelled before walking over.

"Man, give me the remote 'cause I know where the songs are." Domino grabbed at the remote. Terrance pulled it back.

"Dom, we are not listening to no rap. You can't make love to no rap music." Terrance said before putting an elbow in his chest. "Don't you know nothing, young buck?"

"Oh, he knows nothing, T, " Erik agreed.

They bickered back and forth, back and forth, squabbling, changing CDs, leaving me completely unnoticed and virtually forgotten.

I finally yelled, "Do I have to go out and get *another* husband to get some dick up in here?"

Their reaction was instantaneous.

The remote was flipped into the air.

The room shook.

Chandelier swung.

And I smiled . . . as I got stampeded by my three sexy-assed *husbands*.

Yes, love *is* a mind fuck.